Postmarked for Peril

Postmarked for Peril

Eve Barnes

Wandering
Grove

To Yvette for your infinite
cheerleading, positivity, and collaboration.

One

My fingers twitched, itching to flick a crouton at Jess Cooper's forehead. As I arranged my salad into neat rows, I silently chanted a refrain of restrain. "Don't do it girl. Don't do it." In terms of breakups, this had to rank in the top five dullest. Halfway through our food Jess cleared his throat. And adopting the tone of an eighth-grade math teacher, he began his lecture on the cost-saving benefits of ending our relationship.

"I spend thirty dollars for the round trip between your place and mine," he droned. Since Jess lived with his family on their orchard forty miles outside of town, we did our socializing at my place. "Let's say I make that trip three times a week. That's almost four hundred dollars a month or nearly five grand a year in gas alone." He emphasized this last point, making his eyes go extra big. It only made his forehead a more tempting target.

I did a little math of my own, and by my calculations, I had a solid sixty-forty chance of hitting him right between those big brown doe eyes if I launched the crouton now. To give my hands something to do, I stuffed my mouth with a forkful of greens. This breakup was lasting longer than our actual relationship.

Jess and I met a couple of months ago on Tamale Wednesday. We got together because we were both single, roughly the same age, and neither of us actively stockpiled weapons for the Great Reckoning. In a town of eight hundred thirty people, those were some high selling points. So, we figured, why not give it a try?

"Ending things makes total fiscal sense," I agreed, talking around the salad I was still chewing. "It's also better for the environment," I added, hoping to get this over with faster.

"Exactly!" Jess exclaimed a bit too enthusiastically. "I mean, you're a great gal, Maya. There's nothing wrong with you. It's just--"

I raised my hand, signaling him to stop his faint praise. "We're all good, Jess." I didn't need a gentle letdown when I was already standing on the ground floor. And where I didn't see myself dating Jess forever, when you talk to the squirrels in your yard for company, a little human interaction goes a long way. Jess was a nice enough guy. True, he only wanted to watch movies with exploding cars, but at least he brought the pizza.

"Thanks for taking this so well, Maya." The tense crease between Jess's strawberry-blond eyebrows, visible throughout the entire meal, finally eased. And didn't you know, that just pissed me right off more?

Jess scraped his chair along the floor as he stood. "I'm gonna use the restroom then head out, okay?"

I watched him walk to the back of the family bar and restaurant and thought about slipping part of his cold burger into his jacket pocket. I knew it was purely a kick in my pride's keister, but how dare he think I cared more about our lackluster romance than he did?

"Dessert?" Angel, the Oasis's waiter/bartender/sometime cook, asked as he cleared our plates.

I glanced at the empty seat across from me, contemplating the question. If Jess and I were desserts, I would be a hot fudge sundae with sprinkles, and he'd be an oatmeal cookie--without raisins. "Nope." I shook my head. "We're done here."

Since the only remaining question about this relationship was who was buying lunch, I shook my head and handed Angel my card. I wasn't letting Jess Cooper leave thinking I was more upset about our ending than he was. A cheer went up across the place, and the large screens above the bar replayed the Seahawks' touchdown.

The uneven clack of Jess's boots on the wood floor announced his return. I slung an arm over the back of my chair and pretended to watch the game. Slouching a little, I took a sip of my Coke as if I didn't have a care in the world.

"Well," Jess said, standing over me.

I looked up and smiled back. "Well."

Jess reached towards his back pocket for his wallet.

I set my drink down and stopped him. "Lunch is on me. No hard feelings."

"Ah, Maya, you should've let me pay." Jess held out his arm and started leaning down for a hug.

I quickly slapped his open palm. "High-five!" I called. "Take care of yourself, Jess." My cheeks warmed, and I willed him to leave already.

He looked at his hand, slightly confused. "Alright, Maya." He lowered his arm. "I'm sure I'll see you around. Tell Dave and Leigha I'm sorry to miss them."

"Will do. See you around," I called in a disturbingly loud and chipper voice.

He frowned, opened his mouth as if to say something else, and then shook his head. Grabbing up his Carhartt from the back of his seat, Jess turned and exited. Once he was gone, I removed my arm from its uncomfortable position and let out a long sigh. I hadn't seen this coming. It was as if Robin had just dumped Batman. Everyone knew Batman was the one with the muscles and cool toys. Robin was the tag-along runt in a mask. A horrible thought rose like indigestion. What if I was really Robin? I thought of all the nights spent watching burning buildings with Jess on the other end of my sofa, his mouth open, snoring. The memory felt reassuring. Batman probably didn't drool in his sleep.

Instead of leaving when Angel brought my card back, I asked for another Coke and explained I was waiting for Leigha and Dave. At least now I understood why Jess insisted we meet early. With fifteen minutes to kill and wanting to put Jess out of my mind, I pulled out my drawing pad.

I'd finished sketching three ideas for a design project I was working on when I heard my best friend's voice cut through the background noise of the bar.

"There she is." My bestie Leigha Lore pointed to my table. As she walked towards me, her pink glitter eyeshadow sparkled in the light. Her husband Dave, carrying their adorable three-year-old hellspawn Libby, followed behind. Libby bounced excitedly in her father's arms, waving one chubby arm at me and blowing kisses with the other. Leigha took a seat across from me, and Libby, overcome by excitement, launched herself from Dave's grasp and into mine.

"I want to sit with Aunty Maya," she declared at an ear-splitting volume. I loved this kid.

Leigha pulled crayons and a coloring book from her enormous, gold metallic tote for us. "Where's Jess?"

I grimaced. "He left. We just split up."

"Did you break the poor guy's heart?" Dave asked, folding his long Levi-clad legs under the table.

I set him straight, recounting our parting of ways over gas prices.

Leigha smirked. "I bet even after that, you paid for his lunch, didn't you?"

"I had to," I confessed.

"Why?" Dave sounded genuinely outraged. "I can't believe the bast-" he glanced at his daughter, "Uh, banana head let you pay after he ended things. Do you want me to put the boot on his truck the next time he's in town?" I knew he half-joked, but I still appreciated the misguided support. Dave was a county deputy, and all jokes aside, he took his job very seriously. In fact, he took most things important to him seriously, his love for his family, the sanctity of fishing with his buddies, the Seahawks, and keeping people safe. But Dave had another side, a hidden side, that belted out Adele tunes in his truck with the windows rolled up tight.

"Nah," I shrugged. "I paid when he used the bathroom to make a point."

"Which was?" he asked.

"Sweetheart," Leigha patted her husband's forearm, flashing her long pink nails. "A girl has got to save face. It was Maya's power move. Her way of sending him off – pay, wave, and sashay away!" she said, doing her best beauty queen wave.

I smiled. It felt good to be so understood. Dave, amused, gave his wife a look like she was the Catch of the Day. Being with my friends helped smooth my Jess-dented ego. As Libby and I worked on coloring purple and green manes on her My Pretty Ponies coloring pages, Dave's attention drifted to the game on the screens overhead, and Leigha caught me up on the Lore household news.

"This morning, Libby tried flushing Greta's squeaky squirrel toy down the toilet. Thank heavens, it went down head first. I pulled it out by the tail when it got stuck. But it was so disgusting I had to throw it out. Poor Greta, it was her favorite toy."

"Greta eats cat poop," I reminded her. "I think a little Ty D Bol dip for the thing might be an improvement." Greta, the Lores' snaggle-toothed Pomeranian, officially held the title of Claryce Falls' Best Dressed as voted for in the Miner's Dispatch, Best of Claryce Falls edition. She was often seen about town sporting a pink velour tracksuit and painted nails.

"Eating cat poop is yucky," Libby declared as if speaking from experience.

"You two," Leigha shook her finger at us. "That is not the point. And yes, honey, you should not eat cat poop. The point is, I can't wait for my mom to get in tomorrow. The extra set of eyes and hands is going to be a real help. She's been hinting about moving closer, and with Dad gone two years now, I hope she's finally ready for a change."

"Do you really think she'd do it?"

"I think so. We're going to look at property while she's here. And that's also why Libby's gonna be an extra good girl for Nana C, right? And you're going to be an extra good best friend by helping sell my mother on the town's charms."

"Nana's coming!" Libby yelled, holding up a ketchup-limp fry in the air and smearing it around her face before finally getting it into her mouth. She made happy little purring sounds as she chewed.

"Consider me the ambassador to Claryce Falls, covertly promoting the virtues of small-town country living to visiting mothers of the community," I pronounced in my Girl Scout pledge voice. "In fact, why don't you all come by the post office on Saturday? I'm only open until ten. We can go to the farmers market after I close up and get lunch there."

"Let's do that! But wait, you said 'I'm only open...' Does this mean Burt is officially retired?"

"It does," I confirmed. "Tomorrow is my first day flying solo!"

"I feel bad. I wish we'd made him a card or something. He worked there for so long, and he always kept cookies for the dogs." Leigha slapped her hand on the table dramatically and leaned forward. "Maya, you have to keep dog cookies at the post office. Greta will be devastated if she doesn't get her treat when we pick up the mail."

I placed my hand over Leigha's. "Tell Greta not to stress. Burt left me a Costco-sized bag of Mini Milk Bones. The tradition will live on."

I was excited about my new part-time job as Postmaster for Claryce Falls. It meant a small, steady income to supplement my freelance graphic design work, and it would still leave me time to do my own art. I guess now that Jess wouldn't be around, it also meant spending more time with creatures who answered back. I loved hanging with my dog Clover, but her small talk needed work.

Leigha pushed a stack of napkins at me wordlessly, asking me to clean her daughter. But when I turned Libby to face me, she launched a counterattack. Her tiny red hands cupped my cheeks, smearing sticky goop across my face.

I grimaced, and Libby burst into giggles.

"That's it, Missy," Leigha said, scooping her up from my lap. "You're coming with me to wash up." Small kicking legs scissored behind Leigha as she maneuvered Libby around sports fans yelling at the screens.

Dave, momentarily snapped out of his football-induced trance by their departure, looked past me and his face lit up. He waved someone over. I dipped a napkin in my water glass and wiped at my ketchup-smeared cheeks.

"Owen, you all settled in yet?" Dave pushed the chair out next to me with his foot.

"I can make coffee and brush my teeth now, so I'm in the home stretch." A deep, easygoing voice answered from above.

I glanced up and did a double-take, like an honest to goodness double take. The guy was pretty, real pretty, but in a manly sort of way that reeked of splitting wood and mechanical competence. To my absolute horror, a huge grin spread across my face. I tried to stop it, or at least temper it into something less Joker-like and more Martha Stewart, cool and welcoming. Really, I'd settle for anything other than this insane-clown facial paralysis. The guy was an annoying cliché in his tall, dark mane, and blue-eyed handsomeness. Frankly, I disappointed myself for succumbing so easily.

Look away! I commanded myself. Just look away!

"Maya, this is Owen Reece. He's the new head forest ranger for Kittitas County. He moved into a place off Driftwood Bay, near you, a couple months ago. Owen, this is a good friend of ours, Maya Ridgeway."

"Nice to meet you," he barely glanced my way as he took the seat next to me. But my condiment-coated cheeks had him doing the double take now. "You've got a little something right here," he said, motioning with his index finger to his entire face.

Covering my deep mortification with sarcasm, I feigned surprise. "Really?" I turned to Dave and asked, "Why didn't you tell me my face was covered with your child's ketchup handprints? I wonder how long I've been wandering around like this without anyone mentioning it until now." I wiped at my nose, the only condiment-free spot on my face. "Did I get it?" I asked Owen, making sure I didn't make direct eye contact.

"Yep, you got it," he deadpanned.

"Thanks. It's good to know you're the 'you've got spinach in your teeth' sort of guy." I rubbed at my cheeks again with the napkin in earnest this time.

"Count on it," he said with a brief polite smile. Turning back to Dave, his expression went serious. "Actually, I was hoping to talk to you about a work matter. I'm sorry to bring it up on your day off, but do you have a few minutes?"

Dave nodded. "What's on your mind?"

Owen leaned in across the table. "I found the remains of another two elk up the Teanaway Forest yesterday near Mammoth Rock." He tapped the tips of his long fingers rapidly on the tabletop. "It looks like someone processed them somewhere else and dumped the bones and hides up there. That makes six this week."

Dave let out a low whistle of surprise, and he pushed back in his chair. "Six? Really? That many?"

Owen nodded, his jaw clenched. "Yeah, they're getting pretty bold. I want to keep a close eye on the area, but I'll be in Sandstone Creek prepping for a prescribed burn tomorrow. I talked with Russ over at Fish and Game too, but you know how stretched everyone is these days. Do you think maybe you could run somebody up to take a look?"

Dave nodded slowly. "I'll try and send a patrol. Let me know if you see anything else and I'll keep you posted."

Owen's shoulders seemed to relax, and he thanked Dave.

Angel made his way over to our table, setting another Coke down in front of me and a beer in front of Owen. I wasn't going to sleep for a week if I kept sucking these down.

Owen glanced up at Angel. "I didn't order this."

Angel looked back at him wordlessly.

"Another one?" Owen growled.

"Courtesy of the ladies at the other end of the bar this time."

The three of us turned to where Angel pointed towards two women in their early thirties. The one with straight, blonde hair gave an exaggerated wink and finger wiggle as if playing the part of a woman of loose virtues in a silent film. It seemed I wasn't the only one who thought Owen was a pretty man pony. Neither of the women looked familiar, and their casual clothes hung well with the ease of city money.

"Your fan club?" I asked sarcastically.

"Evidently, part of them. The women around here are…" his voice trailed off as he searched for the right word. "Very friendly," he finished politely.

"They look like Moon River weekenders," Dave guessed. Moon River was the nearby resort eight miles outside of town. People from planned communities in Seattle and Bellevue drove an hour and a half over the mountain pass to stay at Moon River Resort, another planned community of luxury rental homes, where they could golf and swim in the resort's pool surrounded by nature.

In addition to folks from Moon River, the town was always popular in the summer with the outdoorsy crowd. I understood the draw. Claryce Falls sat at the base of the Cascade Mountains surrounded by hundreds of miles of accessible hiking, biking, and horse trails. Quaint local businesses fronted by original eighteen-nineties western facades formed the heart of the town's historic four-block downtown.

"You want it?" Owen gestured at the beer towards Dave. "I'm heading home soon."

"No, we're gonna go as soon as Leigha gets back."

"Mia?" Owen tilted the beer towards me.

My indignation flared again. On any other day, I may have politely corrected him, like a normal person, but this was today. My tenderized ego had taken its last swipe for the night. And Mr. Blue Eyes was suddenly a lot less attractive. "It's MaYA. As in My, YA seem charming and oh, so memorable."

"Or, My, YA are so gracious when people mess up your name," Owen quipped back.

"Now, you've got it." Deciding to punctuate the point with a dramatic exit, I picked up the beer, tipped it at him, and took a swig. Then I stood. "Owen, welcome to Claryce Falls." Nodding towards the women at the bar, I added, "I hope our small-town friendliness doesn't drive you away." To Dave, I said, "I'm going to go check on the girls."

In the bathroom, Leigha was rolling a long stream of paper towels back up while Libby repeatedly flushed the toilet in an open stall. Wordlessly, Leigha tore off a towel and ran it under the water for me to get the remaining ketchup off my face. The toilet flushed again. "Do you think the Gremlin King will take her back?" Leigha asked as she rounded to grab her daughter.

"Not a chance." I wiped at my face. "He knows she's destined to lead the revolution."

Two

I felt like a perfectly toasted English muffin lying in bed listening to Clover's light snores. Contentment warmed my bones from the inside out. It was one of those magical mornings when I woke with the early spring sun, fully rested, twenty minutes before the alarm. The coos of doves fluttered through the open window on the crisp air. I curled my legs around my dog and ran my fingers through her fur, careful to leave as much of it attached as possible. Clover, my Husky/Australian mix, was almost perfect except for two things. She shed like a furry confetti cannon, and every day was the fourth of July. She was also a dog with strong opinions. Once judged, you were either friend or foe and if found lacking, there was no appeal for the condemned.

I stretched, releasing a power yawn, and threw back the mottled plum-colored duvet I had attempted to ombre dye. My sweats lay at the ready in a pile beside the bed for easy dressing.

Outside, I cinched my hood tighter against the chill. My feet on the compacted dirt road kept a steady drum beat to the morning melody of bird calls and wind. We walked down the driveway towards a nearby logging road to get in a three-mile walk. My plan was to exhaust Clover so she'd sleep while I was gone. Fueled by first-day jitters, our leisurely stroll turned into a fist-pumping, heavy-breathing power walk.

Even with a long shower, after I finished getting ready, I still had forty-five minutes before work. I decided to ride Broomhilda, my old, but much-loved Trek bike, to work.

I pedaled through the hazy smoke from my neighbor Mr. Dibbon's perpetually smoldering burn pile, his apparent retirement project. It was a mystery how one man had so much to incinerate. Two miles down the road, I veered off the pavement onto the gravel recreation trail leading into Claryce Falls.

The path was a former coal rail line from the nineteen hundreds. Converted into a recreational trail in the eighties, it now acted as a primary artery connecting Claryce Falls with two adjacent towns. In the winter, people used the trail for cross-country skiing and snowmobiling, and in the summer, cyclists, dog walkers, and horseback riders shared the path. The elementary school on the left of the trail signaled my arrival into town. Broomhilda's tires creased the damp grass of the ball field, and I waved at Kinsey, who was opening May's Café for breakfast.

Broomhilda coasted to a stop outside the post office. As I entered the lobby, I struggled to maneuver my bike through the door, unclasp my helmet, and peel the sweat-glued curls off my cheeks. I was so preoccupied with multitasking, I didn't notice the man standing in the corner with his arms crossed, glaring at me.

"It's about time you showed up," he growled.

I emitted an embarrassingly loud, high-pitched shriek. "Burt," I gasped. "What are you doing here?"

"The real question is, why weren't you here?"

I glanced up at the large institutional black and white clock on the wall, seven forty-five. "It's not eight yet, Burt, so I think my question still stands. Saturday was your last day, right?"

"It was. But I drove by this morning to make sure you had everything in hand, and you weren't here."

"Again, Burt, it's still early, but if I don't get back there and change, I will be late." I squeezed past him and unlocked the door to the backrooms. I left Broomhilda in the small yellow kitchen and went down the hall to get cleaned up in the closet-sized bathroom. Back up the hall, I unlocked the steel door securing the mail office from the rest of the building.

The post office was in the town's original mercantile. It was cobbled together from a series of rooms connected by a narrow hallway. The former storefront housed the lobby with the mailboxes, drop-off mail slots, service counter window, and the large cork notice board, which served as the communication hub of Claryce Falls. The lobby was never locked, allowing people to collect their mail when they could. In the winter, school buses also used the P.O. as a pickup spot so kids could wait inside and stay warm. The back of the building, now home to the Unitarian church, used to be the shop's storeroom. It had its own entrance but shared the bathroom and kitchen with the post office.

When I rolled up the metal service counter window at seven fifty-eight, like a persistent wart, Burt was still irritatingly there. He stood at attention in his crisp, blue button-up shirt and neatly trimmed beard, but now he had a cup in his hand. He carried the aroma of newly brewed coffee with him from the kitchen.

"I always arrived at seven-thirty. It gave me time to make coffee and look at the paper. That way you have something to talk to folks about," he schooled.

Turning my back to him, I rolled my eyes. I decided to pretend like he wasn't there and just get on with my job. I pulled the bag of letters and boxes left by the Hillsburg postal hub from the drop box. The mail got sorted first thing every morning in between helping people at the counter.

"You didn't put out the bell," Burt called.

After another eye roll, I decided it wasn't worth arguing over and walked around the corner to place the small metal push bell on the counter.

"Don't forget the sign," Burt commanded.

In silent annoyance, I reached under the counter and set the small sign reading, "I'm in back. Ring for help" next to the bell. It was all an unnecessary ceremony. The place was so small you could hear a fly sniffle. "Burt, you do know retirement means you don't have to come to work anymore?"

"I wanted to make sure you didn't have any problems."

My annoyance warred with my appreciation of his sweet and unwanted thoughtfulness.

"I'll read the paper to you while you work." He made a shooing motion with his hand, taking my silence as agreement, started with the page one headline.

"Blaze Ravages Local Residence. A fire Sunday evening destroyed Linda Thornston's Barn. Thornston, who runs a goat and you-pick berry farm outside Hillsburg, was out feeding her animals when the fire started." Burt looked up. "I don't know why anyone keeps goats. They eat everything, and they're tricky little stinkers. Alpacas, those would be the thing to raise." He started reading where he'd interrupted himself. "Thornston, originally from Lewiston, WA, called 911..." In this manner, Burt plowed through the Hillsburg Times, reading three or four lines of an article, stopping to add commentary, then continuing on. "How you coming back there?" he called after the third article.

"Doing good," I hollered back. At nine, my first patron came in.

I was rounding the corner when Burt tapped the bell. "Customer," he called as if I couldn't see the short, sprightly older woman in flower overalls.

"Burt, what are you doing hanging out on this side?" she asked, setting a box on the counter.

"I retired."

"Did you now?" She gave him an assessing look. "What are you doing here, then?" She slapped his forearm playfully in an exaggerated 'you rascal' gesture.

What a great question, I thought.

"It's Maya's first day, and I wanted to keep an eye on her. You know she was almost late today. First day on the job and everything." He winked at her.

"I was not." My defensiveness made my words spikier than intended, and the lady raised her eyebrows.

"You're going to get yourself in trouble if you aren't careful," she joked.

"Purdy, have you met Maya yet?"

Purdy and I exchanged greetings, and I complimented her on her denim. She posted her package to Alaska, then Burt updated her on the local news highlights. She took it in with the rapt attention of an owl tracking a mouse.

The rest of the morning ran in a steady trickle of customers, with Burt's stream of banter on repeat. I reached my breaking point when George Bentler left after purchasing a sheet of Chief Standing Bear stamps.

"Burt," I tried to sound firm. "Stop telling people I was almost late. I wasn't, and it makes me look bad."

"Don't be late, then I won't tell people."

"I wasn't late," I growled and went back to sorting in a huff. But he didn't mention my near tardiness to anyone again.

At eleven-thirty, Burt put the paper in the recycling bin. "I think you got it covered today. I'm heading out," he announced.

With his imminent departure, I felt a little more gracious and thanked him for keeping me company. The last thirty minutes were a rush of customers, then poof, it was noon, and my first official day as Claryce Falls' new Postmaster was over.

In celebration, I decided to treat myself to a fancy coffee and a new book from Rustic Reads and Perks before I biked home. Rustic Reads and Perks sold hiking guides, outdoor adventure books, and discounted literature titles, pairing them with a coffee bar and a couple of long communal tables. The place was a favorite for book clubs and community group meetings. As I sipped on my latte, I eavesdropped on a couple of resort weekenders. They flipped through the hiking guides and discussed activity options for the week. She wanted to take a glassblowing class at Flameworks Glass Studios.

"You should do it," he said, clearly not interested. "While you do that, I'll take the guy at the Pro Shop up on his offer and go target shooting."

She disagreed. They were supposed to be doing more things together, after all. I never found out who won because I got distracted by a book and lost interest in them.

I settled on Fuzz: When Nature Breaks the Laws by Mary Roach. She was a science humor writer and always good for a laugh. Book in my backpack and latte in hand, I walked out to release Broomhilda shackled outside of Barber & Bark, the men's barbershop and dog grooming salon. In Claryce Falls, it was a fiscal necessity for businesses to cultivate a multiple personality disorder. Leigha ran Glamour Nails & Boogie out of her backyard studio. She did nails on Monday and Tuesday, aired out the building for a day, and taught Country Zoomba workouts on Thursdays and Fridays. Then there was Wade's Bait Shop and Taxes and the Hummingbird Inn and Café. Even

Provisions in the Pines, our local grocery store, sold chicks and chicken feed in the back.

Latte still in my grip, I mounted Broomhilda and headed up the trail for home. As I rode, I cycled through my morning. Any lingering irritation with Burt blew off and dissolved into the shimmering shadows of the quaking aspen leaves. I imagined the hole it would leave to do something for nearly twenty years and then one day be expected to just stop doing it. Without things to keep a person busy, no matter how much you loved living in Claryce Falls, the solitude of the woods could get lonely.

I listed my day's accomplishments and mentally high-fived myself for acing my adulting today. Steering my bike with my knees, I sat up to sip on my latte. I hadn't ridden Broomhilda since last summer, so I gave myself another high-five for my amazing bike skills.

But as someone wise or a sailor, or a wise sailor once said, "Pride is the wind that fills the sails of a ship and also the storm that capsizes it." Suddenly, I was airborne, sailing free of my vessel, over my handlebars, across the dirt, and skidding on my belly. I groaned, assessing my damage. Nothing seemed broken or sprained. Gravel was embedded into my palms, I ripped the left knee of my jeans, and my white t-shirt was wearing my remaining latte. I stood up with the confidence of a newborn foal in roller skates. Feeling sorry for myself, I picked the gravel out of my hands and hobbled over to Broomhilda. Her front wheel was flat. I let loose a long, colorful stream of curse words involving mothers, ducks, and illegitimate children. It made me feel better, so I tried it again, releasing an even longer string. It worked, and I was ready to try making my way home.

As I limped along the side of the road, an unfamiliar white truck pulled up next to me. What the heck now? I thought.

The window rolled down, and a perky chihuahua poked its head out to stare at me curiously. A familiar blue-eyed male face leaned into view. I cringed and let out another string of curses. It didn't work this time.

"You need some help? Looks like you had an accident," Owen said, not bothering to hide his amusement.

I stared back at his forehead, waiting for my childhood wish for powers of invisibility to finally manifest themselves. I took a long breath and let it out. Since my powers didn't seem to be forthcoming, I nodded. "Looks that way," I said flatly.

"You have a... You've got a little something here." He gestured to his torso.

I looked down at the enormous tan stain on my t-shirt. Yep, I looked every inch the disaster I felt. But I was stubborn if not tidy, and I would not show my embarrassment. I stuck to my stoic shtick. "Looks that way," I repeated.

Owen put his truck into gear and started driving away. Relief battled with outrage. What a jerk. The guy was going to leave me here to eat his dust. But before I could get myself too worked up, his truck pulled to the side of the road. Owen got out and walked back. He took Broomhilda from me and put her in his truck bed as I stood mutely watching him.

"Come on, I'll give you a ride home, MyYA," he said, emphasizing the last syllable of my name, clearly a reference to our exchange last night.

I limped to the passenger side, feeling resentful for needing aid. I waited for Owen to move the little dog hanging out the window before getting in. The dog yipped and jumped onto my lap, intensely sniffing my shirt.

"This is Fizzy," Owen said. "She doesn't understand personal space."

I scratched the little runt's head. "Looks that way," I smirked.

Owen gave me a lopsided half-grin, and dang if it didn't just make bad worse. No one had the right to be so stupidly appealing. Seriously, it made me want to take a magic marker to his face, blacken a couple of teeth, and give him an unibrow. Maybe glue some fake hair in his ears, just to even the playing field. Ugh. Fizzy put her paws on my shoulder and gave me a lick on the face. She knew what I was talking about. I patted her butt.

"I don't know where I'm going," Owen prompted.

"Right," I shook myself out of my sulk and gave him directions.

Minutes later, we were sitting in my driveway. Just looking at my little moss green house with its single-slant roof made my body relax. I got out and went to the door to let a very vocal Clover out. Her excited whine went to level eleven when she saw Fizzy. "She's good with other dogs if you want to let your dog out."

Owen opened the truck door and set Fizzy on the ground. She charged Clover and abruptly stopped. Her tiny head moved like a Pez Dispenser, kicking out barks. Clover looked at her curiously, then at me for permission to approach. The two postured for a few minutes and took off chasing each other like old buddies. As the dogs played, Owen unloaded my bike. I offered him a beer to be polite, expecting him to decline, and was shocked when he accepted.

I opened my fridge to look for beer I knew wouldn't be there. "Um, I'm out," I called. "But I can make a margarita."

"That seems like a lot of work. I should probably head out."

He gave me an out, but generations of gendered social conditioning had me reassuring him that it was no bother, instead of just keeping my mouth shut and feeling grateful he wouldn't be staying.

There was a long pause from outside. "Why not? I don't have anything else going on this afternoon," Owen finally said.

"You do know how to make a person feel special," I quipped. "Keep an eye on the dogs while I clean up real quick, will you?"

I ran into my bedroom, swapping my disaster clothes for clean jeans and a cotton henley. I grabbed my flip-flops and glanced in the decorative portal mirror. "Oh, no." I was an electrocuted chia pet. My wavy dark bob stuck out like a drunken octopus, and a bruise had started to form on my chin. I tried smoothing my hair down and gave up after my fourth attempt.

Humming Que Sera Sera, I mixed us margaritas on the rocks. "Let's go sit in the back," I said, handing Owen his glass. I watched him silently check out my art as we walked through my living room. A few of the pieces I had done, while others were paintings by friends or from a small community gallery in my old Seattle neighborhood.

I winced as I lowered myself into the lawn chair. The weight of the day pulled heavily on my limbs.

"What happened to you today?" Owen asked

"A story as old as time," I sighed dramatically, looking off into the yard. "Bicycle showboating and lattes, a lethal combination best left to circus folk and Portland hipsters." Now that I was clean and not in too much pain, I felt ashamed of my earlier surliness. "By the way, thanks for the ride. You saved me from a miserable walk home." I paused. "You know, the day started out so good, then I got to work and it didn't go the way I thought it would." And without prompting or even the slightest expression of interest from Owen, I let roll a full recounting of my Burt-filled morning.

When I finished, we sat in silence watching the dogs play. The embarrassment of oversharing started to knot in my stomach. I glanced at Owen, hoping for some kind of reaction, and saw he was definitely having one. His face was pink, and his body shook slightly.

Rolling my eyes, I groaned, "For heaven's sake, just let it out."

With permission granted, he burst into loud laughter. The single tear sliding down his face made me giggle. When I snorted, the dogs stopped and stared at me in shocked stupefaction. It put me over the edge, and I laughed like a demented hyena until I was holding my stomach in pain and feared peeing my pants. I tried to calm down, taking long, deep breaths and making short "who who who" Lamaze noises when I exhaled. There would not be any more embarrassing accidents for Owen to witness today.

"I think I was a kid the last time I laughed that hard." Owen wiped at his eyes.

"I'm glad my pain can bring you so much joy."

"You really are a piece of work." He shook his head at me.

I didn't know if I liked being a piece of work or not. "You have a lapdog," I accused him. I knew I was being petulant, and yet, I couldn't seem to stop myself. "What kind of manly forest ranger has a chihuahua?"

Owen sobered. "The kind of guy whose girlfriend buys a chihuahua. Besides, there's nothing wrong with Fizzy. She's full of spirit, and I like that."

I couldn't argue with the last point. And of course, Owen had a girlfriend. It was oddly a relief, somehow taking the pressure off. Changing the topic, I asked him how he was settling in. He told me about work, a little more about the poached elk, and how he was trying to track down shed-invading raccoons. Conversation came easily. I even succeeded in making direct eye contact a couple of times without my insides flipping over. At this rate, Owen Reece and I might just become friends.

The next day after work, I picked up Clover and the invitational postcards for the Moon River Golf Tournament. I opened the sunroof and windows as we cruised down the sunny road. Before the resort turnoff, three whitetail deer tranquilly ate grass from the manicured landscaping. I slowed the car to a crawl. "Deer," I whispered.

Clover went rigid. She stuck her head out the window and lost her ever-loving mind. There would be no finding it again until the deer were long out of sight. Instead of trying to quiet her, I joined in, cheering her on. I fully admit we both have a problem. Though the way I figured it, I was also providing a valuable reminder to the wildlife. Stay vigilant. Life is always dangerous if you're a deer.

We waved to the gate guard and wound our way down a paved road through multi-million dollar vacation homes designed to blend in with the natural rustic setting. I followed the signs through the warren of carefully curated parks, walking trails, and wine shops. Moon River Resort was a self-contained community of the visiting wealthy, and one I was happy for them to keep all to themselves. Even though it was on the outskirts of town, it felt like a world apart, which I suppose was the point.

In front of the Pro Shop, two guys in golf carts attempted donuts in the damp grass. I parked Nell under a fir tree and got out to watch their stunt driving. On a particularly spirited turn, one of the drivers cut the angle wrong and the entire cart teetered on one set of wheels, threatening to roll over. When the little vehicle righted itself, both guys hooted and drove towards each other, leaning out to swap passing fist-bumps. I decided to leave them to it and headed for the Pro Shop. As I got closer, they stopped their trick driving and turned to watch me. I waved, and both drivers started up, heading towards me.

"Hi, you Maya?" asked the one in the blue polo shirt and black cap as he pulled up. Both guys were good-looking in the way all healthy people in their twenties are.

"Yep, I have the invitational postcards for the tournament to drop off."

"I'm glad it was you and not one of the guests. I'm Jay."

"And I'm Peter," announced the other, pulling up on my other side. He ran his hand through his wavy blond hair. "You want a ride? I could take you for a spin." He gave me a mischievous smile.

"As tempting as the offer is, I prefer my donuts with coffee, more sugar buzz, and less motion sickness."

"Things get a little slow around here midweek." He winked in acknowledgment of being caught fooling around. "Sometimes we have to liven things up a bit."

The guys parked their carts and joined me in front of the shop. Jay, the one in the blue polo shirt, was a much bigger guy than he seemed sitting down. Over six feet, he was built for heavy lifting. Peter was lankier, and if the flare he used to open the door for me was an indicator, quite the aspiring ladies' man.

Inside, Prospector's Pro Shop was an ostentatious treasure trove of golfing merchandise. Its array of titanium clubs, outrageously priced argyle sweaters, and polo shirts in hues of a psychedelic Nantucket sunset, all made promises to compensate for any skills a golfer may lack. I set the box of postcards on the counter.

"These are lit," Jay said, pulling a card from the box.

"Thanks, I'm pretty happy with how they turned out, too."

The resort hosted an annual golf tournament in June. This was the second year I was doing the design for the event's invitations, posters, and t-shirts. I liked working with the resort manager, Elby. She was easy to collaborate with, and it was nice to have local clients.

"Elby said she would leave a check for me here."

Jay cursed. Elby forgot to leave it before she went on vacation, and she wouldn't be back for a week and a half. He offered to run it by my place when she got back.

"You can drop it off at the post office. I work mornings there. So, any time before noon." I tried to temper my irritation. It wasn't Jay's fault after all. It was, however, a good thing I wasn't counting on the money for something.

"Okay, I'll do it as soon as she's back."

I made a mental note to call and remind Elby. "See you then."

Before I made it to the door Peter stopped me. "You sure I can't interest you in a ride?" He gave me a huge, toothy grin.

"Thanks, but I prefer bigger, um, vehicles," I smiled back.

"I've got an old Silverado, extended cab. Plenty of room in there," he called as the door shut behind me.

Three

"A ttention Littering Bastards" jumped boldly from the flier. "I'm sorry, but you can't hang that in here," I informed the woman clenching her jaw. I glanced again at the paper on the counter and caught the phrase, "Die in a Pit of Your Own Filth." Below the text, a stick figure lay flattened under a mountain of meticulously labeled Miller Lite cans. Its eyes crossed out. Death by lite beer really was tragic.

"Why not? It's a public notice board." She glared at my forehead, and I wondered if I'd accidentally worn my breakfast muffin as a hat. Personally, I loved the flier. It had a strong point of view, a clear message, and the graphics fit the theme. But as a United States Federal Postal Employee, I couldn't let her hang it.

Burt, who walked in moments earlier, stood sentinel in the entry. "There are rules, Janet." He pointed to a laminated paper on the board.

The woman, or Trash Trooper Janet as I decided to affectionately dub her, pushed green glasses up her Roman nose in preparation for an exhaustive regulatory review. She stalked to the board and read aloud, "No profanity. No defamatory language. No political messages. And absolutely no postings of Bigfoot sightings unless accompanied by clear photographic evidence and a sworn affidavit from a sober witness. Oh," she said. "I did not realize that. I'll make a new flier and come back." She collected her paper off the counter and abruptly exited, her graying braids whipping out like the quills of a determined porcupine.

Burt looked at me and shrugged his shoulders. "I brought donut holes," he said in a chipper voice. Luckily, the federal government also had strict rules regarding food at the service counter, so Burt went to the kitchen to eat his pastries and leave me in peace.

The P.O. was only open for two hours on Saturdays, so I hustled to get the post sorted in between customers. I just finished when Libby and Greta blew into the lobby, a hurricane of high-pitched shrieks and barks. Leigha burst in after them, pulling her mother in tow.

"Guess where I found the car keys this morning?" Leigha challenged. "In Greta's dog food bowl, covered in wet kibble."

Since this was one of Libby's staple hiding spots, the real mystery was Leigha's surprise. However, an even bigger shocker was Greta's superpower of dodging choking hazards.

The action drew Burt in from the kitchen, and he held out his hand to me. "Cookie, if you will?"

I compliantly handed over the small milk bone.

"Do you want to give Greta the cookie?" Burt asked Libby, bending down.

She stuck out her arm and the goods swapped hands again.

"Burt, you remember my mother, Carol?" Leigha asked.

"Of course I do." Burt beamed at her. "It's so nice to see you again. How long are you in town for? I hope it will be a long visit." Burt sounded smooth, a little too smooth.

Scrutinizing their exchange, I realized Burt had the hots for Leigha's mom. Even odder, she seemed to like it. I blinked, trying to see them objectively. Carol, not as Leigha's mom or Libby's grandmother, but as the energetic, silver-haired, glitz-loving, sweet woman she was.

As for Burt, it was harder. I struggled not to see an old barnacle with a distressing lack of hobbies. I guess he could be someone's idea of a catch if the fishpond hadn't been stocked for the season. He maintained impeccable hygiene, a straight spine, and some of his hair, even if most of it was on his face. He gave cookies to children and dogs and stayed abreast of the latest news.

Burt asked if we were headed to the market, and before I could spit out some sort of "ladies-only" anti-invite, he was already browsing the first stall with us. To be fair, the market started right outside the post office on Main Street, and my mouth hadn't moved fast enough. Still early in the season, the farmers market only ran for two blocks. By late June though, with the addition of fresh produce, live music, and the adjoining Army and Girl Scout recruitment tents, it would stretch to fill the entire four blocks of downtown Claryce Falls. By then, the event drew crowds, like Alan Jackson fans to a Stetson sale. People flocked to the market to cram in as much nostalgic small-town quaintness as they could get in their baskets.

Luckily, since the wares were still limited to handicrafts, dehydrated meats, and things in jars, the crowding season hadn't started yet. We strolled under the cool spring sun, chatting with vendors, trying samples, and slurping up every last drop of fun.

"Oooh, Buuurt," a voice called from the crowd. "I got something with a little bite you might like."

I cringed at the brazenly blurted double entendre. Flower overall-wearing, Purdy stood behind her table of pickles like a naughty circus barker. Her tent banner read "Purdy Good Pickles." She waved us over, holding out chunks of pickles on toothpicks. "I remember you like the ones with chili flakes in the brine," she wiggled her eyebrows, as smooth as a buttered prune.

Burt took two of the sticks and handed one to Carol.

"The heat is a little too much for me." She fanned her mouth frantically. "But I love the 'Take me away Caraway', with the extra caraway and mustard seeds."

And being the Don Juan in orthopedic shoes he was revealing himself to be, Burt immediately sampled the same flavor and agreed with Carol.

"When did you start selling your pickles at the market?" Burt asked Purdy.

"This is my second time. I'm having a little disagreement with the tax man. He seems to think I owe him money. I don't. To be safe, I thought it'd be a good idea to bring in a little extra cash."

Burt bought two jars of caraway pickles and gave one to Carol. "A welcome-to-town gift."

We pressed on, stopping Carol from buying a rustic wood sign with a porch swing and "Front porch charm, back door welcome" painted on it.

"But it looks just like your porch," Carol tried to cajole Leigha into letting her buy it.

"Mom, I don't want to advertise the charms of my back door," she said, taking the sign and hanging it back up.

I snickered and Carol looked confused. "Leigha will explain later," I stage whispered.

"Out shopping for decorations for your future new home?" an unfamiliar voice behind me purred.

"Chris, hello." A well-groomed man in his early forties stood next to Carol, exuding feigned professional warmth.

His side part looked like it had been measured with a level and held in place with expensive spackling. "Maya, this is Chris Weller. Chris has been showing me properties in the area."

Chris held out his well-moisturized hand. His overly buffed nails made me shudder, but I took his hand anyway and shook it vigorously. I didn't like what my aversion to men with soft hands said about me.

"Found anything promising yet?" I asked pleasantly as I covertly wiped my hand against my jeans.

"There is one I really liked," Carol admitted.

"But we're still early days. I have several beautiful properties to show you before you get your heart set on anything yet," Chris cut in. It seemed odd a realtor would be discouraging a client's enthusiasm.

"I know," Carol said. "But I'm a woman who knows her mind."

"I bet you are." He smiled, but his tone didn't make it sound like a compliment.

I saw Libby reaching for a jar at the next stall and quickly ran to intercept. After that, Libby and I plowed through the next couple of vendors, leaving a sticky trail of jam fingerprints in our wake. We lingered at the goat cheese stand, where the ruddy-cheeked cheesemonger, named Linda, entertained us with stories. Apparently, Miss MaeMae, the goat, and Hillary, the chicken, got into her idling truck. The two knocked it into gear and went joyriding around the pasture. She was just getting to the part where her ranch hand, Jorge, jumped in the slow-moving Dodge when she suddenly stopped.

"Carol Livingston, is that you?"

We all turned to Carol, who blinked back at the woman in confusion.

"Yes," Carol answered, dragging out the word, "but it's Carol Miller now. Sorry, how do we know each other?"

Linda's face lit up as she explained they were high school friends. In no time, they were deep in a game of 'Do you remember so-and-so?' like no time had passed.

Finally, Burt, who was twitching with suppressed inquisitiveness, couldn't stand it any longer and jumped in. "Are you the Thornston whose barn burned down?"

Linda's face clouded. "Unfortunately, yes. But it could have been so much worse." Linda quickly reassured us. "We were lucky. No one was hurt, but the barn and all my cheese-making equipment were destroyed."

"What are you going to do?" Carol asked, her brow furrowing as she leaned in.

Linda said the insurance would cover all of it, but the previously jovial mood was gone.

Libby pulled at my hand. We both wanted to move again. "Who's ready for lunch?" I asked, trying to create a natural transition out of the impending awkwardness.

"Me," called Libby like a good little partner in crime.

"What do you say we go get some tacos from the taco truck?" Leigha asked our group.

"Lunch is on me!" Carol called. The two women said their goodbyes, and we filed off in search of food.

"You know, that's the craziest thing about Linda's barn," Carol mused when we were out of her hearing range. "When we were in high school, her family's dairy burned down. There was gossip her stepfather set fire to it for the insurance money. But who really knows? People didn't like him very much. It was probably all talk."

"But still, what are the odds?" Burt mumbled, wrinkling in speculation like a curious Shar Pei.

When Carol went to pay for lunch, she realized she was missing her basket with her wallet. I volunteered to run back and look for it. Luckily, she'd left it at Linda's stall. And moments later, I returned triumphantly, holding the woven container high in victory.

"Where did you find it?" Carol asked, taking it from me and peering inside.

"It was still sitting on the ground under Linda's table. Everything there?"

Carol quickly dug through it. "What's this?" She pulled out a folded piece of paper. Scrawled in blue ballpoint pen was a message, "Keep away from what isn't yours or else..."

"Sounds like an ominous fortune cookie," I said.

"I wonder where it came from?" Carol turned the paper over, looking for clues.

"Someone probably thought it was a wastebasket," Burt offered.

Carol looked offended on behalf of her cute basket with its polka dot scarf jauntily tied around the handle. She crumpled the note and tossed it in a real waste bin.

After lunch, Burt was just about to finally take his leave when Carol stopped him. "We're having a barbecue at Leigha's tomorrow around one o'clock. Do you want to come?"

Burt looked like he just won the all-around-cowboy prize at the Hillsburg rodeo. "I would love to. I've got some elk burger I got from Gary Becker's boy. I could grill up some good burgers with it."

Leigha easily included Burt in the plans and assured him they had the food covered. She shot me a quick look that said, 'I'm sorry, but she's my mom. What are you going to do?'

I sent her a look that just said, 'Traitor.' Still, watching the bounce in Burt's step, I almost felt guilty for my annoyance. But Sunday was my only day off, and the only Burt-free day I should be guaranteed. Now I'd be spending even more quality time with him. I decided I came by my irritation honestly, so I'd enjoy it.

We parted ways, and I took a shortcut to fetch Broomhilda, cutting across the walkway in front of Flameworks Glass Studio. I jumped back to avoid being trampled by a couple as they pushed out of the building and onto the street. It was the same bickering pair I had seen at the bookstore the other day.

"I don't understand why you couldn't wait. We were almost done," the wife complained while her angry husband dragged her away.

They plowed through the crowd, and I imagined them when they first started dating and wondered how their relationship had unraveled. How did they go from individuals in love to a pair that seemed to barely tolerate each other?

I thought of Scott, my own ex-husband, and how much happier we both were now. Maybe they never belonged together either. I continued letting thoughts of the seemingly unhappy couple dissolve into the crowd.

Getting ready for the barbecue on Sunday morning felt like preparing for a role in The Lion King on Broadway. I bathed in a scented bubble bath, shaved my legs, blow-dried my hair, put makeup on, and even wore a dress. I didn't go all out very often. But like my Subaru Nell, after a dusty mountain drive, my dignity needed some detailing to prove I wasn't always a walking food stain.

My labor was instantly recognized on my arrival when Dave opened the front door and wolf whistled.

Leigha let out a cat call. "Wow, momma is looking gooooood!"

Fruit salad still in hand, I gave a little twirl. I arrived early to help with prep and started making a green salad and slicing vegetables for burgers. Leigha ferried food and plates from the house to the yard. On her restocking trips to the kitchen, we took mini breaks to dramatically sing along to the radio or show off our corny dance moves to each other. Dave often marveled at how we ever got anything done when we were together. But it was our system, and it worked for us.

I was singing along to a Zach Bryan tune, slicing the tops off strawberries, when I felt a buzzing in my body as someone entered. Out of the corner of my eye, I recognized Owen filling the door frame. Of course, Dave had invited him. I let out a resigned huff as if the universe had just delivered a very predictable punchline. Purposefully not turning, I continued decapitating berries as I sensed his progress across the room. He opened the fridge and pulled something out.

"Maya, is that you?"

The surprise in his voice didn't seem flattering. It reminded me of fairy tale transformations of frogs, and I wanted to flick a long, sticky tongue at him. I faced him and mimicked his tone, flipping his question back on him. "Owen, is that you?"

"You're wearing a dress and your hair's straight."

It was unclear from his declarative sentences if he thought this was good or bad. I put effort into my looks today. There should be no question about it.

"This is a fun game. My turn," I said sarcastically. "Owen, you're wearing jeans and a gray t-shirt. Now you. Do you want to tell me what shoes I'm wearing?"

"Sorry," he smiled sheepishly. "I hang out with trees all day. What I meant to say was, hi Maya, you're not covered in food. I didn't recognize you."

I gasped. "Bite your tongue." I pretended to spit on the floor and made vague crossing gestures as if warding away evil. "The afternoon is still young, and there are so many condiments in play today." I looked at the beer he pulled from the fridge. "Doesn't Dave have those outside?"

"You see the woman in the yellow dress there?" He pointed out the kitchen window to the backyard.

"Yeah, Emily Brady. She works at Provisions in the Pines. She's in Leigha's workout classes sometimes. What about her?"

"She keeps following me, giggling, and touching me. I'm hiding from her. Can I just stay in here with you where it's safe?"

For a brief moment I thought, poor guy, then I shook myself. I was feeling sorry for him because he was literally too sexy. I snorted.

"What's funny?"

"I have this image of you strutting down Main Street with 'I'm too sexy,' playing. All the single women of Claryce Falls are lined up and leaping out trying to catch you. They're throwing you love trinkets as you sidestep them." I picked up a carrot and started acting out the scene. I pretended to catch a rose from the air and sniffed it. Raising my foot high, I stepped over a woman who had thrown herself in front of me. "Ladies, please keep your apple pies. Sugar is bad for my pearly whites." I glided sideways, spinning out of reach. I raised my arms and pretended to catch and almost drop something heavy before setting it on the ground.

"What was that supposed to be?"

"A dog. Someone threw you their Rottweiler. It had bad gas, so you set it down."

He snorted. "Okay, okay, can I stay or not?"

I pushed a cutting board and knife in front of him. "Only if you cut the onions."

He picked up the knife and started slicing. "So, I met Burt," Owen said. "He seems like a nice enough guy."

"He is," I fully whined. "But he hung around the post office every day this week. On Friday, he didn't come in until ten-thirty, and I actually worried something happened to him." I gasped. "Do you think I'm developing Stockholm Syndrome?"

He chuckled. "No, but I do think you should talk to him."

I glared back. "I will just as soon as you tell the arm molester in the daisy dress out there to keep her mitts off your - manly forearms," I said the last bit in my best Arnold Schwarzenegger accent while mimicking weightlifter poses. Suddenly, inspiration struck. "I know. You fish, right?"

"Yeah," he answered warily.

"Why don't you ask Burt to take you out and show you some of his favorite fishing holes?"

Owen narrowed his eyes. "First, you don't ask a guy you just met to show you his favorite holes."

I burst out laughing like a twelve-year-old boy.

"Fishing holes," he amended. "Second, I have my own work crazies to deal with. This week, a woman came into the Forest Service office and dumped bags of garbage all over the reception area. She said we weren't cracking down on litterers, and she was going to keep coming back with the trash she picked up until we did something."

I felt the excitement of recognition. "Did she have braids and green glasses?"

"She did. You know her?" Owen sounded shocked.

"I think that's Trash Trooper Janet. She came into the post office today to hang a flier. She's definitely got her own style of doing things. I kind of like it. She's hard to ignore. But I don't know much about her. Burt seems to, though. We can ask him." I made an exaggerated motion of peering out the window. "If you stick close, I'll try and keep you safe from Emily. No promises if she has chocolate. I'm a woman whose favors are easily won. Grab that–" I motioned to the plate of sliced vegetables, and picking up the green salad, we walked outside.

Burt had Dave cornered at the grill. "But her stepfather torched their dairy farm for the insurance. It can't be a coincidence her barn caught fire now too. For all we know, she could have been behind the dairy arson back then, as well." He had obviously over marinated in yesterday's gossip.

"Burt, you can't go around accusing people of things you don't have proof of," Dave said. "A fire investigator is coming out from Seattle next week. If there's any funny business, and there's nothing to indicate there was, then he'll find it. In the meantime, I better not hear you spreading rumors about that poor woman. She's got enough on her plate without you stirring up more."

"Your steak is going to dry out," Burt pouted.

Even though I enjoyed seeing Burt set down, I decided to throw him a rope and interrupted. "Burt, what can you tell us about Trash Trooper Janet?"

"Who?" He looked confused.

"Janet, the lady who tried hanging the cursing litter flier."

"You mean Janet Jackson."

"No way," I gasped. "That's not her real name."

"Why's it so surprising?" Burt looked genuinely perplexed.

"Come on, Burt, even you must've heard of Janet Jackson, as in Michael Jackson's sister."

"Is that her name? Huh." He didn't seem impressed. "What do you want to know?"

Owen explained to the group about her antics at the Forest Service building and her promise to return.

"If she said it, then she will." Burt nodded sagely. "She's not like most folks if you catch my meaning."

"How so?" I asked, clearly not catching his meaning.

"She's got that asparagus. Makes her act a little funny - not great people skills. She gets stuck on things and can't seem to stop herself."

"Do you mean Asperger's?" Owen corrected.

"That's what I said."

"Close enough. How do I get her to stop?"

"Redirect her somehow. Give her a better solution to her problem and put it in logical steps."

I was impressed with Burt's insight, asparagus gaffe aside. Owen thanked him, and we went to check on the dogs.

They were locked in Libby's playhouse with her. Clover's nails were colored red and purple. But poor Fizzy had received the deluxe beauty package. Her face was a rainbow, reflecting the spectrum of the full marker pack. Libby stained her own cheeks and lips blue and purple.

"Leigha," I sang out. "Come here and bring your phone."

"What do you need, M?"

"Just come here, please."

I staged Libby and the dogs like a police lineup in a row.

"Libby, what have you done?" Leigha exclaimed.

"I made them pretty." Libby beamed.

"Photographic evidence," I said. "You can use this later as leverage when she's a teenager."

"We don't color on the doggies, Libby."

I looked down at Greta's professional doggie pedicure, which perfectly matched Leigha, Carol, and Libby's glitter nails. "I blame the mother." I pointed between Greta and Leigha's nails, shaking my head in mock disappointment.

"Owen, I am so sorry." Leigha groveled. "But don't worry, they're washable. It will come right out of Fizzy."

Owen chuckled. "It's alright. A little girl time is probably good for her. This is the most excitement Fizzy's had all week. I leave her alone so much, I feel bad for her."

I spoke up without thinking. "Why don't you drop her off at my house in the morning? Then she and Clover can keep each other company."

"You know, I wouldn't mind walking them with Greta on Mondays and Tuesdays morning." Carol offered. "Leigha's got to work, Libby's in preschool, and I need the exercise."

"Are you serious?" Owen looked back and forth between Carol and me. "If so, I would really appreciate it."

"Burt knows all the great walking trails around town." I offered. "I bet he'd show you." For a moment, things seemed to be looking up. I didn't have to worry about leaving Clover alone, and Burt would be too busy walking the dogs with Carol to bug me. Life felt pretty good just then, standing in the cool sun in my pretty dress - right up until I was hit. From behind. With something cold, and wet, and sticky. "What the heck?" I yelled as liquid soaked my backside.

"I am so sorry," Emily gushed from behind me, a now empty pitcher in hand. "I tripped."

I turned and faced the woman straight on. She looked about as sorry as a bear caught with a mouthful of trout, the triumphant gleam in her eyes betraying her contrition.

"What the heck?" I repeated.

"It was an accident. I don't know what happened. My heel must have caught in the grass."

"It's just a little bit of lemonade. It'll wash right out. No permanent damage done," Carol reassured her.

All my morning efforts, ruined. I stalked out of the back-yard, fighting my urge to push Emily over. Leigha offered to find me something to wear, but my mood would not tolerate shiny pastels.

When I rejoined the barbecue, I felt like an ambrosia salad that had been left out in the sun all afternoon. My new look, courtesy of the Goodwill donation bag in my car I kept forgetting to drop off, featured an oversized t-shirt that proudly proclaimed, 'Tough Titties'—complete with cartoon breasts in sweatbands flexing beefy arms and legs. I'd designed the shirt for a breast cancer fundraiser triathlon several years ago. With this I paired neon bike shorts from an old Halloween costume I'd also pulled from the bag.

"Wow," Owen said, taking in my ensemble. "Would you get mad if I said this seems more like you?"

I felt my cheeks heat. "Nope, definitely not making me feel better." I turned to walk away and was stopped by a pull on my shirt.

Owen gripped the edge, tenting my shirt between us. "Temper, temper," he mocked. "Don't be mad."

"This is your fault anyway. I told you not to jinx me," I shot back, glaring at him.

Dave joined us, cutting off Owen's protest. "The burgers and steaks are almost ready, but I've got to head out." His posture seemed stiff and alert, a dramatic change from the man grilling earlier.

"What happened?" Something was wrong.

"A hiker found a body up the Teanaway off one of the hiking trails."

"Who is it?"

"Want me to go with you?" Owen and I asked over each other.

"We don't know. And no. You both stay here. But don't mention it to the others. Only Leigha knows. Burt's manning the grill. Keep an eye on him and just try to enjoy yourselves."

We exchanged worried looks with Leigha as we rejoined the others. The smokey smells of the barbecue mingled with dark thoughts of death. I felt silly for being so angry over a wet dress. Here we were, together, lucky for each other's company. But the mood had shifted, and I couldn't shake the reminder that none of us were guaranteed a tomorrow.

Four

Nine hundred and ninety-eight bottles of beer on the wall had been taken down and passed around, as I happily hummed and soldered aluminum cans together. My day had been blissfully Burt-free, aside from his quick pit stop at the post office with Carol and the pups for dog biscuits.

Fizzy and Clover contentedly lay next to each other in a patch of sun. Everyone seemed happy with the new dog-walking arrangement. The pups were happy. Burt got to spend time with Carol, so he was happy. I didn't have Burt breathing down my neck, so I was happy. The new setup seemed to be a win-win for everyone.

In fact, my Burt-free morning had proven so inspirational that a brilliant solution to the Trash Trooper Janet problem came to me while sorting the morning's mail in peace. I was so excited by my idea, I'd started working on the prototype as soon as I got home.

The crunch of Owen's truck wheels on the driveway gravel startled the dogs and me. I hadn't realized so much time had passed. Clover and Fizzy jumped up, barking in excited greetings. I stood, stretching out my stiff back, and went to join the welcoming committee.

He shook his head when he saw me in my safety goggles and leather gloves. "Do I even want to know what you're up to?" he asked. He scooped up an ecstatic Fizzy, who tried to frantically lick his face.

"You really do want to know. In fact, you should be thanking me for saving you from Trash Trooper Janet and for being generally dazzling and a delight."

By the skeptical look on his face, no words of gratitude or praise seemed immediately forthcoming.

"Come into my laboratory and see what I'm creating." I explained my vision for the recycling project and how I wanted to coordinate its launch with the opening day of the restored Forest Service campground. And while he never came out and said it, I'm pretty sure Owen thought I was brilliant. At the very least, he seemed curious when I showed him my prototype. He wanted to know how I was holding everything together, so I gave him a demonstration.

"This looks kind of relaxing. If you've got another soldering iron, I could do a few of these with you."

"Who doesn't have a backup soldering iron?" I scoffed, handing him a pair of safety goggles.

He took a seat across from me. As I showed him how to tack cans together, I tried keeping as much physical distance between us as I could to prevent the buzzing sensation I felt when we got too close. I turned Afro-Cuban jazz on in the background, and we worked quietly until Fizzy reminded Owen it was well past her supper time. I closed up the shop and Owen headed out for the night.

The next morning, Burt burst into the P.O. lobby. "Maya, where are you?" he hollered.

I wondered if I'd forgotten to put the sign out again. "Calm down, I'm right here." I rounded the corner into view.

"Why isn't the bell out? Never mind. There's been another note."

"What are you talking about, Burt? Slow down."

"When Carol and I got back to the cars after the dog walk today, there was another threat like the one from the market. Someone put it under her wiper blade this time. There's no doubt it was meant for Carol."

"What did it say?"

He pulled out his phone and showed it to me. In the same blue ink as the previous threat, someone wrote, 'Ignore this at your own risk. Go home before it's too late.'

"Why would anyone threaten Carol? This has to be meant for someone else. It just doesn't make sense."

"Her name was written on the outside, Maya. Someone is trying to run her off. I won't stand by and let it happen. As Leigha's close friend, you shouldn't either. What kind of real friend are you anyway?"

"Hold on, when did I become the bad guy? You just told me about this."

"There's no room for excuses. I know who it is and you're going to help me prove it." Burt laid out his case. First, Carol knew Linda's father burned down her childhood dairy for insurance money. So, if Linda burned her barn down, Carol could make the connection. Second, there was Carol's market basket, where the first threat had been found under Linda's table, and third, there really wasn't another suspect.

I chalked my lapse in judgment up to the earnestness of Burt's concern and his promise of tasty snacks because two hours later, I was riding shotgun in his meticulously maintained, ninety-five Ford Ranger, headed to stake out Linda Thornston's farm.

"Clover, your breath smells like meatloaf." I pushed her panting muzzle out of my face. Burt insisted we bring the dogs for backup, but I still couldn't see how Fizzy was going to be much use in a hand-to-hand combat type of situation. Plus, I had to get Owen's number from Dave to let him know we'd drop Fizzy off when we got back to town. It felt awkward getting Owen's number from someone else, but I didn't want him showing up to an empty house. "Get over it," I muttered to myself and turned up "Jolene" on the cassette player, singing along to silence my anxious thoughts.

We exited the freeway, and I opened my window for the dogs to put their heads out. Even though Hillsburg was only a forty-minute drive from Claryce Falls, the landscape morphed dramatically from dense pine forests to a more arid landscape of sagebrush-covered rolling hills and farms irrigated by the Columbia River.

"You missed the turnoff again," I yelled as Burt passed the dirt road for the second time.

"There's a car up there. I don't want them to see us turn. It'll look suspicious."

"It looks more suspicious if we keep driving back and forth down the same quarter mile of road. Just turn already." I was hangry and the snacks were behind the seats where I couldn't reach them.

On the third pass, he made the turn. Our navigational choices were confirmed by the large, cheerily painted signs for, "You Pick Strawberries - This Way" and "Thornston Farms Goat Cheese a quarter mile. You're almost there." Now that we were nearing our target, I saw a couple of holes in our plan. The biggest one being, we didn't have one. When the farm was visible, I made Burt pull over behind a giant sign of a laughing goat with a wreath of strawberry blossoms around its neck.

"What are we doing here?" I asked Burt. "Are we just going to stroll up and ask, 'Hey Linda, are you leaving threats for Carol because you're scared she'll spill the beans about your childhood dairy burning down? And then everyone will connect the dots and figure out you set your own barn on fire?'" Saying it out loud, I felt how flimsy those straws we were grasping at really were.

"I hadn't gotten that far in the plan."

"You dragged us out here without thinking about what we'd do once we got here?"

"Getting all the food together you made me bring took up a lot of time."

"Fine, I'm going to grab a sandwich and let the dogs out while we figure out what to do next."

Looking into the cooler, I had to admit, Burt ran a tight snack game. Homemade chicken salad sandwiches, chips, sliced apples, string cheese, a jug of water, and coffee, water bowls for the dogs, and cookies. "Did you make these too?" I asked through a mouthful of one of the most delicious chocolate oatmeal cookies I had ever eaten. "They taste so fresh."

"I pulled them out of the oven right before I left," he grumbled.

"They're delicious. These totally make up for your lack of strategy."

"What about you? It's time you pull your weight on this team. You come up with a plan."

"I will, as soon as I finish my lunch." After my second cookie, I sighed and brushed the crumbs off my lap.

"Not in the truck," Burt hollered.

"Alright, calm down." I got out to clean myself off and let the dogs pee on things.

A dusty blue sedan rumbled slowly down the dirt road towards us.

"Incoming, get the dogs and get down," Burt hollered. The sheer urgency in his voice triggered my primal sense of self-preservation. I frantically snatched up Fizzy, slung my arm over Clover, and hunched behind the truck. The Hispanic driver in his late twenties gave me a strange look as he passed.

"He saw me. I made eye contact. What should I do?"

"Get in quick. That's the same car we passed on the road earlier."

I stuffed everything back in the cooler, threw the dogs in, and jumped in after them. Burt started the truck, looked straight ahead, and we sat there unmoving.

"Do you see anything?" he asked, hopefully.

"You can see what I see, fields and this giant sign we're poorly hiding behind. There isn't a way to get up to the farm without being seen. The whole place is surrounded by open fields."

"I've got it," Burt exclaimed. "We'll drive up and tell them you're getting married and you want to see if you can rent out the farm. People are always renting out their farms on those fixer-upper shows for extra cash."

"Her barn just burned down. Charred cinders are hardly the stuff fairy tale weddings are made of. Let's just keep it simple. We'll say we're taking the dogs out for a picnic and a drive. We were out this way, so we thought we'd see if she had more goat cheese left. Then we casually ask her questions about yesterday and see if she has an alibi." I congratulated myself for coming up with a plausible plan.

"I like mine better."

"We're going with my story. Come on, let's move out." After making sure the cooler lid was properly closed, Burt carefully backed out onto the road.

Goats, in addition to having a distinct aroma, were also very loud. Any hope of making a stealthy entrance evaporated as soon as we pulled into the parking area of the farm. Clover, mistaking the goats in their pens for shrunken deer, started barking wildly. This triggered a goat bleating frenzy, which brought two collies running to defend their tribe against our truck. It was a real E-I E-I-O moment. In the end, Linda rescued us all.

"Hi," I said lamely after she called the dogs off. "We're Carol's friends. We met at the market in Claryce Falls."

"I remember you. What can I do for you? The farm isn't open yet. It's too early for berries."

I apologized and explained our fictional outing. "I'm hoping you didn't sell out at the market," I concluded. All in all, I thought it sounded pretty convincing.

"And she's getting married. Maya thought your farm might make a nice place for the ceremony," Burt blurted out.

Groaning inwardly, I wanted to kick Burt in the shins and take away his HGTV for a month.

"Uh, congratulations." Linda turned around as if indicating the hulking remains of her burned-out barn. "They said it will take at least a year to rebuild. I don't think we'd be ready to host a wedding here anytime soon."

"It's okay. We'll probably just elope anyway." I noticed the man from the blue sedan feeding the goats. One particularly spunky goat kept headbutting him in the behind and bouncing away. At the sound of my chuckle, Linda turned to watch the antics as well.

"That's Miss MaeMae, the one I was telling you and Libby about. She's a real handful, but she keeps life interesting. And that's Jorge, he's usually in charge of the dairy. I think he passed you earlier."

"Could be," Burt said noncommittally. Higher-pitched bleating came from a smaller pen. I turned in a semicircle to pinpoint the source.

"Those are the youngsters. Do you want to see them?"

"Yes," I said eagerly. Who didn't love a baby goat? I followed Linda over to a small corral. We passed several minutes watching the adorable little mottled kids bounce around and into each other like popcorn in a hot pan. Their cuteness assault fully absorbed me, and I completely forgot about our mission. The sound of an approaching car engine finally pulled my attention from the frolicking corral of joy. A brown sedan made its way up the road.

"Darn it, I forgot I called the police on you."

"What?" Burt and I both exclaimed.

"Jorge said he saw a suspicious truck driving up and down the road, before parking behind our sign. He said a strange woman, which must have been you, Maya, tried squatting down and hiding behind her dogs when he drove by. We didn't know what you were up to."

"Sorry about that." I cringed. Burt and I would never be 007. "I dropped some stuff when I got out of the truck and didn't want the dogs to run into the road."

"Jorge and I are both jumpy after the barn burned down. He's convinced it was arson. He's so unsettled, he carries a baseball bat with him now, even sleeps with it. Come to think of it, it's pretty lucky he only called the cops."

I cursed under my breath. Behind the wheel of the county sheriff's car was none other than Dave. He got out. His neutral expression shifted into a look of irritation when he saw Burt.

"False alarm," Linda called out. "Sorry to drag you out here."

"No problem, Linda. Glad everything is alright." He faced Burt. "What are you doing here?" His voice was heavy with censure.

"We took the dogs out for a drive and Maya wanted more goat cheese."

I held back my eye roll. Now he decided my cover story was good enough to use.

"Didn't know you were such a fan of goat cheese, Maya."

"Neither did I until recently." I sounded extra cheery. "Now I can't get enough of the stuff."

"Dave, I apologize for dragging you out here. I'm easily spooked since the fire. Maya, how much cheese did you want? I'll go get it for you."

Dave cut in before I could answer. "How much do you have left, Linda?" The slight smile on his face made me nervous.

"I've got a case left of mixed flavors."

"Great, Maya and Burt will take it all. Won't you?"

"We sure will," I chirped, jumping in quickly when I saw Burt open his mouth.

Linda went into the house to get the goods.

As soon as she was out of earshot, Dave turned on us. "Burt, I told you to leave her alone. And Maya, I cannot believe you are encouraging him. I have serious matters I'm dealing with, and I had to drop them to rush out here, only to find you two playing Sherlock Holmes and Watson."

I briefly considered which one of us was Watson. "I'm sorry Dave. We didn't mean to scare anyone." I felt like a chastised teenager.

"I don't want to hear it. This is your one warning. Next time we'll have a real problem." He locked eyes with both of us, making sure his point landed.

Thinking of Dave's other serious issues, I apologized sincerely and asked how things were going.

Dave rubbed his hand down his face, his shoulders sagging. "Not well. We've got nothing right now."

Burt looked like he was about to ask questions when Dave cut him off abruptly at the sound of a screen door slamming against its frame.

"Here we go," Linda called, lifting the large cardboard box in the air like a prize.

"Will I see you at the Oasis tomorrow for tamales with your girls?" Linda asked Dave. "Carol invited me, and I think I'll go. I can't touch anything here until the insurance investigator comes out."

"Gonna try."

"Will that make two or three trips for you into Claryce Falls this week, Linda?" Burt tried to sound casual.

Dave shot him a warning look. "Burt, Maya, don't you need to get back and take Owen's dog to him?" he commanded.

"Right," I agreed. "Thanks for the cheese." I pointed to the enormous box now riding high in the back of the truck. I'd be eating goat cheese with my Corn Flakes for the next year.

Dave stood by Linda and watched us pull out.

"What an expensive waste of time," I grumbled.

"We lost the chance to grill her because you went all soft in the head over those baby goats. I hate goats."

"Come on, Burt, you have to admit they were adorable."

There was a long pause on his side of the truck. "They really were cute little dickens, weren't they," he admitted, finally caving. "Too bad they grow into such dirty beasts. And I suppose we can question Linda at the Oasis."

I guess it was tamales for dinner tomorrow. Burt passed the freeway ramp heading back to Claryce Falls. I wondered if I should do the driving from now on.

"Where are we going?"

"To the Dairy Queen. We need ice cream cones."

Five

"It wouldn't be hot sauce if it wasn't hot." I helpfully pointed out as Burt wiped the tears running down his red face and desperately gestured toward the pitcher of water at the end of the table.

"Here." Carol held out a spoonful of sour cream to him. "The fat will help with the heat."

We sat around two long tables, the Lores on one side, Burt, Owen, and me on the other. Burt had invited Owen to join us when we dropped off Fizzy last night. He said our group needed more men. When Burt finally got his hot sauce histrionics under control, Carol cleared her throat loudly. "Everyone, I have an announcement. I'm going to put an offer on a place!"

"What? That's amazing," I exclaimed. "It happened so fast. Where is it? Tell us everything."

"Calm down and let the woman speak, for Pete's sake."

I picked up the hot sauce and pointed it at Burt. "I will use this on you."

He took the bottle out of my hands with a weary sigh and set it out of my reach. "Please Carol, continue."

"It was the second property I looked at. I saw it last Friday, and it's going to be perfect. The place's been on the market for a while, so I know I can get it for a good price. There's cosmetic work that needs to be done, which I'm sure was scaring off buyers. But it is a real gem." As she described the place, I noticed Burt was beaming as bright as Carol. It was sweet to see him so happy.

"You all enjoying yourselves tonight?"

"Hi, Purdy," Burt greeted.

"You look especially nice tonight," I said, appreciating her eclectic, sexy senior, country, 'more is more' type style. "That blue cowboy hat is everything."

"And your floral dress is so cute," Carol added.

"Thank you, thank you. It's good to know this ol' gal's still got it." She winked at Burt. "How are you liking those pickles?" He assured her he was enjoying them. "If you need anything else, I have a number of tasty things I know you like."

I choked on my soda. Owen whacked me on the back until I could breathe again.

"You know we haven't gotten dinner lately." Purdy's voice dripped honey, baiting her trap. "We should do it again soon."

Burt's ears turned pink, and he stammered noncommittal nonsense.

Purdy looked at Dave. "I'm surprised to see you here socializing. I figured they'd be keeping you busy with that body they found. Do you know who it is yet?" It wasn't surprising Purdy knew about the body. News had a way of getting around town fast.

"Sorry, Purdy, I can't talk about the investigation."

Carol patted her son-in-law's arm. "It feels like this is the first meal this poor man's had the chance to eat with his family since this whole business started."

"I bet," Purdy said. "Should I be worried? Do you think I should start locking my doors?"

Dave assured her there was nothing to suggest the safety of the greater public was at risk, and she should always lock her doors.

"Alrighty then," Purdy knocked on the table. "I'll let you all get back to it."

We watched her disappear into the crowd.

"I think she likes you," Leigha teased Burt.

"Nah," he tried waving the comment off. "We got dinner a couple of times a while ago. The woman is the biggest flirt this side of the Cascades. She'll chat up anything in trousers."

"I don't know, she hasn't hit on me, and I look pretty cute in trousers," I goaded.

"I meant men, Maya. Men in trousers and all men wear trousers. I meant she flirts with all men."

"You know, Burt, that's not actually true. Not all men do wear trousers."

Burt sighed dramatically. He started into a rant about how irritating I was when Angel thankfully interrupted him with a bucket of beers and a platter of tamales. He also set a shot of tequila down in front of Owen.

"I didn't order this."

"It's from the woman in the brown sweater over there." He pointed her out.

"Can you just send it back? I don't want it."

"Man, we're slammed, I don't have time for that."

"I got this." I turned to Owen. "You trust me?"

"Not really."

"You leave Fizzy with me. You have to trust me a little."

"Alright, go ahead," he said, looking dubious.

I picked up the shot and swiveled to face the women. I nodded my head at the women in thanks, gave her an exaggerated wink, and tipped the shot back. Stealing a move from Clover, I ducked my head under Owen's arm propped on the table, so it slid around my shoulders. "Now, bring it home," I commanded, sending instructions from the side of my mouth. "Do something to make it look real."

Owen ran his nose along the side of my neck, playing his part a little too well for my comfort. I squirmed against the avalanche of shivers he triggered and smiled brightly back at the woman. She scowled at me and turned to her friend, who gave me the bird.

"Wow, aren't they a couple of charmers? Do you see the fate I saved you from?" I sat back, feeling hot and smug.

Owen's arm fell from my shoulders and onto the top of the chair. To my great discomfort, he didn't move it. The heat from the contact was distracting. How did he not feel it? I leaned forward, scooting to the edge of my seat to try and escape his nearness.

"I hope you all aren't waiting on me to eat," Linda called as she walked up. She took the open spot next to Burt and looked around the table.

"I think you know everyone but Owen." Carol waved around at the group.

Linda glanced at Owen's arm on the back of my chair and smiled politely. "You must be Maya's fiancé."

The beer in my mouth erupted like Old Faithful, spraying the side of Owen's face. Along with the beer, my soul was forcefully torn from my body by violent mortification.

Owen let out a sound of disgust. And I died.

"Shoot, shoot, shoot." I grabbed a stack of napkins and started blotting his face. "I'm not getting married anymore," I called over my shoulder. "I mean, who needs the hassle? I don't need to be married. Really, if you think about it, marriage is an antiquated system of ownership, and I'm a modern woman. I was married once before, and I don't think I need to do it again."

Owen grabbed my wrists to stop my napkin assault. I looked at him with pleading eyes and shook my head slightly, begging him silently to keep quiet.

"Are you saying Leigha isn't a modern woman?" Dave was troublemaking.

Luckily, I'd already told Leigha and her mom about my recon mission with Burt, and I was sure Dave had heard all the details by now.

I knew I was being baited, and still, I couldn't stop myself from swallowing the hook. "Of course, she's a modern woman. You're both very modern people and traditional too."

Owen came to my rescue. "What Maya's trying to say is, we didn't think. We got carried away in something we didn't really understand. And when we finally stopped and took a moment, it felt like we really never even dated. Next thing I know, we're engaged." Owen released my wrists, and I sagged back in relief. Linda, sensing the topic was better to be dropped, redirected her conversation to Carol.

I decided to avoid adults for the rest of the meal and quickly got up. Libby came with me to play foosball in the back. She moved the handles on the table around as I made the tiny soccer men sing songs from her all-time favorite movie, *Trolls*.

I was on my fourth rendition of "Can't Fight the Feeling" when Leigha came to collect us. "At least you didn't set anyone's hair on fire. And really, who doesn't love an awkward retreat?"

"Stop." I spread my hands over my face, trying to simultaneously block my eyes and ears.

"I thought Owen did an amazing job of rolling with it."

"Yeah, yeah. Owen is amazing. Everyone loooves Owen," I moaned.

"Glad you realize it." The man himself stood behind me with my jacket and a container.

"For heaven's sake. Can you just not be around me when I'm doing or saying something embarrassing for once?"

"Does it ever happen?" he asked.

I punched him in the arm.

"No, seriously." He looked at Leigha. "Does it?"

"Very occasionally, when she's sleeping, she can be cute and harmless."

"Guess I'd have to see it for myself to believe it."

"That's not going to happen." I wondered if embarrassment ever had a bottom. "Are you going already? Libby and I just got the chorus line warmed up," I said, spinning a foosball pole.

"People keep coming to talk to Dave about the body. Not, quite the family night we were hoping for."

Owen handed me my coat and the container. "Come on, I'm giving you a ride home. You drank and didn't eat, so you shouldn't drive."

"I rode Broomhilda. I'm fine."

"Remember, I've seen what happens when you ride while under the influence of caffeine. I can't imagine the public hazard you become after a couple of beers. Sorry pal, you're coming with me. I'll throw your bike in the back, and you can explain how we got engaged on the ride home."

And the well of embarrassment just kept getting deeper and deeper.

By the time we reached my house, I'd finished the entire tale. "You see, I never said I was engaged to you. And it was Burt's half-baked story that got me into this mess."

"Seems to me, you went along pretty willingly."

"If you tasted his chocolate oatmeal cookies, you would go along willingly too."

"That good, huh? Wait, I still have a few questions."

"Ask while I show you all the progress I made on the garbage project." I unlocked the front door, letting out the four-legged enthusiasm committee to join us.

"You know the case for Linda being the note writer is pretty weak, right?"

"That's why we were trying to uncover more evidence."

"Right." He didn't sound convinced.

"What's your other question?" I was feeling so relieved he wasn't mad about the weird engagement thing, I would've told him anything, even where I hid my secret stash of chocolate. I would've even told him why I needed to have a hidden stash of chocolate.

"You were married."

"Not really a question - more of a statement."

"Tell me about it."

"Again, not a question - more of a command."

"Maya," he warned.

"Really not much to tell. We met in college at the UW. Got married. Stayed in Seattle for a bit. Then we moved out here when Scott got the job as the principal of the middle school. He wanted to have kids. I didn't. He thought I'd change my mind. I didn't. So we split up, and he remarried Ms. Simon, the Third-Grade teacher. Now they have two boys."

"He lives here, in Claryce Falls? Now?"

"Hillsburg," I corrected.

"It all sounds way too simple and clean. Endings are never that easy."

"Sure, not at first, but later I realized I probably married him for the wrong reasons, and I was happier without him than I ever was with him. He's with the right person now." I paused, shaking off the past belonging to a different version of me. "Enough about that, what about you?" I hesitated a moment, about to ask questions I may not want the answers to. "Is it hard with your girlfriend being gone for work so much?"

Owen looked confused. "What girlfriend?"

"Fizzy's mom, the flight nurse."

"Ava? We broke up before I moved out here. Why'd you think I was still dating Ava?"

"You have her dog. Why would you have her dog?" I let out a gasp. "Owen, you didn't steal Fizzy, did you?"

"No, Maya, I didn't steal Fizzy," his voice rose with exasperation. "Ava got a flight nurse job that meant Fizzy would be alone for days. She was stressing out about it, so I offered to take her."

Too many thoughts ran through my mind at once. I couldn't imagine giving Clover up. And Owen was single. Would I make things weird between us now? I hoped not. We were becoming actual friends. Owen was like coffee ice cream, I wanted a steady supply of each and both gave me a happy buzz. My brain short-circuited.

"I need more cans, look," I blurted out, pointing at my growing creation.

Owen seemed genuinely surprised with how much progress I'd made.

"I know, it's a lot, right? I can't help myself sometimes. Once I get an idea in my head, it's hard for me to put it down until I'm done."

"You're actually going to make this happen." He sounded impressed.

"Of course," I bristled. "It was never a question. But, there's still a ton of work to do, and I need to collect more cans and work double-time if I want to get them done for the campground opening."

"Speaking of picking up cans, I forgot to tell you, Janet came back to the Forest Service Office today."

"That's Trash Trouper Janet. And why am I just now hearing about it?"

"I was going to tell you over dinner, but you spit beer in my face and hid."

"Okay, fair enough," I admitted. "What happened?"

"I caught her right before she emptied her bags on the floor. I showed her your plan and gave her the list of things you wanted her to do."

"And," I prompted.

"It worked! She agreed to everything and took her trash with her to start sorting."

I pumped my fists. "I told you I was brilliant."

"Starting to look that way." He smirked. "As for the supply problem, what are you doing on Sunday?" Before he took off, we made plans to go scope out some other places Owen knew about.

The next morning, Burt made an exuberant entrance. "Look what I have!" He held up a large piece of cardboard in one hand and a canvas shopping bag in the other. He bubbled with excitement like a freshly shaken Coke.

The woman I was helping glanced over her shoulder. "Hi, Burt."

"Hi, Merna. How are the rabbits doing?"

"Fluffy and prolific. Berry and Fiona had a new litter in time for Easter. If you know anyone who wants one, send them my way. I got a flier up there if they're looking for my number." She gestured to the noticeboard.

"Will do. You need help out with your package?"

Merna shook her head, saying she could manage.

"All right, we'll be seeing you." Burt hurried the woman out. When the door shut behind her, he started again. "Look what I have." He set his bag down on the counter and unfolded the trifold cardboard. It was the kind used in middle school science fairs.

"What am I looking at, Burt?"

He beamed. "Our new suspect board. We can keep it in the back office, fold it, and lock it up in there when you leave." He pointed to my side of the counter.

"I thought we only had one suspect."

"True, but it will help us keep our thoughts organized, and we can use it when we present our case to Dave."

I considered it briefly. I did love a good art project. "Alright, I'm in. Show me the rest of it. What's in the bag?"

"A berry and goat cheese cobbler I made this morning and the paper. I suppose it's too much to hope you've been reading the news without me?"

"It really is, Burt," I said somberly. "But I made you coffee." I figured he'd be in sooner rather than later to tell me what he learned from Linda last night. He seemed pleased with my initiative. "Don't get used to it," I warned. "So, what did you find out from Linda?"

He walked back in from the kitchen with a cup of coffee in one hand, several stacks of sticky notes in the other, and a Sharpie tucked behind his ear. He methodically unwrapped the brightly-colored pads, handing me the cellophane. Next, he placed them in a neat row according to color. I watched him work with rapt attention, oddly fascinated by his process.

"Green will be for suspects' potential alibis, got it?" He said, tapping the pile of green sticky notes for emphasis.

"Sure, whatever. Now tell me what you found out from Linda."

He uncapped the marker slowly and peeled off a green sticky note. He was moving with the speed of a pre-global warming glacier.

"Tell me already."

"If you stayed at the table and helped me last night, you'd already know, wouldn't you? Do you know how much harder it was getting information from Linda with Dave glaring at me and interrupting me the entire time?"

"If you hadn't told her I was engaged in the first place, the entire awkward scene never would have happened, and I wouldn't have needed to turn tail and run."

"You know, sometimes you talk a lot of nonsense."

"I know. Now spill it."

"Linda said she and Jorge were deworming the goats Tuesday. I looked it up on the internet. Their story's plausible. It's the right time of year."

"How can we confirm if she was really there or not, though?"

"Ah," Burt looked excited again. "I've already thought of that. Linda mentioned the vet came out to look at one of the goats. Carol and I made an appointment for Greta with the same vet for tomorrow."

"Does that mean Carol thinks Linda' behind the notes too?"

"No, but she agreed to try and rule her out. She's such a sweet woman. Carol's inclined to think the best of everyone."

"What are you going to say is wrong with Greta?"

"We had a real stroke of luck there. Libby's been feeding Greta her vegetables, and they gave her diarrhea." Burt carefully wrote on the sticky note 'Goat Worming.' "I'm going to move this to the kitchen where I have more room to work." He collected the office supplies and quietly disappeared. An hour passed before I heard from him again. "Can you draw?"

"I can. Why?"

"I need a drawing of Linda for the suspect board. Can you draw something?" he called from the kitchen.

Luckily, things were pretty slow, and the place was empty except for us. I thought for a moment, "I'm on it," I called back.

"That isn't Linda," he complained when he came to collect my drawing.

I held up my sketch of a baby goat framed in a wreath of strawberries. "But it's sooo cute."

"Suspect boards aren't supposed to be cute."

"Old men pouting aren't cute, either," I pointed out.

"I'm not pouting, and I'm not old. I'm mature."

I scoffed. "Your moping would indicate otherwise."

He grabbed the picture from my hands and stomped back to the kitchen.

At noon, I closed the counter and joined Burt for cobbler and to check out his craft project. "This is good. You can hardly taste the goat cheese," I said.

Burt's board was impressive too. He divided the trifold into three color-coordinated rows: Suspects, Alibis, and Evidence. Taped under evidence was a printed picture of the second threat and a drawing for the first one. Next to each, written in neat handwriting, Burt listed the date, time, and location of their discovery. My goat drawing with 'Linda Thornston' written under it was taped in the center of the 'Suspects' row.

Burt pulled out the newspaper, preparing to read to me as I ate. "Oh no." All the color drained from his face and the paper shook in his hands. "This is awful."

"What is it?"

"It's Peter, Gary Becker's boy. He's the one they found in the Teanaway."

"Peter Becker, not the young guy who works at the Pro Shop, good-looking, lanky build, blond hair, early twenties?

Burt nodded solemnly. "Sounds like Peter."

"But I just talked to him last week. He was goofing around in a golf cart and flirting." My brain tried to catch up with this new reality, one with a missing playful, Peter-shaped hole. "What happened?"

Burt picked up the paper and began reading in a raspy voice: "Kittitas County law enforcement is investigating the death of a man found in Teanaway State Forest on Sunday. The man, identified as Peter Becker, twenty-two of Claryce Falls, WA, was found by a hiker's dog around one-thirty p.m. that afternoon. Authorities withheld the victim's name from the public until the deceased relatives could be notified. Becker's parents returned from Arizona on Wednesday. Kittitas County Sheriff Davis Burk said the incident is being investigated as a homicide. Law enforcement urges the public to provide any pertinent information regarding the incident. A funeral service will be held for the friends and family of Becker on March twenty-seventh at the Hillsburg Eagles Lodge."

"That's this Wednesday," I said, stunned.

"This is going to break his parents." Burt set his reading glasses down on the table and rubbed his eyes. "The kid was always up to something. Not bad, just entrepreneurial with enough disregard for the rules to get himself into trouble. I liked him. It was hard not to." He clenched his fist on the table and inspected the back of it. "Gary told me about this time, Peter was maybe thirteen. One night, while Gary slept, Peter took his dad's pickup to one of the orchards and loaded the bed with windfall apples. The next day, he got hold of his mom's press and went door to door at the resort, selling jugs of fresh apple cider. Lucky, he didn't give everyone salmonella or worse."

I smiled sadly, easily imagining the young guy spinning wheelies doing something like that. And now he was just gone. "Why would someone want to kill him?"

Burt shook his head. "I don't know, but for his family's sake, I hope it wasn't something he got himself mixed up in."

Six

We rock stepped our way up the wood floor of Glamour Nails and Boogie, a chorus line of Lycra-coated Skittles in cowboy boots. "Isn't this so much fun?" Carol puffed beside me. "And Leigha is such a good teacher."

I nodded enthusiastically, trying not to miss the shuffle, turn, shuffle this time. "Ouch!"

Emily Brady's elbow connected with my left side as she swung wide on the turn. "Sorry," she singsonged. This wasn't Emily's first misstep into me today.

"I think the poor thing has two left feet," Carol whispered. "Do you want to switch places?"

"Thanks, but I'm okay. Class is almost done." I ducked to avoid being decapitated by Emily's over enthusiastic air lasso. Four more grapevines and a couple shuffle kicks later and Leigha was congratulating us for our hard work.

"Do you have time for a coffee after this?" Carol zipped up her pink velour hoodie, the mate to her matching leggings. "Leigha's going to pick up Libby from preschool."

"Mind if I join?" Emily linked her arm around Carol's.

"Honey, normally I'd love it if you came, but I have a few private things I need to talk with Maya about today," she said, extricating her arm.

"Some of us go out for coffee or a snack after class sometimes," Emily explained.

"That does sound nice. Maybe, we can try for next week," Carol placated.

"Alright, I'll hold you to it." Emily smiled sweetly at Carol.

"Let me change my shoes, and I'll be ready to go." I walked over to the row of benches and pulled my sneakers and a towel from my bag.

"So, you snapped up Owen, and now you're getting all buddy-buddy with Carol too," someone hissed. I looked up at Emily looming over me.

"I beg your pardon?"

"Don't play dumb. I'm on to you. I heard you're engaged to Owen. You sure work fast. He's been in town less than four months."

"Where'd you hear that?" Emily was giving off some strong Tonya Harding vibes. I instinctively covered my knees.

"I have my sources, and they saw you kissing on him at the Oasis Wednesday. They also overheard you bragging about how you're engaged. As if that wasn't enough, now you're cozying up to Carol to get tighter with Leigha." She looked around to make sure no one was listening. "You know, Leigha and I haven't hung out once since her mother's been in town. I tried to be nice to Carol at the barbecue, but she only wanted to play with her granddaughter and talk to Burt. I can't wait until she goes home."

I didn't know where to start with this woman. For Owen's sake, I decided to start there. "First, not that it is any of your business, but I'm not engaged to Owen or anyone else."

"Do you promise?"

"We are not engaged."

"And do you promise to keep it that way?" Emily demanded.

"I don't need to promise you anything. And another thing, Carol isn't going anywhere. She's moving here, so you'd better change your attitude."

"What? She's staying. I thought she'd leave for sure. We'll have to wait and see about that. Won't we?"

"You leave Carol alone." An angry heat rose up in my belly. "You better not pull any of this crazy crap on her."

"Do you promise to leave Owen alone?"

"Owen and I are just friends," I growled.

A smile bloomed across Emily's face. "Is that so? Good, make sure it stays that way." She twirled around and skated out of the studio with icy self-satisfaction.

I stared after her, dumbfounded. It was hard to believe people like Emily existed in real life. I thought they were only the stuff of reality TV and movies about high school girls.

"You ready Hon?" Carol broke my trance. "I need to check in with Chris. I haven't heard back from him about the offer I made on the house. Would you mind if we did that first, or would you prefer to meet me at Rustic Reads?"

"I'll come with you." We called our goodbyes to Leigha and headed out of her backyard studio. The Lores' house sat three blocks up from Main Street on a steep hill overlooking the valley. I loved the view of the town framed by the mountains from here. In the summer, Leigha and I sat on her deck with a cold drink, our feet propped up on the railing, and watched the people in town move around like actors on a set. I stomped down the happy daffodil-lined path from Leigha's studio to her front gate.

All day, my center had been leaning south of steady. Everyone who came to get their mail today wanted to talk about Peter's death. The community was shocked, and they needed someone to talk to about it. Burt's persistent presence, normally unwanted, lent a much-needed steady support as people tried to make sense of the loss. And now, with the Emily encounter, I was in hair-pulling gladiator mode.

Carol commented on my speed-walking, so I slowed my pace. We made our way down the hill at a more sedate amble to Chris Weller's office. Located in part of the old grain mill, the building housed several small businesses including Flameworks Glass Studio, a craft collective, a used furniture shop, and an outdoor gear rental place. I briefly ran my graphic design business out of one of the smaller offices, but the agonizing cries coming from the neighboring, and now-defunct tattoo parlor didn't help my concentration.

Chris sat enthroned in a large leather desk chair, dominating his compact office. His formal blazer, which screamed Fortune Five-Hundred ambitions, rebelled against the small town's lethargy. "Carol, I didn't know you were coming in." Chris set the scissors and magazine cut out of a yacht down on his desk. "Updating the ol' vision board. You've got to dream big first before you can achieve it."

"It's important to have aspirations," Carol agreed. "Speaking of which, I wanted to see if you heard anything from the sellers yet."

His brows drew together in a look of disappointment, more simulated than sincere. "Unfortunately, they didn't accept the offer."

"Why? Did they counter?"

"No, I told you they are very touchy. Easily offended. Remember, I did warn you this might happen. This is why I selected several other beautiful properties for you to look at."

"What if Carol calls their agent and tries talking to them herself?" I asked. "After all, this is her big dream we are trying to achieve." I tapped the paper yacht on the desk meaningfully.

"It's being sold directly by the owner, and they only want to talk to agents."

I wasn't giving up easily. There was still fuel burning in my tank from the Emily encounter. "Carol's got nothing to lose if she talks to them. Does she?"

"Great idea," Carol agreed. "Can I get their number from you?"

Ridges formed on Chris's forehead like a roman blind. "Sorry, no, that's confidential information."

The iPhone on his desk conjured a fantasy of a grab and dash. I could be fast when I needed to be. But it probably had a passcode, so it wouldn't do me any good. "If it's being sold by the owners, wouldn't they expect people to call them? Why go through an agent? Doesn't that defeat the whole purpose of selling it yourself?"

Chris looked around the room as if searching for an answer. "The number is private, and I could be risking my license if I give it to you."

"Which law specifically would you be violating?" I was fired up. I believed the guy about as far as I could throw his slender, yet dense-looking frame.

"It's okay," Carol cut in. "It's disappointing, but there'll be other houses. I have the listings Chris sent me." She stood up and looked at me pointedly.

"Fine." I unobtrusively moved Chris's water glass off its coaster. I hoped it left a mark.

Back on the street, Carol grabbed my arm. "You were right in there. Something's not adding up, and we're going to figure it out."

I was fuming. "Whatever you're thinking, I'm in. What should we do?"

"Right now I think we forget the coffee and get a margarita. Then we talk about what comes next."

I took us to Pioneering Pies, a place notorious for its over-priced pizza and famous for its strong margaritas. The plastic red-and-white checkered tablecloths clashed with the large sepia-toned photos of pioneer cowboys and women, each awkwardly holding a digitally added, full-color slice of pizza. I ordered the Misfire Margarita, a tasty drink served with salted jalapeño and crystallized mango on the rim. After our waiter left, Carol pushed up the sleeves of her velour hoodie and leaned over the table.

"What I'm about to tell you, you can't tell Leigha."

I hesitated. "I don't know if I can do it. What if you're about to tell me something like William isn't really Leigha's father? That's something she should know first."

"For heaven's sake, where do you even come up with this stuff? I think I'm starting to see what Burt is talking about with you."

"What does Burt say about me?" I asked defensively.

"Maya, focus. Just promise me, or I won't tell you. Leigha and Dave have enough on their plates with the murder investigation and everything else without worrying about me."

"It seems like people want me to make a lot of weird promises today," I grumbled. Caving into my curiosity, I leaned in. "Fine, I will promise as long as there's, I don't know, a time limit on it, like a month."

"Fine, fine, everything should be sorted by then anyway. Keep your promise for a month."

"Done, now tell me what it is."

"Someone slashed my tire."

"What? On purpose?"

"When I went to take Greta to the vet this morning, there was a screwdriver sticking out of one of my car's wheels and a new note. It just said, 'Leave town.' I only told Leigha and Dave I got a flat."

"That's horrible," I gasped. "And also incredibly short-sighted. It's a lot harder to leave town with a flat tire. But these threats are escalating. Why wouldn't you tell them? This could be dangerous."

"Dave's so busy with work. They don't have any suspects yet, and the pressure is really on him to find the killer. He's putting in long hours and Leigha is stressed. I will not add to their burden. Besides, none of this makes a lick of sense. But, between you, Burt, and me, I know we can figure it out."

I didn't feel as confident in our abilities as Carol seemed to. "As of right now, we have one suspect. And I think she's a long shot."

"Which reminds me, you don't know what we found out today. The long shot just got longer. The vet confirmed Linda and Jorge were both at the farm when she went out on Tuesday."

"So, that's it then. It's not Linda."

"Burt thinks she may still have had enough time to drive in and leave the note. But I don't like Linda for this, either."

"It's just so strange. Who would want you to leave town?" We sat silently for a beat, running unlikely scenarios through our heads. Then we both turned to each other and spoke at the same time.

"Emily," I half shouted.

"Chris," Carol stated. "Let's lay this out logically. You first."

I cleared my throat. "To start with, Emily obviously has jealousy issues. First, she admitted to trying to cozy up to you at the barbecue and feeling thwarted. Second, she said Leigha hasn't spent time with her since you've been in town, and third, she admitted she couldn't wait for you to go home."

"She sounds more lonely and socially misguided. Hardly conclusive." Carol played devil's advocate.

"The woman's a sociopath," I protested. "Anyone who throws beverages on a person's good dress and tries to make said dress wearer promise not to marry other people, is unpredictable high drama." I saw the skepticism on Carol's face. "She is going up on the board." I was resolute. I defended my case, filling in the details of the story I left out.

"It seems like her problem is more with you than me. But we can put her on the board."

"Thank you." I felt like Carol was still minimizing the potential menace that was Emily.

"Let's talk about Chris. I'm not sure what he's up to, but we both felt like something wasn't right earlier. And when I went to view the property with him, he was so negative. He pointed out every rotting fence post and faded paint spot. He even complained about the animal smell in the barn. It's a barn, they're supposed to smell that way. It was almost as if he didn't want me to buy the place."

"Then why did he show it to you?"

"I was the one who found it and asked him to take me to see it." Carol's voice rose excitedly. "And remember, he was at the farmers market when I got the first note. Shoot, I wish Burt was here to talk this through with us."

I kept my smirk to myself. Carol and Burt seemed to be getting along quite well. "Why don't you both come by the P.O. tomorrow at closing? We'll add everyone to the suspect board and formulate a plan."

"It's a date," Carol declared, raising her margarita in toast.

A couple of hours later, I had learned the painful lesson that soldering and distraction didn't mix. I sat sunbathing under a throw blanket with my hand submerged in a bowl of ice water. I was taking a break from my trash project to tend my blistered fingers.

"Where are you all?" A now-familiar voice called.

The dogs stirred from their dozing positions next to me.

"We're in back." It had only been a week since Owen started leaving Fizzy at my house, and I was already used to the evening dog retrieval routine. "Get yourself something to drink if you want. There's tea on the counter," I called.

Owen took the chair next to me, iced tea in one hand and Fizzy in the other. He eyed my bowl and gave me a look. "It's not so bad," I said, taking my hand out of the freezing water and showing him the red burns on my thumb and index finger. "It could have been so much worse."

"With you, I have no doubt." He shook his head. "Do you have any aloe?"

"You don't get to help me if you're going to be rude."

He pushed himself up. "Truth hurts. Now, tell me where it is, so I can come back and relax." Knowing when to concede a fight I didn't want to win, I gave him location instructions.

"You have a lot of first aid supplies," he said, handing the aloe to me. He paused as if in deep contemplation. "Yep, that tracks. I'm sure they get used."

"Hahaha," I laughed sarcastically. "If you're going to mock my pain, you can take your dog and go."

"Now, don't make poor Fizzy pay for your bad attitude. Besides, would you change your mind if you found out I picked up King salmon to grill?"

"Who's doing the cooking?" I asked suspiciously.

"I will. You're injured, after all."

"Alright," I sighed as if I was doing him a huge favor. "You can make me dinner." But I felt like a benched player watching him cook. So, with the knife skills of a three-toed sloth, I carefully made a salad and set the patio table while Owen grilled squash with the fish. The blissfully domestic scene drew unwanted thoughts like flies to horse manure. A vision of Owen sliding his arms around my waist as I tossed the salad buzzed through my brain. Zap! I mentally electrocuted the scene, like the bug zapper hanging in my yard. I imagined his breath in my ear as he whispered, "Are you ready?" Zap!

"Maya, are you about ready? The fish is done."

"Right, yeah, ready," I stammered. I needed to turn up the voltage on the dang zapper if I wanted to make it through the meal without embarrassing myself. To my great satisfaction, Owen overcooked the salmon. It was good to know that he wasn't good at everything.

After dinner, while we cleared up dinner, Owen spotted the cribbage board on my bookshelf and challenged me to a game. I have many virtues and a few flaws. My family and the friends who will still play board games with me might argue my somewhat over-healthy competitiveness might qualify as one of my flaws. "If you can handle my smack talk and losing, then I'm up for a game," I warned.

"Are you sure, I wouldn't want you to hurt yourself again, tripping over that confidence when you lose?"

"It's on, Mr. Reece." I moved the pegs to their starting positions and shuffled the deck.

"If you can play cards as well as you can collect bruises, then it should be an interesting game." His eyes went wide, and his mouth made a big "O" shape.

I pushed the deck in front of him. "Cut the cards pretty boy and play."

Two hours later, I was gloating. "If this had been a beauty contest, you may have had a chance against me. Sad for you, it wasn't."

"You warned me you were competitive, but you didn't mention what a poor winner you are, too."

I smiled brightly, flush with the cockiness of my victory. "I know it must be confusing for you since scoring points with cards is different than scoring points with ladies." I wiggled my eyebrows. "Maybe Fizzy can give you some tips in case we play again."

"Maya, you were at The Oasis with me. As long as there're ladies from Moon River, I don't have to try to score." He smiled wickedly. "And we are definitely going to play again."

Seven

It was like an International House of Pancakes on UN Day but without ethnic diversity or pancakes. Burt, Carol, Trash Trouper Janet, and Bev, the Unitarian minister for the church the P.O. shared the building with, convened in the kitchen drinking coffee and stuffing themselves on Burt's goat cheese scones.

"It sounds like a party in here." Purdy walked in carrying a stack of large manila envelopes. I indicated the sign taped to the wall with a big arrow pointing into the hall, 'Burt's Kitchen - Fresh Baked Scones & Coffee'. Under it, a smiling Burt-like figure with a closely cut beard was holding a coffee pot and a plate of scones. This was the second edition of the sign. In the first version, I intentionally exaggerated Burt's girth. He insisted I redraw him to represent his proportions more accurately.

At first, I'd refused, telling him to think of it as a cautionary drawing of what he could look like if he ate too many of his own baked goods. He said it was a good thing I wouldn't have to worry since I wouldn't be eating any more of them.

I thought of those cookies he'd made for our stakeout. The threat was effective, and I immediately redrew the sign.

"I'll have to go try one when I'm done here." Purdy patted her mail stack. "Can you get me a couple priority envelopes? The kind that don't bend."

I pointed to the rack against the wall she'd walked by.

"I had a photo shoot done, of the boudoir variety, in Hillsburg. Very classy, but real sexy. I'm sending these to some gentlemen friends." She winked at me.

"I didn't know there was a place in Hillsburg that did those kinds of photos."

"Sure, Frontier Frames. You know, the studio where you can dress up in frontier costumes and get those old-timey looking pictures."

"The place for tourists?"

"That's the one. I know the photographer's grandad, and for an extra twenty bucks, Josh will stay late for a private 'saloon girl' shoot."

"I'll have to remember that." I tried putting the image of Purdy in a corset and half boots out of my head.

"These are all going to Alaska." She handed me four priority envelopes. "I don't want them bent."

I took them from her. "They should get there no later than next Wednesday."

"Great, great. I think I'll go get one of those scones. I've been starving myself all week for the photo shoot. Maybe I'll trade Burt a picture of my goods for one of his goodies." She threw her head back and cackled. Part of me wanted to applaud Purdy's liberated spirit, but my other part felt like I'd just walked in on my grandparents' square dancing in the buff. I wasn't sure if I wanted to scour my eyes or clap along.

At ten a.m., I closed the service counter window, locked the door to the P.O. back room, and joined the others. "I think

I like the savory ones better," I said through a mouthful of scone. "You are doing some amazing things with Linda's goat cheese."

"Is this from Thornston Farms?" Bev asked.

I nodded.

"Did you hear about that goat of hers? There's an article in this week's Miner's Dispatch that just came out." Bev dug through her enormous patchwork bag and pulled out the paper. "Here," she said. The chunky silver rings on her fingers knocked against the table as she patted the article.

'Lights Out On Thornston Farm Fire Investigation: Appetite for Mayhem Proves the Culprit'.

"One of her goats got into the cheese-making room and chewed through the machinery wires and started the fire." She gave us the article highlights. "The same little bugger chewed through the extension cords the Fire Investigator was using to light the barn and left everyone in the dark."

"Does it say which goat it was?" I asked eagerly. "Was it Ms. MaeMae?"

"Let me see." Bev scanned the article. "You're right! 'The goat known as Ms. MaeMae has a reputation as the farm's troublemaker.'"

"I never liked goats and here's another reason not to," Burt said, vindicated.

As much as I was enjoying the scones and social time in the kitchen, I was also anxious to talk with Burt and Carol privately. "Why don't we get started?" I suggested.

Purdy checked the wall clock and abruptly left, probably late to a burlesque dance audition. I needed to quickly wrap up the litter project meeting and get rid of Janet and Bev.

We discussed the new recycling bins installed outside the church, and Bev's update on the bike pull event logistics.

"I made these." I put a stack of posters and signs on the table. "I already hung one up on the notice board."

Bev divided the posters and assigned us a distribution area.

"Trash Trou- sorry, I mean Janet, how's the rest of your work coming?" Janet turned out to be remarkably effective and accomplished much more than expected. The event was set, and we were solidly on track.

"I'll start cleaning up," Burt announced, clearing the remaining scones and trying to socially nudge the women out.

Bev stood. The tiny bells on her charm bracelet tinkled as she stretched and released a loud yawn. "I've a talk to prepare for tomorrow. I'd better get started." She untangled her long skirt from between her legs and slung her tote over her head. "Come on." She freed her straight gray hair from under her bag strap and motioned to Janet. "We can hang these signs by the recycling containers on our way out."

"I thought they'd never leave," Burt muttered.

I grabbed the trifold from its hiding place inside the P.O. back room. Burt laid out the brightly-colored sticky notes. 'Ms. MaeMae Fire Starter - No Motive,' he neatly wrote on one.

I did two sketches for the empty suspect spaces, one of a chair with a crown on the seat and the other of an ice skate with blood dripping off of its blade.

"I don't understand the pictures," Burt said after I taped them to our board under Chris and Emily's names, respectively. "I think you're being too hard on Emily," Burt admonished after I explained the Tonya Harding reference.

"This isn't so far-fetched. Tonya used a crowbar on a knee, and Carol's stalker put a screwdriver in her tire. Who knows what they'll do next?"

"Gosh, do you think someone would actually hurt me?" Carol paled, and I immediately regretted my thoughtlessness.

"No," Burt reassured. "Maya is exaggerating the threat because she doesn't like competition for Owen." He gave me a dirty look.

"What?" I exclaimed, offended. "First, Owen and I are just friends. Second, he hid from her at the barbecue. She wouldn't be competition anyway." I could feel myself getting worked up again and took a breath. "But Burt is right, Carol. I did get carried away. I think whoever is leaving you these notes wants to scare you away, not injure you."

"We should focus on Chris and what his motive is," Burt said, stepping back and looking at the board.

"It has to be tied to the property on Lupine Lane I want to buy. I wish we had the owner's number so we could just call them."

Burt looked like he might combust with excitement. "That's the Stevens' place. I can do better than a phone number. They're friends of mine. Let's drive over and talk to them in person."

"Chris said they're touchy," Carol said, concerned. "Are you sure they won't get angry if we just show up?"

Burt frowned. "I've never known Ben Stevens to be touchy."

"Can I come too?" I didn't want to be left out of the action.

"I wish you would. You're part of the team, after all." Carol squeezed my hand. We piled into Nell since we all wouldn't fit comfortably in Burt's truck and headed out.

The house was a cute, if slightly rundown farmhouse situated in the middle of a giant meadow. There was a small barn with tractor tires in front filled with bright flowers, and a horse grazed in the adjoining field. It was quite a tranquil pastoral picture, rivaling any velvet waterwheel painting. "It's so peaceful, Carol. And I see what you mean, with a little paint this will be an absolute gem." A round golden potato with fur and legs waddled out to welcome us. His tail moved in double time, helping his forward progression.

"Hello there, Buddy," Burt said, scratching the top of the Labrador's head.

The pasture grass smelled sweet on the breeze. Carol sighed, "I absolutely love this place."

A stooped older man wearing a John Deere cap and a pair of loose jeans with suspenders came out of the house and stood on the porch looking at us.

"Afternoon Ben."

The man raised his hand to shade his eyes from the bright sun. "That you Burt?"

"Sure is."

"Haven't seen you in a while. What can I do for ya?"

"We're hoping to talk to you about the offer this lady here made on your place." Burt gestured towards Carol.

The man looked confused. "First I'm hearing about it. You all better come inside and have a cup of coffee." Spring weeds threatened to obscure the flagstone path winding lazily from the driveway to the porch.

"Nancy, we got company," Ben yelled over his shoulder. "Woman's going deaf. Watch the step there, it's coming loose."

We gingerly made our way up the stairs, which were solid except for the wonky one. The front of the house looked like it had a bad case of mange, with patches of bare wood exposed where loose paint had been scraped off. Someone had prepped the house for a new coat but never got around to finishing the job.

"I would paint it a beautiful blue with cream trim," Carol whispered when she saw me eyeing the bald patches. "And I have two white wicker rockers that would go perfectly on the porch over there." She pointed surreptitiously to the other side.

I held up my crossed fingers to show her I was rooting for her.

"Nancy, company!" Ben yelled again. Inside the house, the musty air smelled of mentholated cream. Like the exterior, the interior showed signs of home improvement projects half completed. A plaster patch on a wall meticulously filled and sanded but never repainted, an old dishwasher sat in the entryway poised for a dump run, and a curtain rod drooped low from where the holder had been pulled from the wall. "Grab a seat in there, I'm moving slowly these days, so I'll follow you."

In the living room, large picture windows overlooked the meadow, which ended in pine trees. It was the single restful vista in a room where every square inch of wall and flat surface was covered by photos of smiling adults and children. A short woman with a closely cut frizz of curly hair teetered in. She adjusted her sweatshirt with running horses circling her middle.

"Why didn't you tell me we had company?" She lowered herself slowly into a recliner, letting out a "huh" when her body dropped the last couple of inches.

"Turn your hearing aids on," Ben hollered.

"Hold on, I can't hear you," she called back, fiddling with her ears. "Burt, it's been forever. How you getting along without Patty these days?"

"Patricia's been gone three years ago, Nancy," Ben reminded at top volume.

"No need to scream, I'm sitting right here." She leaned back, looking at Burt. "I'm sorry about Patty. She was always up for a gab. I used to say to Ben, she missed her calling. Patty should've been a reporter like Barbara Walters. She could pry a secret out of a stone. You know, I gave her my recipe for blackberry pie, and I never gave it to anyone. And boy could she crochet. That over there–." She pointed to a throw on the back of a chair in unattractive shades of green, yellow, and brown. "That's one of hers."

Patricia may've been handy with needles, but she may also have been color-blind.

"Patty was a great lady. We had a lot of fun together," Burt murmured. "I miss those Saturdays the four of us would take a picnic up to the lake and Ben and I would fish."

"Used to be good trout fishing there," Ben said. "They still biting like they used to?"

"I haven't been fishing in a couple of years, but all this talk is making me want to break out the old rod." Burt turned to Carol. "Do you fish?"

"I grew up fishing, but I haven't in a long time. It might be fun to try it again." Facing Ben and Nancy, Carol motioned to herself. "I'm Carol." She put a hand on my arm. "And this is Maya."

"Sorry about my lack of manners." Burt did a round of introductions and finished with the reason for our visit.

"And you say he told you we rejected the offer?" Nancy clarified.

Carol nodded in confirmation. "He said you were very touchy and only wanted to work through agents."

"Why, that sneaking snake." Nancy slapped the arm of the recliner. "I told you not to work with him, Ben. Didn't I tell you?"

"You also said you were leaving at the end of the month with or without me, so what was I supposed to do?" He turned to us. "I had a stroke six months ago, and I can't keep up with the place. We were planning on moving down to be with our kids, but the stroke pushed the move up. I put the for sale sign up two months ago, and we hadn't gotten a single offer. Then Chris showed up and said he'd help us. He said he'd list it on the internet. He knew we wanted to be out of here by the end of the month. Chris said he couldn't afford the asking price and offered us $80,000 less. I told him if at the end of the month we still hadn't sold the house, then we'd take anything reasonable."

I was having a hard time sitting still, I was so angry. That shiny-haired rat was trying to swindle these old people.

"He was taking advantage of you," Carol echoed my thoughts aloud. "I absolutely love your house. It's charming, and I can just feel your love in the place." She looked out the window longingly. "I can see my granddaughter playing out front in the field of wildflowers you planted. I would be honored if you sold me your house at full asking price."

Nancy slapped her hands against her legs. "I knew today was going to be a good day. Didn't I tell you, Ben? I said I got a feeling we should buy a lottery ticket today."

Ben wiped his eye with the back of his hand. "You say that every time the jackpot gets over five million." He shook his head and turned to Carol. "I can't tell you what a relief this is. We loved raising our family here. It was breaking my heart not being able to take care of it the way I used to." He sat back and took a sip of his coffee. "Getting old isn't fun."

"I will take good care of it," Carol promised.

I felt myself tearing up and tried to discreetly wipe the moisture from my own eyes.

"The only worry left now is Buddy." We all looked at the Lab lying on Burt's feet. "The youngest grandkid is horribly allergic. We need to find him a new home with someone we trust and know will look after him." Ben looked meaningfully at Burt.

"Nope, I don't want a dog." Burt shook his hands in protest.

"You're retired now. Not that you'd know it." I mumbled the last part to myself. "What else are you going to do? You're already walking Clover and Fizzy, what's one more?" I loved Buddy for Burt. If he had a dog, he would spend less time at the post office. It was true, I was sort of getting used to him, but it would be nice to see less of him.

Burt looked down at Buddy, who, sensing he was the topic of conversation, looked up into Burt's face and thumped his tail on the floor. I knew Burt was a goner.

"Pat was allergic to dogs too, so we never had one. I don't know how to take care of him."

"It's easy, and I'll help," I prodded.

"He is a good dog." Burt leaned over and scratched Buddy on the head.

"Why don't you take Buddy for a walk when you and Carol go on Monday and try it out?" I persisted.

"There's a path down there that lets out onto the coal miner trail. You could park your car at the house and walk from here," Ben suggested.

I liked that Ben and I were on the same program.

"That's a lot of dogs," Burt protested.

"But they can all be off-leash. Right?" I looked for confirmation from Nancy and Ben.

"Buddy is well-trained. He'll listen to you," Ben confirmed.

"Alright, we'll go for a walk on Monday, but I'm not making any promises beyond that."

I hid my grin. I knew victory when I saw it.

We said our farewells and headed out.

"I can't wait to tell Leigha I'm getting the house! It's going to be so nice to be close to my girls and Dave. I can't wait!" Carol clapped her hands in excitement.

"You already have friends, and you don't even live here yet." Burt beamed.

"That was a real unexpected bonus. I think I'm going to be very happy in Claryce Falls."

With the excitement over, I realized my stomach didn't feel so good. I rolled down the window and Burt complained about the wind in his face. I told him it was either the wind or me being sick. He could choose.

"It was probably all those scones you ate before we left." Burt chastised. "It was like watching a one-woman eating competition."

"Are you food shaming me?"

"If food shaming means you made yourself sick because you ate three scones in the amount of time a normal person would eat one, then the shame is all yours." I didn't have a ready comeback because it was true. "You know what this means, though?" Burt scooted to the edge of the backseat to lean in between Carol and me.

"That Maya should chew her food slower so she doesn't get sick," Carol offered.

"No. I mean, yes, she should do that, or she'll end up choking on a pickle like that singer, Mama Cass."

"It was a ham sandwich, and she actually died of heart failure," I corrected.

"Really? I thought it was a pickle. You learn something new every day." Burt mused.

"You two are sounding like one another," Carol said.

"Don't say that," we both said in unison, only proving the point. Gah! We all needed Burt to take Buddy.

"But that's not what I'm talking about, either. I mean, Chris, he has a very strong motive for scaring Carol off."

Carol nodded, "I agree, the only part that doesn't sit right with me is that I am definitely going to buy a house and does Chris strike you as someone who would want to lose out on the commission?"

"Not if he could avoid it," I agreed.

"He's proven to be completely untrustworthy and motivated by greed," Burt reasoned.

"True, but I'm with Carol. If Chris could get the Stevens' place and sell Carol another house so he gets her commission, I think he'd try for that first."

"He is still a solid suspect," Burt insisted. "We need to establish if he has an alibi for any of the times when notes were left."

"Maybe we should just confront him and see what he does," I reasoned. "Once Carol buys the house, and he realizes we're onto his little scheme, he wouldn't dare leave another threat. If they do stop, then we'll know it was Chris."

"It's not conclusive. Let's get a confession. Threaten to sue him if he doesn't come clean."

"Burt, we can't blackmail him," Carol objected. "But I'm contacting the State Realtor Association. What he did to me was dirty business, but what he tried with the Stevens is fraud. Let's wait to do anything until I get the offer letter signed. My lawyer should have it ready by Tuesday."

We synchronized our calendars and locked in Wednesday for the ultimate real estate smackdown.

Eight

The creek water felt like ice piranhas gnawing on my toes with tiny frozen teeth. "That's cold," I yelped.

"It's spring, they're fed by the snow melt right now." Owen scoffed. "What did you expect?"

"I know, but there's a theoretical knowing and there's the physical, 'my feet may shatter into a million pieces if I step on them' knowing." As if to call me out for being a wimp, Clover pranced into the stream to lap up the frigid water. Watching her made me even colder and yet I still let out yawn.

"What's going on with you today? Usually, your chatter button is stuck to 'on'. But that's like the seventh or eighth yawn you've let rip since we started hiking, and I'm not even counting the ones on the ride to the trail."

"Will you pass me my backpack?" I was sitting on a log, barefoot, on the edge of the creek. I took out a thermos and two travel mugs. "Do you want some coffee?" Owen nodded and I passed him a filled mug. "I slept really poorly last night. I was hoping dunking my feet in the creek would wake me up, but I'd have to go full polar bear plunge this morning. And I'm pretty sure that would give me a heart attack. Then, Clover would be motherless, and you'd have to leave my body here to be eaten by bears."

"Tired and cheery, I see. What kept you up? Were you working on the cans all night? I said I'd help you this week."

"No." I yawned again and took a long pull on the warm coffee. "I was saving kittens and baby turtles from burning yachts all night."

"Uh, explain please." Owen reached for the metal cup of coffee I held out for him and sat on the log next to me.

I felt his body heat against my chill and fought the urge to lean into him. "There's a realtor in town trying to swindle a sweet elderly couple by keeping offers for their property from them. He's waiting for them to get desperate so he can buy the place for cheap."

"Did you report him?"

"Not yet, but Carol is going to this week."

"But how is this related to kittens and burning yachts?"

"Stress dream-saving the innocent from the forces of greed and evil trying to destroy them."

Owen nodded as if it all made sense.

"What's going to happen to the elderly couple?"

I moved down to the ground so I could lean my back against the log. It was colder in the forest, but the weak sun still felt good on my face. Closing my eyes, I willed it into my pores and soaked in the sounds of the wind blowing through the pines and the dogs splashing in the creek. I took another sip of coffee and told Owen about yesterday's trip to the Stevens, leaving out any mention of Carol's notes.

"Sounds like it will all work out in the end."

"I suppose." I hesitated. "It's not just Chris; it's also Peter Becker's death and other stuff. I don't understand how people can be so horrible."

A large hand rested on my shoulder. "Not all people are. Some are actually pretty sweet."

I glanced up at him. Owen gazed down at me with a look that felt as warm as the sun on my face. I involuntarily returned it, and we held eye contact until he cleared his throat and stood up.

He pulled a bandana from his bag and handed it to me. "Dry your feet off and let's head back to the trailhead. It's another twenty-minute drive until we get to the other target practice sites. We'll get your cans, clean up the trash, then let's grab a pizza in Hillsburg on the way back."

My stomach gurgled loudly at the mention of food.

"I'll take that as an agreement."

"Depends. How do you feel about pineapple on your pizza?" It was a trick question. There was only one right answer. It's delicious. For the rest of the hike, we debated the merits of different pizza topping combinations.

It was novel riding down the forest roads as a passenger. I'd taken Clover up here hiking many times and used to come with Leigha before Libby. I almost always drove, so I decided to enjoy the experience. Sweet, yellow buttercups dotted the side of the road, with the occasional white trillium making a showing. Patches of snow in deeply shaded areas fought the encroachment of spring. Along the way, Owen pointed out different projects underway to help restore the fish habitat and manage the watershed.

"See those logs over there." He pointed to a log jam across the stream. "We put those there about two months ago, and you can already see the pool forming. Helps with erosion and creates better fish habitat." Listening to Owen talk, it was clear how much he loved what he did. "This is the turnoff." He maneuvered the truck onto a path which seemed more like a deer track than a road.

The path deadened into a dirt embankment. White and blue Miller Lite cans lay scattered around the ground, interspersed with crinkled chip bags and candy wrappers. Small piles of rifle casings glinted in the dirt.

"Wow, Trash Trooper Janet's head would explode if she saw this. How did you even know this was here?"

"It's my job to know these woods." Owen sounded very official.

"Understood, Sir." I stood at attention and saluted him. "Should I get the buckets or will you, Sir?"

He picked up a pine cone and hucked it at me.

"No maiming the help." I grabbed an empty bucket from the back of his truck and put on the leather work gloves he handed me. "I haven't heard you mention the poachers. Have you found any more dead elk?"

"Not for about a week. Hopefully, they stopped. But it's more likely they're dumping the carcasses somewhere new we haven't found yet."

"Man, someone really likes Cool Ranch Doritos and Butterfingers." I stuffed another candy wrapper into my bucket of non-recyclable garbage. "Do you think they ate them all on the same day? I mean, there'd need to be like ten guys to eat this many chips."

Owen straightened, holding up a couple of shell casings to the light. "They're probably from a couple of different trips. It looks like a lot of the shells are from the same rifle, probably from multiple practice sessions."

"How can you tell?"

"For starters, all the casings are from a seven-millimeter rifle." He pointed to a spot on a casing. "See this tiny mark on the edge on this one and this one?" He handed them to me for closer inspection. "The marks are in the same place, which means they're from the same rifle, but I picked them up from different piles, and you can tell these are older because of the dirt and discoloration."

"Very observant. You sound like you could be on one of those CSI shows - CSI Claryce Falls." I tossed the casings in with the others.

We continued sorting the trash into buckets by categories, cans, non-recyclable garbage, plastic bottles, and shell casings. When we were done, I was ready to eat my weight in dough and cheese.

Good news for my arteries, when we got to Zeke's in Hillsburg there was a twenty-minute wait so we decided to pick up Thai and bring it back to my place. Now, admiring the fresh rolls, chicken satay, two noodle dishes, and the yellow curry laid out on the table, I realized Owen was right when he warned me I was over ordering.

"You're thinking I was right, aren't you?" He nudged me in the ribs.

"I was thinking how much I love leftovers, and I'm really glad we'll have some."

Owen's sudden bark of laughter startled Fizzy, who yipped in reproach. "You're never going to let me win, are you?"

"Not intentionally." I felt like being really comfortable, so I suggested we fill our plates and take them to the couch. Even though it wasn't cold enough to warrant a fire, I started one anyway. My bones ached from lack of sleep. "I get cold when I'm tired. If you start to feel like a roasted chicken, we'll open the door and let in some air." I picked up my phone and put on Leon Bridges in the background. "You okay with this music?"

"I like it." Owen inhaled a spring roll in three bites. "Man, I didn't realize how hungry I was."

"Food is the best after a hike," I agreed. We ate in determined silence. As I ripped chicken off a skewer, I felt like a tiger with food aggression. The thought sparked a memory of my brother Michael and me as kids. When we were little, I loved tater tots, but we'd only get them when my mother was away at a conference. I'd scarfed mine down first, then pretend to be a lion, getting Michael to toss me his tots. I used to think I was really outsmarting him, but years later when I confessed, he said he knew all along. He just liked playing with me more than he liked tater tots. Michael had been on my mind a lot lately. Peter's recent death stirred up a lot of memories, but I pushed them aside and focused on the man on my couch.

"I know you have a brother and a sister, Jason and Katie, right? Where do you fall in the order?" I asked.

"I'm the middle, Jason is the oldest, and Katie is the baby by eight years."

"Are you all close?"

He looked over at my painting of an old truck parked in a wheat field dominated by a massive open blue sky and contemplated the question. "We all love each other, but we don't see one another very often. I talk to Katie more than Jason. She's got two girls, Zoe and Emma. I video chat with them about once a month. Ava and I drove over and spent last Thanksgiving with them in Idaho. They're in Boise. Jason and I smack talk about football over text, usually when the Cowboys or Seahawks lose. He's married too and has three kids, but he's down in Texas and pretty involved with his wife's family. I could be better about making an effort, but I know he's happy and that's good enough for me. What about you? I haven't heard you talk about any siblings."

A familiar knot tightened. I set my plate down on the coffee table and curled my feet up on the couch. "My brother Michael was three years older." I pointed to a photo on my bookshelf of us grinning into the camera. "He died ten years ago. Michael was the best, gentlest guy. He had a horrible sense of humor, an endless supply of dad jokes, I mean really, the worst. And I adored him. I adore him," I corrected. The ache from Michael's absence dulled with time but his loss was woven into me. It was always there, like an ear or chin—not something I thought about every day, but part of me.

Owen reached over and held my foot in comfort.

"He was killed in a car accident. A mom in a minivan was trying to pull Cheerios out of her bag and she ran through the stop light." I breathed in deeply, then exhaled slowly. "I was in a rough place for a long time. Scott helped me through the worst of it, and that's when we got married. After I came out of my grief, I was a different person. I didn't need Scott in the same way. It was hard for him." I shook my head to clear memories I'd rather not hold onto. "Enough of that, tell me about something that makes you happy."

Owen thought for a moment. "My photography."

"What! You've been holding out on me. I didn't know you were a photographer."

"It's just a hobby. With camera phones, everyone's a photographer, right?"

"A picture of a breakfast burrito with a blurry background does not make you a photographer. Show me some of your photos."

"I don't really share them with people. I'm not a real artist like you."

"Whatever." I batted the comment away. "Please show me your photos." Begrudgingly, Owen pulled his phone out, opened an album, and handed it to me. He pulled back into the couch corner to watch me from a distance.

My mouth dropped open. "These are incredible. The lighting is so dramatic. Is this photoshopped?"

"Nope, that's one hundred percent Mother Nature. When you spend as much time as I do in the woods, you have a lot of opportunities to see some incredible stuff." The digital album was a jaw-dropping collection of dramatically lit vistas and close-ups of insects caught in battle or trout leaping into the air.

"These should be in National Geographic. I can't believe you took them. I love this one. What is happening?"

Owen scooted closer to see what I was looking at. His shoulder brushed mine, warm and comforting.

"It was the craziest thing. I was in town and a murder of crows surrounded this moving truck and silently followed it for blocks. They kept it surrounded, even turning around corners. It was like something out of the old Hitchcock film *The Birds*. I happened to have my camera out, and I got the picture."

"I wonder what they were doing. It's such a cool photo, and it looks so eerie in black and white. I love it."

"Thanks." He moved back to his side of the couch.

As we continued to chat, the warmth of the fire in combination with a full stomach proved to be too much. I must have fallen asleep when Owen went to the bathroom because when I woke up, he was gone. I was lying on the couch, a blanket over me, and Clover curled up next to my feet.

The thought of getting up and putting the leftovers away made me snuggle deeper into the couch in protest. Sitting up slowly, I tried not to disturb Clover. The table was already clear. Owen, the magical fairy, put everything away before he left. I sighed contentedly and snuggled back into the cushions to dream of bright mountain skies and blue eyes.

Nine

I loved getting paid. Or rather, I loved it when clients paid me when they said they would. Everyone was always in a rush to get their designs, but when it came time to pay up, clients were a lot more relaxed. Jay trudged into the P.O. with my check from the resort. His weighted steps battled gravity, which looked about to crumple him. I stopped the happy money dance I was doing behind the counter and sobered.

"Elby said to apologize for forgetting to leave your check before she left. She put in a little bonus to make up for it." And that was why it was great working with Elby. "I also have the specs for the t-shirts and caps. She said she'll need them next week." I thanked him and tucked everything behind the counter.

"Jay, I'm so sorry about Peter. He seemed like such a fun, spirited guy."

"He was, man. Peter was the best friend anyone could have." Jay looked like he was about to cry, and I reached for the box of tissues under the counter. "I can't believe he's gone and never coming back. It was like one second he was here, bam, the next second he wasn't. I don't know how to deal with all this." Dark circles rimmed Jay's deep-set brown eyes.

"I'm really sorry for your loss."

"Yeah, thanks." He straightened his shoulders, clearly done talking about Peter with a relative stranger. "Do you know any of those church people?" He indicated the back of the building with his thumb.

"Sure, why?"

"I parked in the back lot and accidentally knocked over one of their garbage containers. I picked everything up, but I dented it. Will you tell them I'll pay for it if they want? I don't need to tick off God right now."

"I think you're more likely to tick off Janet before God," I murmured.

"Why are there so many of them anyway? It looks like a barrel race arena."

Hoping to lift Jay's spirits, I launched into a story about Trash Trouper Janet's trash "capades" and the campground event we were planning. "Janet wasn't wrong, though. I was up the Teanaway this weekend with a friend, cleaning out this spot someone was using as their personal target practice range. You wouldn't believe all the cans, junk food wrappers, and cartridge casings we picked up. On the upside, I can use everything but the Doritos bags and Butterfingers wrappers for the trash project. Unfortunately, my poor garage is starting to smell like The Oasis bar at the end of a Friday night."

Jay looked grim. "That's pretty bad. Hey, I gotta get back to the Pro Shop. Elby's covering for me since there's no one else now." His chest rose and fell in a dramatic stagger as his breath caught.

"Thank Elby for me and tell her I'll call her to arrange a time to drop everything off."

Jay nodded and left.

Just before noon, Carol, Burt, and the dogs came in for their post-walk cookies. "How did it go with Buddy?" I reached down and pulled out the biscuits.

"He's a good dog," Burt admitted grudgingly.

"He's a sweetheart," Carol cooed. "If Burt doesn't take him, I will."

"We'll see," is all Burt said.

Changing the subject, I asked Carol if she got a hold of her lawyer.

She clapped her hands in an enthusiastic staccato burst, her purple metallic nails reflecting off the fluorescent lights. "I'll have the paperwork tomorrow morning. We'll head over to the Stevens in the afternoon to sign and make it official!"

"I'm so happy for you," I gushed. "It's going to be great to have you here permanently." I threw my arms up and did a little chant and dance, "Carol's moving to Claryce Falls! Hey! Carol's moving to Claryce Falls! Ho." My song got the dogs excited, and they barked along.

"You're still working. You should act like it," Burt scolded.

I stuck my tongue out at him as I rolled down the service counter window.

I didn't feel like heading home yet, so after I set up Clover and Fizzy with water and chew toys in the back of Nell, I walked over to the library. Off the main road leading into Claryce Falls, the library lived in the old City Hall Building. Originally only occupying a ten by twenty-five foot room, the library stayed that size for almost sixty years until the Gates Foundation gave Washington libraries a bunch of money in early two thousand.

Now the library spanned the entire ground floor and served as a community center, holding a weekly stitching circle, after-school chess club, and hosting a monthly birding lecture series in addition to more standard programs like book clubs and reading tutoring. The sun-filled back wall lined with communal work tables was one of my favorite places to spend an afternoon looking through books and sketching out ideas.

"Hey, stranger," Jason called. "Where've you been? I haven't seen you around lately. I've been holding a couple of books I think you'll like, but I was starting to think I'd have to put them out on the shelves if you didn't turn up soon."

As the Lead Librarian, Jason Carter was a walking exclamation mark of enthusiasm and height. His short strawberry blond hair perpetually stuck out in different directions, as if he just emerged from a whirlwind. For me, Jason was synonymous with his infinite collection of sweater vests. Last summer, after the first time I saw him in a polo shirt, I immediately left the library and bought a package of t-shirts. I dug out my old silk screen equipment and printed sweater vests on all the shirts for him. He wore them the rest of the summer, and we'd been buddies ever since.

Jason pulled out the books. After we finished quietly catching up, he pointed me in the direction of the photography section. "I know you don't really care about birds, but Fred Anthony is giving this month's lecture tonight about his trip to South Africa, and he'll be talking about all kinds of wildlife. I've seen some of his photos. They are incredible."

"First, it's not like I'm the chairman of Death to Avian Life Incorporated with my own team of kitten assassins. I'm just not getting up at five a.m. to go squat in the cold and creep on Woodpeckers like a Peeping Tom with you and Maggie. Second, it sounds interesting, so count me in."

"Great!" He smiled broadly. "Mags will be excited to see you."

"Me too," I agreed. I found a couple more books on nature photography before forcing myself to leave while I could still carry everything back to the car.

"Why are you dressed up?" Owen asked suspiciously when I opened the door for him that afternoon. "And why does your house smell like cotton candy?"

"Hello, Owen, nice to see you too. I look pretty? Why thank you." I motioned him in.

"Yeah, yeah, you know you're pretty and all the rest. Aren't we working on the cans tonight?" He walked into the kitchen and looked around as if searching for clues. His eyes landed on the menagerie of rice crispy treat animals wearing iced accessories in the colors of the South African flag. "What are those for and can I have one?"

"Manners," I chastised as my inside voice sang to me, "He thinks I'm pretty. He thinks I'm pretty."

"Sorry, may I please have a rice crispy treat?"

"Eat one, for heaven's sake."

Owen stalked over to the table and bit the head off a polar bear wearing a jauntily frosted tie. Jason asked me to bring a dessert for the reception after the lecture and I'd gone all out with the cookie cutters, decorative icing, and Rice Krispies. My kitchen might resemble an Easy-Bake Oven explosion, but the treats looked like blue ribbon winners at a bake-off.

"I'm so hungry. We cleared deadfall all day, and Raccoons or something stole my lunch from the back of the truck."

I steered Owen to the leftover curry and joined him at the table with a cup of tea.

"So, what's with the fancy outfit anyway?" He covered his mouth with the back of his hand to hide the mouthful he was talking around.

My stain-free jeans, button-up cotton blouse, and a pair of dangling earrings hardly seemed fancy. True, I was more groomed than usual. My dark waves were actually staying in place for once. I'd rimmed my brown eyes with liner, along with my usual mascara, aiming for large, open doe-eyes. But

I may have overshot the mark and hit shocked owl instead. Either way, I was hardly dressed for an evening at the Opera. However, it did make me wonder what I usually looked like if my outfit was so noteworthy.

I told Owen about the library lecture and invited him.

"I'd like to go, but I'm pretty wiped out," he said.

"What if I drive, and we leave right at eight?" We negotiated the specifics, Owen changed into a clean t-shirt he kept in his truck, and we were off again.

"Thank heavens, you're here." Maggie Carter threw her arms around me. Maggie, Jason's pint-sized wife and all-around badass, was Claryce Falls' reigning Lumberjack Days Speed Pole Climbing Champion. At five feet even, she was half squirrel, known to climb any vertical surface.

"I'm happy to see you too."

Maggie's bear hug pinned my arms, so I could only use my forearms to return her hug. I felt like a harbor seal hugging a chipmunk. She released me and stepped back. "Owen, I didn't know you knew Maya."

I looked between the two. For only being in town less than six months, Owen knew quite a few people.

"Maggie is on the community forest's citizen advisory board," Owen explained.

"Of course you are," I said, shaking my head in awe of her boundless energy. "Wow, your hair is getting so long." I playfully pulled her blonde ponytail.

"Where should I put these?" Owen held up the platter of covered treats.

Maggie pointed to a folding table in back. "Over there, but keep them wrapped. Last month, someone started eating early and kept crunching carrots during the talk. It drove me crazy. If that happens again, I can't be held responsible for my actions. So, let's uncover the food at the end."

Owen nodded and headed to the table.

"How do you know Owen?" Maggie asked suggestively.

I rolled my eyes at her. "It's not like that. He leaves his dog at my place with Clover during the day, so neither of them gets lonely now that I'm working mornings at the P.O."

"Right, I forgot you're working there. We are overdue for a catchup, but right now I need you to run over to Provisions and pick up a box of cups and coffee for the reception. I'd go, but the projector broke, and I'm trying to fix it. Everything's already paid for."

"I'm on it."

Owen came with me in case I needed help carrying anything.

"Welcome to Provisions in the Pines." Summoned by the bell jingle, Emily's perky voice greeted us from behind a shelf.

If I'd remembered she might be working, I would've insisted Owen stay behind. I ducked below a display of locally made huckleberry jam and pulled Owen's arm down with me. Mid-crouch, I changed my mind and started shooing him away. "Go! Wait outside for me," I whispered frantically, hoping desperately there was still time for him to leave unseen.

He stared down at me. "What? Why?"

We weren't fast enough.

"Owen, hi! What a wonderful surprise to see you here. How can I help you?"

"We're picking up the order for the library event tonight," he answered.

"We?" Emily questioned.

I rose, feeling like a Whac-A-Mole critter emerging from the safety of my preserve barricade. I really hoped Emily didn't have a mallet. "Hey," I said sheepishly.

Emily's jaw clenched in acknowledgment. "You're going to the talk tonight?" Not removing her gaze from Owen, she attempted to make small talk.

"Yeah, Maya and I are picking up a box for Maggie."

She giggled. "That is so sweet of you to do. I just love the library. I was thinking of going over there myself when I finish up here. Maybe I'll see you there."

I wanted to barf. "Can we just get the stuff already?" I didn't know how much more of this I could stomach, literally.

"Here." She shoved the box across the counter. I went to take it from her, but she held on. Leaning towards me, she looked me in the eyes. "I deserve to have the love and life I want," she whispered.

"Okay." I pulled back from the crazy lady in the pink "Pacific Northwest Girl" sweatshirt.

"Like Maya said, we gotta get this back to Maggie before the talk starts." Owen picked up the supplies.

"It was nice seeing you again, Owen."

I could feel the death daggers Emily was throwing at me as we quickly exited.

"What was that?" Owen asked when we cleared the block.

"If I were you, I would keep track of all my loose hair and toenails because that gal is one voodoo doll away from selling her soul to become Mrs. Owen Reese."

"Doesn't everyone in town think we're engaged?"

"What?" I squawked.

"Three women I barely know came up and congratulated me after dinner at the Oasis last week."

"That's crazy. I hope you set them straight."

"Nope, I thanked them and carried on."

"Why would you do that?"

"I don't owe them an explanation and if I'm being honest, I thought maybe it would get women to back off a little. The ladies are thirsty in this town."

I wanted to make fun of him, but part of me, despite being mortified by this dang lie that wouldn't die, was oddly pleased that the thought of us being engaged repelled Owen less than being aggressively hunted by single women.

"I'd think with Emily working at the grocery store, she'd heard about us."

My chest squeezed at Owen's use of "us". I was really happy he wasn't a mind reader. For a brief, irrational moment, panic speared me. What if he could read minds? Then he'd know I was as Owen-crazed as every other single woman and some of the men in Claryce Falls. "Quick, what number am I thinking of?" I blurted out.

He looked at me with an expression of confusion. "What?"

"Nothing, never mind. So, yeah, she did hear." I told Owen about my Emily daytime drama episode at Glamour Nails and Boogie.

"You have to be exaggerating. She sounds genuinely deranged. Do I need to be worried for you?"

"Thank you!" I exclaimed. "Burt and Carol keep acting like I'm blowing this up because I'm jealous."

"Jealous of what?"

"This was my point."

Owen was really getting me right now. We didn't have time to finish the conversation because Maggie grabbed us as we entered the library. She took the box from Owen and told us to grab a seat. Jason announced Fred Anthony, and the lights dimmed. Fifteen minutes in, I was hooked. I was in love with South Africa. A quiet snore came from my left. Owen's head was propped up on the wall and his eyes were closed. I gently shook his leg. He roused enough to sit up and fall back to sleep.

Moments later, his body tipped and my shoulder became his new pillow. The angle of his neck looked very uncomfortable, but I was selfishly enjoying the contact too much to wake him again. My chest filled with contentment as I breathed in

Owen while falling under the enchantment of lush wineries, dry rocky desert landscapes, elephant herds bathing in mud, and blue whales in clear aqua waters.

A sharp poke in my back pricked me from my daze. "You said you were just friends," a voice hissed in my right ear. I slowly turned, trying not to disturb Owen. Emily sat behind me, glaring. She jabbed her finger at me and silently mouthed "You," and stabbed her finger towards Owen, "Him" she continued with the pantomime. Holding up her two index fingers, she smashed the tips together, moving them back and forth while making kissing motions with her lips as the two fingers made out. Violently, she flung them apart and brought them back together to form an 'x' sign. If her aggression hadn't been directed at me, I would've applauded the emotive performance she was able to extract from her fingers. Maybe I was seeing the birth of a new art form.

But it was directed at me, so I rolled my eyes and mouthed, "Go away." I turned back to the projector show and pretended to ignore her. Emily didn't poke me again, but I heard her muttering something over and over. I only caught a few stray words, "love," and "deserve." I really hoped she wasn't trying to hex me back there. Eventually, she went silent. When the lights turned on, Owen woke, and Emily and her troupe of thespian digits were gone.

Ten

Sitting at Leigha's kitchen table, we were as buoyant as the giant "Congratulations" balloon Libby chased around with the dogs. The entire room was lit with cheer, from the yellow gingham curtains to the whitewashed wood slat walls, to the matching yellow mugs we drank our celebratory cocoa from. The signed offer letter for the Stevens' house lay in the middle of the table in pride of place.

"We agreed that they could have two months to move out, which works out perfectly since we both have so much to pack."

"You know what this means?" Leigha was buzzing with excitement.

"Antique shopping!" Mother and daughter sang in unison.

"We can do a girls' weekend to La Conner and go poke around the shops."

"I love it." Carol beamed. "I'm ready to pare down my old things to make room for the new. Which reminds me, the Stevens are moving in with their kids and need to get rid of a lot of stuff. With your girls' help, I was hoping we could have a garage sale for them. Maya, you saw them. I don't think they can do it on their own."

"Of course," I agreed.

"The only thing is, we're in a bit of a time crunch because I leave for home in just over two weeks, right after Maya's event. We won't clear them out, but it will help," Carol cajoled.

I ran through my mental to-do list, the designs for the Pro Shop tournament were due soon, and there was still a lot of work left on the can sculptures before the campground opening. But, as far as I knew, you only lived once. "I'm in," I declared and wiped my cocoa mustache on the back of my hand.

Clover, Fizzy, and I headed down Main Street to where I'd left Nell parked outside the P.O. The good mood from the kitchen clung to me like pollen to a bee and tasted sweet. I battled my urge to skip in public but lost the fight every third or fourth step. I was also thinking about my first giant aluminum can sculpture I would hopefully finish today. It was twelve feet tall and so far seemed like it could stand on its own. I was so preoccupied with resisting skipping and thoughts of my cans, I didn't notice Chris Weller storming down the street until he was almost fifteen paces away. We made eye contact, and I stopped abruptly. I felt like Wyatt Earp about to shoot it out with Billy Clanton. Except in this version, Billy's hair was perfectly pomaded into place and his brown loafers gleamed with a high shine.

"You," he shouted. "You are the reason this is happening."

Clover growled low, and Chris stopped.

"Get your dog under control. If that mongrel so much as slobbers on me, I will have it put down."

Instantly, my guns were loaded with fury and ready to fire. Nobody threatens my dog. "Get yourself under control," I shot back.

"I got a call from Ben Stevens today. Guess what he said. They sold their house. It seems someone paid them a little visit behind my back. You did that. Carol never would have double-crossed me on her own if you hadn't put her up to it. So, you owe me."

It had just turned into a spaghetti western if the fool thought I owed him anything! "You were trying to swindle senior citizens out of their property. You're lucky you haven't been arrested and your license suspended. But if I have anything to say about that, you will."

"How dare you." Spit flew from his mouth. "I am at least owed the commission on the sale. I am her realtor."

"I'm pretty sure you've been fired." Some people just couldn't read between the lines.

"That commission is mine and one way or another someone will pay."

"They will," I quipped back. "But it won't be us. It will be the guy trying to steal from the elderly."

Chris took a step closer. Clover's hackles went up, and she moved in between us. Her growl rose into menacing barks.

"I'm calling the police on that out-of-control beast."

"Please, go right ahead. I'd love to tell them all about you."

Chris glared at me, emanating hate. "This isn't finished," he said, before turning and storming back down the street towards his office.

Wally from Wally's Tools and Supplies opened the door to his store. "You okay Maya?"

My insides felt shaky, but I nodded.

"What was all that about?"

"Real estate." I didn't feel like explaining myself. All I wanted to do was get away from people and get rid of some of my excess confrontation adrenaline.

On the way home, I pulled off on one of the steep logging roads with the dogs to power-walk my feelings out. Fizzy was tired from her morning with Burt and Carol, so I carried her on my shoulders, draping her around my neck like a puppy stole. The fast four-mile therapy session did its job, and by the time we reached the house, I felt calm.

Owen texted saying he'd be late. Perfect. I set myself the challenge of finishing one of the sculptures before he arrived. As soon as I let Clover out, she went on high alert, nose to the ground, tracing the invisible trail of invading deer or coyotes. The garbage cans were knocked over, lids flung off. I usually didn't put trash in them until collection day for this reason. A full garbage can was like an Open Table reservation to bears and other scavengers. I picked up the lids and righted the bins.

Clover circled my workshop, sniffing and growling. I opened the doors and carefully maneuvered the giant can through the door. It was a nice day to work outside, and I needed the head clearance. I secured the sculpture to a hook on the side of the building and propped the ladder in front of the workshop entrance where the ground was level.

Clover was still on the hunt. I wanted to focus and not worry about breaking up a rumble between her and a pack of raccoons, so I put both her and Fizzy in the backyard. Stromae's dance hip-hop pumped from my speakers, fueling my progress, losing myself in the rhythm of soldering. I worked intensely, only taking short breaks for intermittent dance sessions when my soldering hand cramped. It was nearly finished—just a few more touches before my first piece would be complete.

Inside my workshop, something crashed. My heart leaped, causing the ladder to shiver beneath me. I shut off the music, the sudden silence rang in my ears. Every nerve was on edge as I strained to listen. Nothing. It was possible a critter had gotten inside again. Last month, a pack rat had taken up residence and chewed through the cord of my miter saw before I rehomed it farther out in the woods. Maybe the raccoon Clover had been hunting was inside, hiding all along. Or more likely, I'd pushed something too close to the edge when I moved the sculpture.

I stayed still for a few more minutes before shaking off my unease and getting back to it. Turning the music on again, I lowered the volume. The can was so close to being done. From the top of the ladder, I stretched to reach the far side of the sculpture when movement caught my eye.

The hair on the back of my neck stood up and I recoiled. A figure in a black hoodie emerged from the workshop's shadow, moving towards me fast. My mind blanked, panic surging as the stranger charged the ladder.

The rungs tilted beneath me. I grabbed at the side of the building, trying desperately not to fall. In the background, Clover barked, wildly. My fingernails dug into the top of the door frame. For a brief moment, I thought I'd saved myself. But hands grabbed my legs and pulled hard. Wood splintered as my nails ripped free.

"Don't hurt the can," I yelled as I plummeted. My head hit the ground and the world went dark.

"Maya! Maya!" A panicked voice called my name. "No, Clover, give her space," he commanded. "Maya, are you okay?"

"No," I groaned. "I hurt."

"Where?"

"Everywhere."

Clover whined.

"It's okay, let her come here."

"No, you're covered in blood. Stay still." I felt a cloth pressed to the back of my head.

"I'm okay girl. It's okay." I winced. I tried sitting up, but Owen held me down.

"Dang it! Stay still for a minute. I have a neck brace in the back of my truck, let me get it. Don't move. Promise me."

"I'm fine."

"Maya, say it or I can't leave you."

I promised. Owen returned and secured a large brace around my neck before turning me on my side. "It looks like you cut your head on a rock when you hit it. It's not too big, but it's bleeding a lot. I'm gonna wrap a bandage around it before I move you."

After my head was bandaged, I tried sitting.

"Let me help you." He slipped his hands under my head and back and slowly eased me up. "You've got to be more careful. I thought you were dead. Clover busted through the fence to get to you. You scared the crap out of us."

"This wasn't my fault," I groaned as I tried to move my arm. A pain shot up my shoulder. "There was a person. They pushed me over. Didn't you see them?"

"No, we need to take you to the hospital. You clearly have a concussion."

"No, I mean yeah, probably, but there was a person in a black hoodie. They pushed me off my ladder."

"Come on, we're heading to the ER in Hillsburg."

"No, I'm fine."

"We're going, no argument. Can you walk?"

"I think so." I got on my hands and knees to try and push myself to my feet. My head went fuzzy, and I threw up on the ground.

"That's it. Put your arm around my neck." He wrapped one arm under my thighs and the other around my back and hoisted me up.

I started to feel sick again. "Wait, hold still for a sec." When the nausea passed, I gave him the 'okay,' and he put me in his truck. He locked the dogs inside and got in. I closed my eyes.

"Don't go to sleep, Maya," Owen said, shaking my leg.

"Don't do that," I protested. Every jostle and rut felt like a nail going through my brain. I heard Owen on the phone.

"Dave, I'm taking Maya to the hospital in Hillsburg. She fell and hit her head."

"Someone pushed me," I groaned.

"Yeah, that was her. She said someone pushed her, but I don't know if it really happened or if it's the concussion talking." He silently listened for a few minutes. "That would be a good idea. Thanks. See you soon." He hung up. "How you doing over there?"

"I feel like a puffer fish that's been turned inside out, and my needles keep poking my own brain."

"You're sounding more like yourself. That's something."

The ride was unpleasant, and the ER even more so. At the hospital, they insisted I leave the neck collar on until I got X-rays. Waiting in the tiny room with Owen, I felt like a dog who'd lost a fight, forced into a cone of shame. A series of assistants, nurses, and doctors came in and out to poke at me and hear my story.

After three hours, I had three stitches in my head, was diagnosed with a concussion, and put on a twenty-four-hour watch. My left cheek, shoulder, and hip were bruised, but nothing was broken.

When the doctor left to get the discharge nurse, Owen started unbuttoning his work shirt revealing his cotton undershirt.

"What are you doing? I asked incredulously.

"You're covered in dried blood. I'm giving you my uniform shirt, so you don't freak out your friends in the waiting room."

"Wait, people are here? Do I really look that bad?"

"Yes," he said flatly. He shrugged out of the button-up and handed it to me. "It may reek of sweat. Sorry. But it's better than what you're wearing. Do you need help changing?"

I shook my head.

"I'll wait outside, holler when you're done."

Owen's body heat lingered on his shirt. His warmth and smell slipped protectively around me as I slowly and painfully replaced my top. I lifted the stiff fabric to my nose, inhaling his comforting scent.

A soft knock on the door brought me out of my fog. When the nurse wheeled me into the waiting room, I was met by a chorus of worried faces. Dave, Leigha, and Burt jumped up when they saw me.

"Are you alright? Is she alright?" Leigha frantically looked between Owen and me. "Why is she wearing your shirt? What happened to her clothes?"

"I'm fine," I reassured them. "Just a bump on the head and a bruise or two. You didn't all need to come."

"I don't understand what happened," Leigha still sounded scared.

As I was wheeled out the door, I gave them the highlights real of the evening. Leigha and Burt had so many more questions, but I was too tired to answer them.

"She's lucky," Owen said. "But someone needs to stay with her for the next twenty-four hours."

"What about work?" I panicked.

"Don't worry, I'll take care of it," Burt reassured me. The group worked out a babysitting schedule as I sat in Owen's truck, feeling pathetic.

"I'm going to come by tomorrow, Maya and get an official statement from you. Okay?" Dave asked.

"Sure, thanks again for coming." I felt guilty and loved. The pain meds the hospital gave me were kicking in, and as long as I didn't move my head too quickly, it didn't hurt much.

"I'm going to get Maya home and to bed," Owen announced. "Burt, Leigha, I'll see you both in the morning."

I must have dozed most of the way home because it felt like no time had passed before I was tucked in my own bed. I halfheartedly tried to convince Owen to go home, but he told me to quit fighting him and go to sleep. So, I did.

The low murmur of voices and the smell of coffee roused me from an unpleasant dream of elk struggling to free themselves from a net of plastic bags and beer cans. I really needed to stop playing with garbage. My head felt much better. I only had a slight ache behind my eyes. Slowly, I swung my legs around and sat. Everything stayed in place, so I tried standing. When the world continued to stay still, I grabbed my enormous cotton robe and tottered out.

Owen, Burt, Dave, Leigha, and Carol all sat around my kitchen table. "Good morning," Leigha greeted me with sunshine in her voice. "How you doing this morning?"

I joined the others and took a chair next to Leigha, who slung her arm around my shoulders and hugged me gently.

"I'm not bad, actually."

"That thick head of yours was finally good for something," Burt teased.

Owen filled my cup with steaming coffee, and Burt pushed a plate of flaky-looking pastries at me. "My version of a Danish made with goat cheese."

I thanked them and took a big gulp of coffee.

"You know, I think I'm feeling good enough to go to work."

A round of protests went round the table. "Not going to happen," Owen said. "You're staying here with Leigha and Carol this morning. Burt will be here after he closes the P.O. at noon. I'm going to have dinner with you. After that, we'll see how you're feeling."

"You know you're very bossy," I said but smiled and squeezed his forearm in appreciation.

"Alrighty, I better go open things up." Burt pushed his chair away from the table. "Let me grab the keys from you, Maya."

I pointed at the hook by the door. "You think I'll ever get them back?" I asked as the door closed behind him. "Now that he's behind the counter again, he may never leave."

"He was very worried about you," Carol lightly chided. "We all were."

I stared down into my coffee. "I was pretty scared myself for a minute there."

"About that," Dave said. "Do you feel like answering a few questions now?"

I nodded.

"Describe to me what happened. Give me rough times and everything you can remember. Even if it doesn't seem important."

I ran through the evening in as much detail as I could. I told him about Clover being on high alert as soon as we got home, so I didn't think it was someone we knew. I explained how they must have been lurking in the shed the whole time, which made everything creepier. They watched me dance and sing, waiting for their moment. I hadn't seen much. Just a figure in a dark hoodie rushing me.

Dave asked if I thought it was a man or a woman, and I wasn't sure. It all happened so fast. "You really wouldn't have to be that strong to pull me off the door frame. I was only hanging on by my fingertips," I tried to answer thoughtfully.

"But why would someone be hiding in your workshop in the first place?" Leigha broke in.

Dave raised an eyebrow at his wife.

"Sorry, I'll try and let you ask the questions, but it's very hard."

"Would anyone want to hurt you?" Dave asked.

I took a deep breath and let it out slowly. "I've been ticking people off lately." I started with my showdown with Chris Weller yesterday. When I told them about Emily, Leigha let out a surprised gasp.

"That just doesn't sound like her. She's usually so sweet and kind of shy."

"Those aren't the words I'd use to describe her," I said.

"Yeah, me either," Owen agreed.

"Maybe you're the cause, Owen," I joked. "Maybe your pheromones triggered some sort of chemical reaction that flipped her switch. Turned her from American Sweetheart to American Psycho."

"Anyone else?" Dave tried to get me back on track.

"Do you think the person leaving me the notes could know we're investigating them?" Carol asked.

"What? What do you mean notes, plural?" Leigha asked, outraged.

"And what do you mean you're investigating them?" Dave seemed equally upset.

"What notes? You mean there's more?" Owen was just as incredulous.

"I think it's time we told them," I said.

Carol reluctantly related most of the story of the notes but gratefully glossed over our suspect board.

"Carol, why didn't you tell us?" Dave tried to keep his voice calm through clenched teeth.

"I didn't want to add to your burden. I'm here to help, not pile onto your worries. And I figured Maya, Burt, and I could handle it."

"How could you keep this from me?" Leigha turned on me.

Before I could say anything, Carol came to my defense. "I made her promise not to say anything, or I said I wouldn't tell her. This isn't Maya's fault."

"We're not done talking about this," Leigha said to me with a little less heat in her voice.

"Anyone else I should know about?" Dave sounded weary as if we had broken him.

"Nope, I think that's everyone who would want to push me off something high or run Carol out of town."

"I did a walk-through of your garage." Dave ignored my attempt to lighten the mood. "Was it, um, messy before?"

"I have a lot of cans and stuff in there, but they're all sorted in bins. Is that what you mean?"

It wasn't. Dave asked me to take a look with him, and what I saw made me groan. It looked like a drunk black bear had been square dancing in my workspace. All the recycling bins were upended, many of my tools lay on the ground, and screws and nails were scattered everywhere.

"Can you tell if anything's missing?" Dave seemed doubtful.

"Not until I pick up."

"Walk me through what happened again." This time, physically take me to where you were." We went through everything again. "Is this where Clover broke through?" Dave asked, pointing at the splintered fence board. Love swelled in my heart for her.

"Looks like it. It wasn't like that before. Uh, I'll have to fix that today."

Dave picked something up from the ground with a pen. "Does this look familiar? Do you know what it is?"

I walked over and peered at the crusty black material. "No idea, it looks like..." my voice trailed off. "Do you think Clover got my attacker? It looks like a piece of a hoodie."

"Could be," Dave admitted. "This might be blood, but it's too hard to be certain just by looking at it."

A real clue. Excitement zinged through me. "Will you send it in for analysis?"

"Unfortunately, this kind of incident doesn't get approval for that kind of expense yet."

"Yet, what do you mean yet?"

"Things would have to escalate before the department could justify the cost. We barely have a budget. It's not like what Hollywood makes it look like."

I pointed at the fabric. "So, you'd have to find me dead before they'd let you get an analysis on that?" I felt frustrated by my own uncertainty of what to do next. Action was my answer to most uncomfortable feelings, even when I was doing the wrong thing, I still preferred that to being afraid or angry.

Dave tilted his head and pressed his lips into a thin line. "Pretty much. But I'll find the guy long before it comes to that, Maya."

"We're going to find him," I mumbled under my breath. I'd never done passive victim before, and I wasn't about to start now. We went through all the things I kept in my garage, looking for missing items as we slowly made the circuit. My expensive tools were all there and besides those, there wasn't anything else of value. Dave took pictures, and he and Owen headed out to work.

The walkthrough with Dave tired me out. I was thankful for Carol and Leigha's company. After my noontime nap, I wandered outside to find a work party winding down. Burt had joined the ladies, and they were all finishing the last of the cleanup.

Burt eyed the giant can standing as an ineffectual sentinel in my yard. "Tell me what you're planning on doing with this thing again."

I brightened and patted my aluminum creation fondly. "I am so glad you asked. Picture it…" I painted the scene for him with enthusiastic brushstrokes.

"That head of yours sure is an interesting place?" Burt said.

"It's a wondrous and magical world in there," I teased.

"It sure is." Carol patted me on the back, and I warmed to her easy affection.

Watch duty shifted again. My house felt like a community relay race and I was the baton. Leigha and Carol went to pick Libby up from preschool, which left me with Burt until Owen got off work.

Burt swung a change of dress clothes from his hand. "We should get ready now and pay our respects early."

I had no idea what he was talking about and said as much.

"Peter's memorial service, it's today. Do you think you're up for it?" He gave me a once over, assessing my fitness for himself.

"Crap, that's today?" I exclaimed. I wanted to go, but I also felt my claim to Peter was tenuous at best. Grief felt private, and I didn't want to intrude where I had no right. I thought about my brother Michael's funeral and how my dad and I tried to avoid everyone, staying close to each other. But for my mom, seeing all the people who showed up for Michael's service was proof of just how well-loved he was, and it comforted her. I changed my mind, thinking of her. "Okay, give me ten minutes, and I'll be ready."

He looked me over. "I think you better take twenty."

When we were both presentable, we headed down to the Fraternity of the Eagles Lodge for the service. Burt brought a lasagna and a pie, so we'd each have something to carry in.

The lodge was in a plain, rectangular brick building. It looked like the front for an insurance office or a rug cleaning shop, except for the blue and white swooping eagle sign hanging above the door. Its personality inside matched the blah exterior.

The main room was cream-colored with low ceilings. Tables draped in black cloth were scattered around the space.

On the back wall, a large TV played snapshots from Peter's life: him as a child, screaming in delight from a sled; a teenage Peter in camo and hunter's orange, posed with an older version of himself—likely his dad—beside the deer they'd bagged; Peter as a kid again, standing in a river with a fishing pole in one hand and a sandwich in the other. For a guy who seemed anything but bland, the service felt flat.

I followed Burt over to a long folding table loaded with food, where we set down his offerings.

"That's Gary and Suzanne over there." Burt pointed out the man from the photo, his dirty blond hair now mostly gray, and an equally slim woman with a grim expression.

We made our way over to them, and Burt embraced them both, wordlessly giving his condolences and support. He introduced me, and I told them how the last time I'd seen Peter, he was joyriding in a golf cart. His mother smiled and wiped away tears in her eyes.

"That boy could turn two sticks and a rock into a good time," his dad said, his voice wistful.

Burt squeezed Gary's shoulder and hugged Suzanne again. A woman stood close behind me waiting for her turn, so we took the hint and moved on.

"What do we do now?" I asked.

"We drink a cup of coffee, sit for a minute, and I get you back home."

I nodded, feeling uncharacteristically compliant. Looking for a place to sit, I spotted Jay by himself at a table in the corner. He looked even worse than when I'd seen him the other day—dull, greasy hair, swollen eyes, and pale skin. His gaze was locked on the slideshow, unblinking. When I pulled the chair out next to him, he jumped, startled by our presence.

He glanced at the bruise on my cheek and quickly returned his focus to the screen.

"Have you eaten? Can I get you some food?" I offered.

"We've been best friends since we were eight, you know," Jay said, ignoring my question.

There was nothing I could do to make things better, so I joined him in silently watching the slideshow. Another picture of a grinning Peter on a successful hunting trip. He held up a string of dead birds, his rifle slung over his shoulder.

"Why would anyone want to kill Peter?" I murmured. "Seemed like everyone liked him."

"They did," Jay said, his jaw tightening.

"Did he have any side hustles you knew about?" I asked.

Jay glanced at me again. "Why do you want to know?"

"I was just telling Maya about how entrepreneurial Peter was," Burt said, cutting in. "Like when he sold cider as a kid."

Jay's expression softened. "Last summer, he got a couple of busted jet skis for free. We got them running, but one over-heated after an hour and the other had a slow leak we couldn't track down. Peter had this idea to rent them out an hour at a time, with a big fine for going over. We'd let the one cool off and drain the other before renting them out again. We spent all summer out on the lake and made bank."

"He sounds very clever," I said. "Did he have anything like that going on recently?"

Jay shook his head. "Nah, not that I know of." He rubbed his thumb back and forth over a crease in the tablecloth.

A picture of teenage Peter and Jay floating in inner tubes filled the TV frame.

A tear rolled down Jay's cheek onto the table, and he curled his hand into a fist. I reached out, giving his arm a gentle pat.

He pulled back and abruptly stood, his chair scraping against the floor. "I've got to go." He headed for the exit.

We stared after him—a man trying to escape his grief.

When we got back to my house, Owen was pulling the second lasagna Burt had made for dinner out of the oven. Although Burt didn't want to stay and eat with us, he insisted on making a salad before he left. He even set the table and filled water glasses.

"I would've gotten a concussion sooner if I'd known that's all it took to get you to clean and cook for me," I joked. Burt bent to set the silverware on napkins, and I glimpsed the skin on the top of his head through his thinning hair. Oddly, it made him seem vulnerable, and the sight triggered a tsunami of gratitude for him. I spontaneously hugged him. Burt stiffened before patting me awkwardly on the back. His discomfort amused me, and I released him.

"Get some sleep," he commanded before leaving.

Owen dished up the lasagna, and we took our places at the table. The house felt pleasantly empty. The day's stir of people and activity started to settle. There was a deep comfort in the silence as we ate. Neither of us felt the need to fill the air with meaningless words, and our tired brains and bodies could just rest near one another. I pushed my plate back and rested my chin in my palm.

Reaching out, I touched Owen's forearm. "Thank you for everything you did. I don't know what I would've done if you hadn't been here."

He gave me a warm smile and placed his hand over mine. "I'm glad I could help."

I pulled my hand back. "You know, you're pretty good at this nursemaid stuff."

But instead of laughing like I expected, Owen seemed to grow even more pensive and serious. "I had a lot of practice growing up," he said quietly. He lapsed into silence as if weighing whether to go on or not.

I leaned in, quietly waiting for him to decide.

"My mom was diagnosed with M.S. after Katie was born." His eyes followed the path of his finger as it traced the wood grain on the table. "I spent a lot of my childhood helping take care of my little sister and, later, my mom when she got sicker."

I did the math in my head, realizing how young he must have been. "You were just a kid," I said softly, my heart aching for the younger version of him. "That must have been incredibly tough."

He nodded, a distant look in his eyes. "I suppose it was. At first, I was focused on helping, you know? But as I got older, and her illness became the norm, I felt like I was missing a lot. My friends were out having fun, and I was at home, worrying about my mom and taking care of my sister."

We sat in silence for a moment, the weight of his words hanging in the air. I wanted to reach out, to comfort him, but instead, I blurted out, "I'm sorry if taking care of me made you feel like that again."

He shook his head, a small smile tugging at the corners of his mouth. "No, it's different with you," he said, his tone lighter now. "Back then, I didn't have a choice. But now... now I'm here because I want to be. And honestly, I've made peace with all that stuff. I've got a great relationship with my mom now, and I don't spend time thinking about what might have been."

His words eased some of my guilt, and I felt a warmth spread through me. "I'm glad you're here," I said, returning his smile. "You're a good man, Owen Reece."

He glanced at me, a spark of something more in his eyes. "Thanks," he replied, his voice soft. "I'm glad I'm here, too."

I put my hand back on Owen's forearm resting on the table. "So you know, I don't plan on making this a habit."

He nodded. "Good. And just so you know, I never mind helping out the people I care about."

He stood, signaling the end of the conversation. "Someone's gotta clean up this mess now that Burt's gone."

Eleven

I got up from the floor and flexed. I might not have been hoisting anyone over my head like a WWE Bella sister, but these little arms could still knock out the push-ups. It felt good to be back at work. Both Burt and Owen tried convincing me to take another day off, but I was in good spirits and upright. No ladder pusher was going to keep me down. If they wanted me, I would be ready for them. And if there was a next time, Clover wasn't the only one who'd take a piece out of them. No one was pushing me around or over anymore.

"Morning, Burt here today?" Purdy asked as she walked into the lobby. Her bright pink, over-plumped lips looked stuck on like a Mrs. Potato Head. Her eyelashes spiked out in clumps of mascara, and her perfume punched me in the sinuses. It was like Purdy was playing the role of a washed-up Vegas showgirl in a B horror flick.

"Wow, Purdy!" The exclamation just escaped.

"I know." Purdy parted the fuchsia banana slugs on her face. She tapped her lips together, making a smacking sound. "I just had them done. Don't I look thirty years younger? A gal's got to invest in herself. Right?" Luckily, she wasn't looking for a reply. "Burt here today?"

"No, he filled in for me yesterday."

"Darn it. I'll pop in again later to see him."

"I don't think he's coming in today." I wasn't sure if that was true or not, but I feared permanent brain damage from prolonged toxic fume exposure if she returned.

"If you see him, tell him I was looking for him."

I agreed if only to hurry her along. Unfortunately, her olfactory napalm hung around long after she departed. It made my eyes water. I took a wedge to the front door and propped it open to clear the place out.

Maggie Carter bounced down the sidewalk with a large canvas bag slung over her arm.

"Hey there." I waved.

"I am so glad to see you. I heard what happened and was so worried. I brought you some soothing chamomile and peppermint tea straight from my own garden." Maggie gave me one of her crushing hugs, apologizing when I winced. She rooted around in her bag, pushing aside cardboard tubes and file folders. "I'm working on an exhibit for the library of Claryce Falls through the ages. I'm going through old archive photos. There isn't a lot there, but what I did find is pretty amazing." She pulled out the mason jar of tea and handed it to me. "I want to hear what really happened and how I can help."

Maggie wasn't the only one to hear about the attack. Some people came to check on me, while more came to collect the gossip. Leigha and Carol both popped in around ten, but I was with customers, so they just gave me a thumbs up, which I returned, and they left. All in all, it was a very social, if somewhat exhausting, morning. Close to noon, one of the last people I wanted to see walked through the door. Emily, I sighed and thought of all the push-ups I'd done that morning.

"Hello." She walked to the counter, her squared shoulders broadcasting determination. "Please put this letter in Owen Reece's mailbox," she instructed, her voice all business.

I looked down at the plain white envelope with only Owen's name written on it. "I can't do that without the full address," I said.

"But I don't know his box number, and I need to get this to him. It's important he gets it today."

"Officially, I can't take it without a complete address. Sorry." I pushed the envelope back to her, not feeling the least bit remorseful.

"Then tell me what his box number is, and I'll write the address in." She was scowling at me now.

"First, I don't know everyone's box number off the top of my head, and second, I can't give you that information." This woman didn't know when to quit. Well, she was about to find out that I could be just as stubborn.

Emily's voice rose to a high-pitched whine. "But it has to get to him today. It has to. You're an obstacle in the path to the life I deserve. I will not let you stop me."

Something that had been bending inside me all week finally snapped. I was done. Done with Chris's angry showdowns. Done with creepy people in hoodies shoving me over. And done with Emily's weird nonsense. The last one stopped now. There was a counter between us and pepper spray within reach if she came for me.

I narrowed my eyes and used my sternest tone. "Was that a threat? Because things won't go well for you if it was. You're in the post office threatening a federal employee, which is a federal offense."

Emily's mouth dropped open to protest, but I wasn't done.

"I don't know what your problem is, but I won't let you hurt me or Carol or anyone else I care about." I was full of righteous fury. "Also, Owen is not yours to claim. You made your interest abundantly clear, and if he wanted to date you, he would've asked you out. And another thing, I don't know what this crap is about what you deserve, but I am not your or anyone else's obstacle. You and your bat poop-crazy behavior is your obstacle. Quit pointing the finger at other people and pick up a dang mirror because you're what's in your way." Finally finished, I stared at Emily, my body coiled for the fallout.

Silence stretched, then Emily's bottom lip started quivering, and she burst into tears. "I would never hurt anyone. I can't believe you thought I'd do that." Clearly, she'd forgotten about her toe-crushin' spree during Country Zumba class last week. Emily's sobs shook her body. "It's that stupid book. I kept trying to do what it said, and now everyone is mad at me. Leigha yelled at me. You yelled at me. And I hate being yelled at." She looked pathetic, but I wasn't buying it. "And I deserve it. I've been horrible." She wailed, releasing another loud wave of sobs like a soap opera star whose contract was just canceled.

Behind her, Burt cautiously walked into the lobby. I put up a hand, silently telling him to keep his distance from whatever was happening in front of me. I didn't trust Emily's Jekyll and Hyde theatrics. Burt shook his head at me as if blaming me for her meltdown.

Emily stood stiff, continuing to leak tears all over the floor as I waited. Annoyed I'd have to mop the lobby soon, I moderated my tone and suggested she head into the kitchen, where I would join her after I closed up. "You can tell me what this is all about, then."

She didn't move.

"I have some soothing tea I'll make." I pulled out a box of tissues and handed them to her. "Burt's here too. I bet he can find you a cookie."

"That would be nice," she said shakily.

I quickly locked everything up and joined them, making sure to shut the door between the lobby and the hall. Emily sat at the table, hunched over a plate of cookies like they were her only allies, as Burt patted her on the back.

A bright yellow book with red lettering screamed Get Outta My Way: A Guide to Bulldozing Obstacles that Keep You from Living Your Dreams. "All I want is a boyfriend to take to my sister's wedding. I thought if I did what the book said, I'd be happy. But I'm miserable." A new round of tears hit. At this rate, I'd need a life raft just to make it out of the kitchen.

I picked up the book and paged through it. "Chapter One: Shout It Loud and Proud: Dare to dream at ear-piercing decibels; Chapter Three: Blueprints and Blowhorns: Plow the path to the life you deserve; Chapter Six: No Means 'Not Yet': Stop being a doormat and ring destiny's doorbell" Yikes, if this was the advice Emily was following, it was lucky I hadn't gotten a brick through a window or worse. A stray thought ran ice through me. What if she had done worse? What if Emily was the person in the hoodie? She could be the one threatening Carol. I made a cup of tea and set it in front of her.

"Thank you." She loudly blew her nose into a tissue. "You are being so nice to me, and I don't deserve it."

"That's probably true," I muttered. Burt shot me a dirty look and patted Emily on the back again. So, it was like that, was it?

"Why don't you start at the beginning," Burt suggested. "I'm sure it's not all that bad."

Emily cleared out her sinuses again, sounding like an angry moose with a head cold.

She straightened and sipped the tea. "This is really nice." Clearly stalling, she daintily picked up a cookie, took three small, precise bites, chewed slowly, and sipped her tea. When it looked like she was going in for a fourth bite, I readied myself to knock the cookie out of her hand, but she saved herself.

Sighing, she set it down. "My ex, Noah, and I had been dating for over a year, and everything was going great. Then, my younger sister, Ella, got engaged to a guy she met online. He's really cute." Emily sighed again. "Anyway, at Thanksgiving, while we were eating pie, Mom joked about Noah and me having a double wedding with Ella."

Emily's voice started to wobble, and I held a cookie up in her face to distract her.

She shook her head. "Thanks, but I got this. Noah said he wasn't ready for marriage. And I asked why not?" The tears started falling again.

I gave up hope they'd ever end and just ate the cookie myself. Emily shakily described Noah's confession. He planned on breaking up with her after the holidays, but she'd forced his hand.

"Then he got up and left me there. My dad had to drive me home after he'd finished his pie. It was so embarrassing."

My face felt like the "eek" emoji, my teeth gritted and lips pulled back in sympathetic horror at Emily's telenovela of heartbreak. "I can't believe he did that in front of your family. That's terrible."

"I know. My mom said it's because I'm too passive, too nice."

"If it makes you feel any better, I would never describe you that way."

Burt frowned and shook his head at me again.

"Thanks, it does."

I sent him an answering smirk that said, "See, so stick that in your pipe and smoke it."

"My mom gave me that book," she said, the last two words with contempt, "for Christmas and made me promise I would try it. I wasn't going to, but then Owen moved to town, and I thought it was a sign. I promised myself I would give it four months and follow the book exactly."

"Did the book tell you to throw cold beverages on me?" I asked skeptically.

"Maya, I am so sorry about that. I panicked. Owen was obviously having fun hanging out with you, and the lemonade was sitting on the table and... I was, you know. I saw you as an obstacle I needed to remove. I will totally pay to dry clean your dress."

"So, it wasn't an accident?" I wanted her to repeat that last part for Burt so I could savor my vindication a little longer.

"No, I'm so, so sorry, really. But it's over now. I told myself I'd follow the book for four months and if nothing changed, I'd give it away. And today is the last day." She pulled the letter with Owen's name on it out of her bag and tore it in two. "I'm done. I'll just go to my sister's wedding alone, and my mother can deal with it."

"When you say you're sorry for everything, what exactly do you mean by everything?" I wasn't ready to let Emily off the hook quite yet.

"There was the lemonade at Leigha's." Emily held up one finger, keeping track of her crimes. "I spread the rumor that you and Owen were engaged so no one else would go after him." Two fingers pointed in the air as she paused, collecting her thoughts. "I was rude to you and ran into you a lot at Zumba." Emily cringed. "And I may have told a few people I overheard you talking to your doctor on the phone and that you..." Emily whispered, "have Chlamydia."

"What?" I was outraged. Everyone thought I had an STD rampant among college campuses and Koala bears.

"I'm sorry, it wasn't me, it was the book. I swear."

I caught Burt chuckling on the other side of Emily.

"I'm pretty sure you were the one doing the talking." I was so annoyed. Just when I started to feel bad for her, she went and ruined it by giving me a disease.

"What can I do to make it up to you? I'll do anything."

"Okay, start by telling me where you were Tuesday night between five and seven p.m.?"

"Why?" Emily seemed confused.

"Just answer the question," I said, feeling like a TV detective.

"I worked the last shift at Provisions in the Pines. I was there until closing at nine."

"Can anyone verify that?"

"Sure, lots of people. Sue Parker came in around five-fifteen for chocolate and wine." Emily named several more people and what they bought. She was like an elephant on brain-boosting mushrooms; she never forgot a purchase.

I made a mental note not to buy anything incriminating from her. I noticed Burt was discreetly taking notes. Good. One of us would follow up with her alleged alibi.

She may not be the one who knocked me over, but she still could be the note perp. Since Emily was in a confessing mood, I decided to go the direct route. "Did you leave threats for Carol?"

She gasped, "What? No! Why would I do that? I've been trying to get Carol to like me. Wait, has someone been leaving her threats? What did they say?" It seemed Emily wasn't immune to the allure of gossip because she looked measurably better.

"Someone left Carol several notes threatening her to leave town or else," Burt explained.

"Or else what?" Emily seemed very interested now.

"We don't really know." Burt rubbed his eyebrow. "They're vague in their menacing."

"And you think I wrote those notes? Why would I?"

"You said Leigha hasn't spent any time with you since Carol's been in town, and you couldn't wait for her to leave. It sounds like you saw Carol as an obstacle too." I reminded her.

"Oh man, I did say that, didn't I? I was really feeling sorry for myself that day. But I didn't leave her any notes." She brightened and clapped her hand like she'd just won a year's supply of Burt's cookies. "I know. Do you have one of the notes here? We can compare my handwriting."

"How can we be sure you won't alter your handwriting to throw us off track?" It'd take more than a few tears and an aggressively misleading self-help book to convince me to cross Emily off our suspect list.

"We can use this." She held up the torn letter to Owen. "Just, don't read it, okay? It's embarrassing."

We agreed, and I went to get the printout of the note from our suspect board.

"Okay, here it is," I said, slapping it down on the table in front of Emily.

"Remember, don't read it, just look at the handwriting." I thought she might make us pinky swear. She pulled the torn letter from half of the envelope. Side by side, the handwriting couldn't be more different. Emily's letters were round, neat, and precise. The handwriting on the threat was sloppy, the letters pointy, and the lines anything but precise. They were definitely written by two different people.

"Is it okay if I take a picture of this?" Burt asked. "I would like to keep it for our files. I'll make sure to only photograph from here to here." He pointed to a non-incriminating section of text.

Emily nodded.

Dang it, I groaned inwardly. It would be easy enough to confirm Emily's alibi for the time of my ladder assault, and her handwriting ruled her out for Carol's crime. That meant Emily was simply a small-town girl following the wrong advice on her quest for love.

"Do you believe me now?" she asked hopefully.

I nodded.

"Maya, I hope someday you'll be able to forgive me and that maybe we'll even be friends."

"Sure," I said. "If you promise never to tell anyone I've got STDs again."

"I can do that," she promised.

Emily and I may not be besties anytime soon, but I didn't think I'd have to worry about her flying elbow in workout class anymore.

Twelve

Other people's good intentions were exhausting. Everyone had invited themselves over to keep me company and feed me. I sat in the lounger, half dozing, half watching Burt grill elk burgers. Smoke from the fire kept fogging his glasses, setting off an elaborate spectacle cleaning routine. First, Burt removed his glasses, then untucked his white t-shirt from under his button-up that he used to wipe the lenses. Next, he held them up to the light for inspection, before putting them back on and re-tucking his shirt. The whole cycle was both comical and oddly soothing.

Libby snuggled by my side, pretending to read me stories from her picture books. All three dogs lay around our lounger, sleepy after a bout of energetic play. I was surrounded by a cuddly barricade of cuteness.

Carol and Leigha came in and out of my house with plates of food, dishes, and drinks. The rhinestone heart on Leigha's hoodie scattered rainbows around the yard as she walked back inside. If I wasn't so tired, I would've felt guilty about sitting on my butt while everyone worked. But, I reminded myself, they weren't invited. So, I decided to let them shower me with care, since there didn't seem to be anything I could do about it. I felt a blanket drape over my legs, and I opened my eyes to see Owen standing over me. His dark hair was flattened to his head from a ball cap he'd worn, and his skin was already starting to tan. My insides purred.

"How you feeling?"

"Like an abandoned bear cub—everyone wants to come look at me, check on me, and give me snacks. But I'm telling you right now, I draw the line at bottle-feeding."

"I should probably tell Burt to return that case of formula I saw in the back of his truck?" Owen grinned.

And I shuddered. "Some things are just too wrong to joke about, and I think we found one of them." I tried hard to shut out the disturbing images trying to take shape in my brain.

"Shhh - I'm reading a story to Auntie Maya," Libby admonished Owen.

He apologized and held up his hands in supplication. As he retreated, he mouthed, "Talk later."

I nodded and went back to Libby's story of the monster-fighting princess.

There must be some primal draw to an open flame in the outdoors that men are particularly susceptible to. Burt, Owen, and now Dave, holding Libby, were all crowded around my grill watching the burgers cook. Vegetable kebabs lined the top rack like tidy sacrifices to the gods of grilling. My stomach growled in reaction. I rose stiffly from the lounger with more effort than it should have taken, only to walk ten feet and plop myself back down at the patio table. I felt like a sore, lumpy mound of potato salad.

Carol came and sat next to me. "How you doing Honey?" She cupped the back of my head and smoothed my hair down.

"I'm doing good," I exaggerated.

"Burt mentioned you had an eventful morning."

I agreed, but before I could tell Carol about it, Leigha shouted from the kitchen for me to hold off because she wanted to hear it too. Instead, I asked Carol if she'd heard anything from Chris Weller.

"I've got an update on that," Dave said, setting down a plate mounded high with kebabs. Burt brought the burgers over and all conversation paused as we constructed our meals.

Once everyone was settled, the conversation resumed. "I paid a visit to Chris after I left here this morning," Dave said. "He wasn't the person who assaulted Maya."

"How do you know?" I didn't believe him.

"Because there are five witnesses who swore he was singing 'Tainted Love' at the Lucky Dragon's karaoke night in Hillsburg."

"I was pushed sometime between five and six. How early did the karaoke start? Also, Chris was furious after our fight. What kind of person gets mad, then drives to another town forty-five minutes away to angry sing 'Tainted Love'?"

"Evidently, Chris Weller does," Dave answered. "It sounded strange to me too, but I verified his entire timeline. He left soon after your encounter on the street. He said singing made him feel better. The bartender confirmed Chris was a regular, and on Tuesday, he got there around four p.m. and stayed until close to nine. He was sure it was four because karaoke didn't start until five, and Chris loaded up their jukebox and sang the same three songs at the bar until it started."

"That wouldn't be annoying at all," I observed sarcastically. "Suspiciously annoying. What if he was trying to be obvious?"

"Is the bartender sure Chris was there the whole time?" Owen asked. "That's a whole lot of 'Tainted Love'."

"I checked the video footage myself. He was there."

"Darn it. What did he say about Carol's threats? He could still be the one leaving those." I wasn't ready to let Chris off the hook yet.

"He denied knowing anything about the threats. Chris admitted to trying to encourage Carol to look at other properties, but he seemed genuinely surprised when I showed him the notes. He said he'd been counting on Carol's commission for a down payment on a new boat. He definitely didn't want her to leave before she bought a house."

"And you believed him? Did you at least get a sample of his handwriting?" I didn't let up.

"I did believe him. And he's not required to give me a sample of his writing. I didn't pursue it. I don't want you to, either. In fact, I want you all to leave him alone. He's pretty ticked off and isn't going to be any happier once he gets wind of Carol reporting him." He looked around the table, making intense eye contact with each of us, so we knew he was serious. "Okay?"

We nodded.

"Nope, not good enough. I want to hear you all say you will not go and talk to him?"

We all mumbled "Okay" and Dave seemed satisfied.

"If it's not Chris, and it's not Emily, then who would want to mess with me?"

Leigha wanted to know how I knew it wasn't Emily, and so Burt and I tag-teamed the retelling of the morning's soap opera.

"Wow! You really are a people person, aren't you," Owen teased.

"I think this one is more on you than me mister, 'I'm Owen, handsome forest ranger, female magnet.'"

"It's that crazy book's fault and the mother who gave it to her," Burt added his two cents. "Why do women read that nonsense anyway?"

I felt like I needed to defend the highly suggestible Emily and all womankind from Burt, but before I could, Carol jumped in.

"Wanting love is perfectly natural. It speaks well of Emily that she's willing to put herself out there. Maybe she didn't follow the best advice, but she's young, and hopefully, she's learned from it. Now, we can be better role models for her."

I didn't think I was qualified to be anyone's role model, but it was nice seeing Burt put in his place.

Getting back to my original question, I voiced my thoughts aloud again. "If it isn't Emily or Chris, then who was it and why?"

"Maybe it has something to do with your trash project," Leigha offered. "They did trash - no pun intended - your workspace with your recycling bins. Maybe it was an anti-environmentalist. You know, those guys you see around town with the enormous trucks who leave them running to burn gas in protest of global warming. I mean, they are pretty nutty."

"I've heard of them, but do you actually know any personally?" I asked. "Still, it's not like we have other options." Taking a bite of the elk burger, I savored the rich, slightly-gamey flavor while trying to connect the dots between the garbage and being knocked out. "Burt, this elk burger is tasty. Where'd you say you got it again?"

"From Gary Becker's son..." Burt's voice trailed off. "I guess this will be the last of the burger I'll get from Peter."

Poor Peter. A whisper of an idea blew across my thoughts. I put the burger down and considered it. "Owen, have you found any more poached elk since Peter's death?"

Owen shook his head.

"What if Peter was the one poaching elk, and his death is somehow related to it?"

"But what does that have to do with someone trying to hurt you?" Leigha asked.

"Probably nothing. I don't know if the two are related. It's just a thought. But, Burt, you told me Peter was always engaged in some kind of money-making scheme. What if selling elk meat was one of those schemes? If he was, it would make sense why Owen hasn't found any more dead elk."

"It's a new angle and worth seeing if anything comes of it," Dave acknowledged. "Owen, do you have time tomorrow to take me to the sites where you found dumped carcasses?"

"Sure, I can shuffle a few things in the morning and be ready by ten to take you up."

With that decided, the conversation shifted to lighter topics. Leigha, Carol, and I agreed to meet at the Stevens on Monday after Leigha and I were done with work.

"How's your can project coming along?" Leigha asked. "Did the one you finished get damaged?"

"It's still standing strong. Luckily, it was tied down pretty well."

Owen jumped in. "It looks great. You should go take a look at it after dinner. I told people at the Forest Service office about it, and now they're all excited too." Owen turned his megawatt smile on me.

I melted. My cheeks warmed, and I looked away.

"Maya is really clever and funny," Leigha chimed in.

"And cute as a button," Carol added. I knew my entire face was definitely red now.

"And stubborn as a mule, argumentative with tendencies towards tardiness," Burt added.

My head whipped around, and he winked at me. "What can I say? Some people bring out the best in me." I gave him a toothy grin.

Soon we were full, and with the whole crew working, the cleanup was over quickly. All evidence of the impromptu dinner party was either wrapped or in the dishwasher.

After everyone went out to admire my giant can, they headed for their own homes, except for Owen who lingered. "Are you okay? I mean, really okay?"

We walked back into my house.

"I'm fine." The annoyance evident in my tone. "I've been asked that like eight hundred times today."

"Yeah, but I was there, remember? I get to ask. Plus, you had an intense afternoon with Emily."

I immediately felt bad. "You're right, I'm sorry. It was a zoo all day with people wanting the scoop. And even though everyone's been sweet, I just want some time alone. You know what I mean?"

"I do," he agreed. "Fizzy and I will head out and let you have some quiet time."

He didn't sound offended, and I added this to the growing list that made Owen great. Impulsively, I turned and wrapped my arms around his middle. "Thank you for everything," I mumbled into his chest. "You're the best."

After half a second, Owen wrapped his arms around me and rested his chin on the top of my head. "You're welcome."

It felt so good to be nuzzled in the scent and feel of him. I stayed there until awkwardness crept in, and I finally pulled away. "See you tomorrow."

The door shut behind Owen. The silence swirled around the house, still churning from the evening's activities. I turned the kettle on, put Billie Holiday on low, and lit a few candles. I made myself cozy on the couch with a fuzzy throw and a cup of Maggie's chamomile and peppermint tea. Clover curled around my legs as Billie sang Solitude. And I spent the next couple of hours absorbed in my book. When I finally crawled into bed, every hair on me was exhausted. I closed my eyes and was out.

My phone yanked me from the dark emptiness of restful sleep. "I've been robbed," an unfamiliar voice said flatly.

"Who is this?" I croaked, barely awake.

"It's Janet, I've been robbed."

I sat up and rubbed my forehead, trying to clear the sleep away. "Janet? You know this is Maya, right? Not the police."

"Of course, I know who I called," the woman snapped. "Someone tried to steal our litter."

"What?" I was alert now. "Start at the beginning." I flipped my bedside light on. Clover blinked at me from the foot of the bed, and I apologized to her.

"My motion sensor lights woke me. I thought it was the coyotes trying to get into my garbage again. I got my air horn and pepper spray and snuck out to the back porch. I've made a hunting blind back there. That way, I can watch the little shits from my window and scare them without having to put shoes on. But it wasn't coyotes. It was some bastard with a sweatshirt pulled over his head. He was making a real mess, throwing all the garbage and recycling onto the ground."

Janet made an odd "hu-hu-hu" noise, and I realized she was laughing.

"That blowhorn worked just as good on him as it did the coyotes. I've never seen anyone jump that high before."

"What did he do?"

"He ran, slipped on some of the bottles, fell over, got up, and ran off." Janet let out more machine-gun laughter.

"Did you call the police?" I asked.

"Yes."

"What did they say?" I prompted.

"They said they'd send someone to drive around to make sure he was gone. But I already know he left because I heard his truck drive off."

"Are you scared?" I asked, not sure what else she wanted me to do in the middle of the night.

"Of what?"

"Of the man going through your garbage."

"I'm not scared of him because he's not here," Janet answered matter-of-factly.

"Do you need help cleaning the mess tomorrow?" I offered.

"No."

"Can we talk about this later?"

"Why? What else is there to talk about? I thought you'd want to know someone tried to steal our litter."

"Okay." I paused, wondering if there was more. "Thanks for letting me know, I guess. I'll see you Saturday for our next meeting."

Janet hung up without saying goodbye. Somebody thought we had something they wanted. If we could figure out what it was, then maybe we'd figure out who it was. I wasn't going to solve this tonight. I started reading, hoping to find sleep again soon.

Thirteen

Sometimes you just can't dance the blues away. Which would be true for me if that dancing was line dancing, and you substituted blues with exhaustion. Sitting outside Glamour Nails and Boogie, I was trying to remember why I'd thought it'd be a good idea to come to workout class today. My alarm rudely asserted itself just as I was finally dozing off, shortly after dawn. The great propellant properties of caffeine were the only thing keeping me moving. I folded my arms on the wrought iron table and laid my head down to rest. I would've headed home, except Carol asked to talk to me after class. But, the longer I waited, the harder it was getting to resist the siren song of my couch calling me to nap.

"What are you doing out here? Is class over already?" Burt was standing over me with two cups in his hands.

I caught the waft of temporary salvation. "Do I smell artificial hazelnut flavor? If you let me have one of those, I'll be your best friend forever." I gave him my most winning smile.

"No, and I already have a best friend."

"Wait, who's your best friend? You only hang out with us."

"His name is Dennis Beackman, and he lives in Westport."

"Are you sure he's real?"

"Of course he is. We go deep sea fishing together once a year. What kind of question is that?" Burt sounded exasperated. He took the seat across from me at the round table, setting the coffees down on it.

"What's that?" I asked, excitedly pointing behind him. When he turned to look, I swiped one of the coffees and took a big swig.

"That was for Carol."

"I need it more than her. It's the thought that counts anyway. I'll tell her how thoughtful you were." I made a production of licking around the coffee lid in case he was tempted to take it back.

"You're an animal." He grimaced.

"Desperation isn't pretty," I agreed. I told Burt about my late-night call that kept me up.

"That's good news. It means your attack was related to the recycling project and wasn't personal."

"Do you think it's an anti-environmentalist, like Leigha suggested?"

Burt thought for a moment. "No, if it'd been someone trying to make a statement, wouldn't they paint a message, leave an angry banner, something to declare their cause?"

"Maybe, but the person got scared off in both cases. Clover chased them from my house and Janet scared them off with her air horn. So, maybe they didn't have a chance to leave a message." The whole anti-environmentalist angle still felt like a stretch.

The doors opened to the studio and women started to trickle out.

Carol saw us at the table and waved. "Burt, thank you for coming."

I realized I hadn't even questioned why he was in Leigha's backyard. Burt was like a grouchy garden gnome. His constant presence made you forget he wasn't really supposed to be there.

"He brought you this." I held the paper cup of sweet preservation in the air. "But I drank it because I really needed it."

"That's okay, Honey." Carol patted my shoulder. "Burt, thank you. It was very thoughtful."

"Told you so," I muttered under my breath to him. After another big gulp, I asked Carol what she wanted to talk about. But she wanted to wait for Leigha first.

"I'm making a goat cheese, honey, and pistachio cheesecake for the recycling meeting tomorrow. You can come by the P.O. before we meet for a slice." Burt offered Carol. Burt recently joined our trash project as the team's refreshment committee.

"Is the goat cheese almost gone yet?" I asked, trying to calculate how much I thought should be left.

"Not even close. We still have over half a case."

Carol wanted to know why we had so much goat cheese. We told her about Dave's revenge.

"He showed you, didn't he?" she laughed. "Honestly, I've been so worried about him with all these long hours and the pressure to find out what happened to that poor boy, it makes me happy he still has a little mischief left in him."

Movement from Glamour Nails and Boogie made me look up. Leigha was turning the lights out and locking the door of her studio, Emily by her side.

"Hi everyone." Emily looked timid as she approached. "I wanted to apologize again for the way I acted. I feel so stupid. I'd do anything to make it up to all of you. Is there anything I can do? Really?"

"Honey, we forgive you. You don't need to do anything." Carol exuded maternal warmth.

It was easier to forgive someone when you weren't the one with smashed toes and the rumor of an STD clinging to you.

"If you think of anything, you let me know. I'll do it."

The unrestricted nature of Emily's vow made me flinch. This girl had no sense of self-preservation. We reassured her we were all good and waited for her to leave, but she didn't.

"What are you all doing?" Emily looked at us, hopefully.

"We have a bit of a private issue we're trying to work out," Carol offered.

"Is this about those notes you've been getting? Have you found anything out? I mean, since you've ruled me out?" Emily asked in rapid fire succession.

I looked at Carol and shrugged. Emily was obviously not going to take a hint.

"It is," Carol said and gave Emily a stern look. "But if you're going to stay, you have to promise not to speak a word of this to anyone."

Like an anxious puppy, Emily barely contained her excitement at being included. She bounced on her toes. "I swear, nothing and no one could pry your secret from me."

Carol looked resigned. "Leigha and I were talking, and we think we should determine if Chris is leaving me the notes before I file my complaint. If he's willing to slash my tire, there's no telling what he'll do when he finds out I reported him."

"Who slashed your tire, and why are you filing a complaint?" Emily asked.

"It's on a need-to-know basis," I interjected before Carol could answer. "Just listen for now, okay?"

"Sure thing." Emily smiled, demonstrating she could follow instructions.

"We need a way to rule him out once and for all," Carol continued.

"You could compare his handwriting like you did mine," Emily offered.

"We could, but how would we get it?" I asked. "All of us are persona non grata. Chris would run us off before we even got close to his office. Not to mention, Dave would kill us if he found out we were still investigating him."

Emily shot her hand in the air like a third-grader volunteering for show-and-tell. "I'll do it! Whatever you need, I'm in. I'll get the handwriting sample from Chris, whoever he is."

I exchanged dubious looks with the rest of the Scooby team.

"That is very brave of you and a great idea," Burt said, making the decision for us. "How well do you know Chris Weller?"

"The fancy-dressed real estate guy?" Emily asked. "The guy who's always out cleaning his sign hanging on the horse corral fence where a lot of the local businesses advertise as you drive into town." Emily lowered her chin. "Chris Weller, Don't Buy a House, Buy into the Dream," she said in a deep announcer voice.

"That's the one," I cringed. The man clearly needed to work on his marketing along with his morals.

"Sometimes he comes into Provisions in the Pines and buys Red Bull and protein bars, but he never talks much. Just in and out."

"That's perfect. It'll make this a lot easier." Burt rubbed his hands together, savoring the plan he was cooking up.

"What are you thinking?" I asked. "Have Emily pose as a potential client. Ask to look at some listings, maybe have him write something down for her or take a sample of his writing when he's distracted?"

"That was exactly what I was thinking," Burt said, annoyed with me for stealing his thunder.

"I can do that." Emily once again bounced with excitement. "I can pretend to be Casandra Kissing, a rich computer engineer from Seattle, looking to buy a fancy vacation home in Claryce Falls."

I tried to hold in my eye roll. "He knows who you are, remember? You'll go in as yourself."

"You're looking to buy your first starter home," Burt added. "Something modest so he doesn't get too excited."

Emily looked disappointed but nodded her head in understanding. We spent ten more minutes working through the details. When we were finished, we had a pretty straightforward plan with minimal risk. Unfortunately, we'd have to wait for Emily, who was working for the next three days. We agreed to reconvene on Monday at Glamour Nails and Boogie before our group dispersed.

Owen must have gotten off early because there was a note on the table and Fizzy was gone when I got home. It said he'd see me Sunday afternoon to work on the cans and to call if I needed anything. I crumpled the note, disappointed I wouldn't see him. I really wanted to hear if he and Dave found anything and to get his thoughts about Janet's late night recycling bandit. Truth be told, I looked forward to our evening chats and sharing the highlights of our day with one another. I liked him in my routine. My tired brain wanted to read more into his absence, but instead, I put on a mystery podcast and went to bed early.

The next morning, Burt jumped out of his truck when I coasted Broomhilda to a stop in front of the P.O.

"Burt, why are you here so early?" I was not in the mood for a lecture. I woke up grumpy, and I intended to stay that way.

"I made you a breakfast sandwich. I wanted you to have time to eat before you open."

"I'm capable of feeding myself." I wasn't in a frame of mind to want to appreciate anything.

Burt seemed immune to my bad temper though, which only annoyed me more.

"But did you eat this morning?"

I kept quiet because I had in fact stayed in bed too long and hadn't had time to eat.

"Just as I thought." Burt sounded smug. "I'll make coffee while you get ready."

I unlocked the door to the back rooms and pushed my bike in without acknowledging what he'd said. With ten minutes left before I needed to open the customer counter, my body fell into the kitchen chair with a cup of coffee and a breakfast sandwich already sitting in front of it.

I took a swig of my coffee before biting into the sandwich. The bread was perfectly crunchy, and the eggs were still warm. I cursed silently. "This is good," I said begrudgingly. "Why are you trying to ruin my bad mood?"

"Why are you in a bad mood?" Burt asked, unwrapping his own breakfast sandwich.

"Sometimes a person just wakes up grumpy. It doesn't happen a lot, so let me wallow a little." All night, I'd dreamed about a panicked Peter climbing an endless ladder to save himself from drowning in trash. I woke up exhausted. If I told Burt, though, I knew he'd fuss.

Instead, he looked at me like I was just crazy.

"Don't bring your sunshine to my thunderstorm. Let me eat this delicious, perfectly cooked breakfast in a gloomy cloud of discontent."

Without any further comment, Burt picked up the paper and ignored me for the next eight and a half minutes. But it was too late, his easy compliance and my full belly ruined my funk. I rinsed my mug and headed in to sort mail in much better spirits.

"What's going on in there?" Lynell Reynolds, local business mogul and self-elected Town Gossip President, asked.

I pointed at the "Burt's Kitchen" sign he'd saved and rehung from last week.

"What is that?" she demanded.

A round of laughter answered her.

"Who's all in there?"

I told her Burt made cheesecake, and she was welcome to join them for a slice and coffee. Without thanking me, she gathered her packages and hurried back. In her yellow-and-black-check shirt and gray, permed hair sticking out behind her, Lynell reminded me of a bossy hen getting ready to rule the roost.

I knew we were in for trouble when I heard Lynell loudly declare, "This is where you all are! We missed you over at the café this morning." As if predicting my own doom, moments later, she was standing back in front of me. "You need to close that down immediately. You're running an illegal restaurant. And if you don't shut that down, I'll report you to the post office."

"Come again?" I was confused by the intensity of her venom.

"Two of my Saturday regulars are back there instead of at my place." She pointed an accusing finger towards the kitchen. "You are stealing my customers, and I demand you shut your unsanctioned social club down immediately, or I'll report you."

Lynell's irritation must have carried into the other room because Burt wandered in and looked between Lynell and me. "Hold on, Maya has nothing to do with me sharing cheesecake with a couple of friends," Burt defended me.

"Then why is that there?" She pointed to the Burt's Kitchen drawing taped to the wall."

Burt walked over and pulled the sign down. "There, now it's not. Problem solved."

"Hardly, you're still socializing in the post office, and she isn't supposed to do that."

"Actually, it's the church's kitchen too," Bev said, coming in as added backup. "And I'm here as the church minister, so, this is a church event."

Carmen, Bev's short, Puerto Rican wife, joined Bev sliding her arm around her waist and blocking the doorway.

"I'm a small business owner," Lynell persisted, even though she was clearly outnumbered. "I can't have my regulars coming here instead of my café. Business doesn't pick up until the campgrounds open."

I didn't like giving in to bullies, but I was still new and couldn't afford to have Lynell complain about me. I tried to come up with a compromise. "You're closed on Monday and Tuesday, right?"

"We are, but what does that have to do with anything?"

"What if Burt agrees only to bring in baked goods on days when you're closed until business picks up? That way, he, I mean the church, can still have its coffee time, and it won't interfere with your café."

Lynell sputtered and clucked, working herself down from the high horse she'd flown up on. "I suppose that could work. But you can't hang that sign in the post office, since it's a church event."

I really didn't see how it mattered, but if my agreement meant she went away sooner, then she had it. I nodded.

"Alright, as long as Burt's Kitchen is only open on days when the Hummingbird is closed, I don't see any harm."

I wanted to remind her that Burt's Kitchen wasn't a real restaurant, but I also didn't want to provoke her, so I just agreed. Burt, though clearly annoyed, also agreed.

Satisfied, Lynell turned sunny. "You all should come by for breakfast tomorrow. We're doing a special on pecan French toast. It is delicious! And Maya, you should bring the Lores. I haven't seen that cute little girl of Leigha's in ages." She waved cheerily. "See you tomorrow."

"That woman is not all there," Carmen said, clearly expressing the sentiment of the group.

At noon, I joined the gathering. Carol briefly stopped by but was already gone. Carmen, Bev, Burt, and Purdy, were the only ones left.

"Janet's on her way," Bev said as I walked in. "I've got some great news about the progress the church is making on the bottle nets."

"Well, gals and handsome gentleman, as fun as playing with trash sounds, I've got a hair appointment in Hillsburg," Purdy said. "I'm going platinum, and this blonde is definitely going to have more fun." She grabbed the deck of cards from the table. "Remember, you promised to play next week," she said to Burt, knocking the deck on the counter twice. "And if you're extra good, maybe we'll play for kisses instead of money." She blew him an air kiss, and he dodged, stretching to swipe an invisible crumb off the table.

"That woman's flirting is out of control," Burt declared as soon as she was out of earshot. "I don't know what to do about it. She won't take a hint, and I don't want people getting the wrong idea."

I was pretty sure that by 'people' he meant Carol, but I wasn't going to call him out in front of Bev and Carmen. "If it's making you that uncomfortable, maybe you'll need to be direct and ask her to stop flirting."

Bev steered the conversation away from Purdy and to the subject we were here to discuss. She wanted to know just how much more recycling we needed to collect because the bins out back were becoming a lot of work. People kept backing into them. "And last night, someone upended all of them. It was a huge mess." Bev blamed it on bored drunk kids, but I wasn't so sure.

"All the garbage and recycling bins were upended? Did it look like someone was looking for something?" I asked.

"I couldn't tell you. Trash was strewn everywhere."

As if summoned, Janet burst in like a triumphant Valkyrie holding her phone high. "I got the little weasel on the trap cam."

"You got who on what?" I understood her words, but not their meaning.

"The recycling thief. I caught him on a trap camera I use to watch the animals around the house."

Carmen looked as confused as I felt. "What would anyone want with your recycling?" she asked.

"How should I know?" Janet answered.

"Can you see who it is?" Burt straightened in his chair.

"He covered his face, so I don't know who he is."

"Do you have the video? Can we watch it now?" I asked, reaching out for the phone.

We passed it around, each of us taking a turn. The video quality was low, and the screen was so small it was hard to make out details, but a few things stood out. The figure looked big. It was almost certainly a male, and by the way he was rummaging through the buckets, he was definitely looking for something.

"Have you shown it to the police yet? I asked.

"I gave it to them this morning."

I asked what they said, and Janet curled her lip in disgust.

"All they said was they would look at it."

"I just don't get it." Carmen looked around the table as if one of us understood more than she did. "Why would someone want to go through all your trash?"

We speculated for a few more minutes on motives, but nothing felt right. With no real resolution, we left the topic and moved on to updates.

The biodegradable nets were ready to be stuffed with the plastic bottles we'd collected. Sherman of Evergreen Wrecking & Demolition agreed to man his old wrecking ball, and four food trucks signed on to work the event. Things were coming together. I was riding the high of our accomplishments.

Before heading home, I swung by Provisions in the Pines. I was in the mood for a classic grilled cheese and tomato soup, but I was out of cheese and soup. Last minute grocery shopping was so much easier now that I didn't have to avoid Emily. The bell above the door jingled as I entered. Emily sat behind the cash register looking at her phone. In the split second it took for her brain to recognize me, the solicitous smile on her face fell. I looked around for a display to duck behind, my old instincts kicking in.

"Oh, Maya," Emily slurred the words in one long exhalation of dismay. "Oh, Maya," she said again. "I am so sorry."

My thoughts raced through a flip chart of all the things Emily could be sorry for. Did she fake her self-help confessional and was still hunting me? Had she started a new rumor about me and this time given me herpes?

"What's up?" I asked wearily, fearing the answer.

"Come here." She waved me over like a tightly wound wind-up toy, her wrist reeling me closer at hyper speed. When I reached the counter, she grabbed my hand and gave me sympathetic puppy eyes. "Maya, he played both of us for fools, and I am so sorry."

"Back up a second." I slipped my hand from hers. "What are you talking about?"

"Owen!" she said, as if it should be obvious. "He was in here early this morning buying food for a picnic, and he was with another woman," she hissed. "And she was all over him, holding onto his arm, calling him 'O', like she'd known him forever! And Maya, she was so pretty, I mean like model pretty. She had long, curly, red hair and the most perfect skin. I hate her." Emily sighed dramatically, shaking her head in disbelief. "I never thought Owen was the type of guy to cheat like that. I guess the good-looking ones always do. All I can say is, I'm glad we found out now before we wasted any more time on him."

Words kept bubbling from Emily's mouth in a groundswell of support, but I had temporarily lost the ability to hear. I felt like someone punched me in the solar plexus. Pain burned my chest and my breath shortened. My instincts had been right. Something was up when he got Fizzy early. Why didn't I trust my intuition? But did it really matter anyway? It wasn't like he was my boyfriend or like we were even dating. I just thought, hoped it was leading in that direction. I pulled myself together.

"And what kind of name is Ava anyway, like she's some kind of old-time movie star," Emily said in an oddly flattering insult. "I mean, she's pretty enough to be one, but still. Just for you, I charged them double for their bottled waters. And I made sure to ask Owen how you were doing."

An ice shard chilled my insides. Ava was the name of Owen's ex. Was that who he was with? I forced myself to act normal and not ask her what he said when she asked about me. I hated that I was dying to know. "Emily, it's okay. Remember, Owen and I are just friends. We've never even been on a date. He isn't cheating."

Emily pinched her lips and drew her head back as if tasting something sour. "You can tell me that story all day long, but I know you like him more than a friend. And it's obvious he likes you too. Don't let that homewrecker steal your guy."

She sounded like a country western cliché, and I wondered if she'd thrown the self-help book away yet.

"I appreciate your loyalty, but you shouldn't overcharge them next time. I wouldn't want you to get into trouble on my account."

"I do it all the time. If people catch me, I just apologize and say, 'Good catch. Let me fix that for you'. I never get in trouble." She smiled sweetly.

I was definitely glad Emily was on my side these days. I paid for my cheese and said I'd see her Monday. "Chin up," she called after me. "We'll get your man back."

Fourteen

The dust bunnies in my hair wore dust bunnies in their hair. Leigha and I were filthy from combing through the accumulation of a family's lifetime. Dave's pickup bed was already full of broken, dump-bound relics, and we hadn't even cleared half of the Stevens' small barn. My arm muscles burned from heavy lifting and hard work, but I was thankful for the distraction. Owen texted last night to see how I was feeling and to confirm he was still coming over at two. I stayed up very late last night working on the cans, trying to get them finished, so I'd have a legitimate excuse to back out of our plans. I didn't trust myself not to be weird around him. As it was, I responded to him with only the flamenco dancer emoji.

His answering text said, "I'll take that as a yes?"

I sent back a thumbs up emoji. What would happen when I had to use actual words?

"Maya, we need some help over here," Leigha called, pulling on a stained recliner.

I hurried over. Between the two of us, we managed to drag it to the truck and hoist it in.

"Phew, I'm going to be feeling this tomorrow." Leigha panted, wiping the sweat off her forehead with her gloved hand. Even in work clothes, Leigha looked like an adorable farm girl with her blonde braided pigtails, navy cotton overalls, and a matching handkerchief tied over her head. "I think that's a load," she declared, eyeing the tower with satisfaction.

Every year the garbage company sent out coupons for half-off garbage dump day, and this year we were getting our money's worth. The dump line tended to be long on coupon day, so we had a plan. Leigha made a karaoke mix, and I was in charge of the gas station snack run on the way there. Carol had several magazines for us in case we got tired of singing, as if that could happen.

"I'll go get Carol, then it's off to the gas station for junk food!" I ran up the Stevens' steps, making sure to jump over the rotten one. "Carol, we're ready for you," I called, poking my head into the house.

"Maya, come look at these."

I wiped my boots, double-checking them for barn muck. Carol and Nancy sat on the couch looking at old sepia-toned photos. "Some of these pictures are almost as old as the town!"

"I hate to get rid of them, but I can't take them all with me," Nancy said, stroking a large image of a man and three children standing in front of an old plow. "This here was my Great Grandpa Gerald. He was a farmer and also worked in the mines right here in Claryce Falls. I've got to keep this one." She set the photograph on top of an already tall pile. On her other side was the considerably smaller throwaway stack.

"These are amazing," I agreed. I hovered, afraid to touch anything with my dusty clothes. "You know Maggie, Jason the librarian's wife, is putting together a photo history of the area. Would you be willing to let her take a look and maybe donate some of them to the library?"

"Do you think she could use them?" Nancy asked, hopeful.

"I don't know why not. Would it be okay if I gave her your number?"

Nancy agreed and I shot Maggie a quick text. "We're all loaded up and ready for the dump."

"Did you get it all?" Nancy asked.

"We made a good start." I tried to sound optimistic.

"These girls sure can work," Ben said, walking up and clapping a hand on my shoulder. "Buddy and I just sat on our butts like a couple of warts on a toad and bossed them around."

"You were very decisive, which helped a lot." It was true, Ben was quick to tell us what stuff should be saved for the sale and what should be tossed. He wasn't overly sentimental about much of it, so the sorting went fast.

"Remind me what we're paying you again?" he joked.

"The friends and family rate, coffee and pie." I smiled back.

"In that case, you're worth double your earnings." He squeezed my shoulder affectionately and let go.

Carol stood, taking a moment to stretch her stiff legs. "We're off to the dump. I'll be here tomorrow around two, and the girls and I will be over again Wednesday afternoon."

Nancy asked Carol to bring Libby with her.

"I will," Carol said. "I don't know how much we'll get done, but things will be lively."

I grabbed the handle and pulled myself up into Dave's pickup. "This thing is a beast," I said, climbing into the back seat of the extended cab. "I'm impressed Dave let you drive his baby."

"You and I both know he doesn't 'let' me do anything. And besides," she leaned over and covered her mom's ears. "Dave thinks it's sexy when I drive it. Especially when we're towing the boat. He loves a capable woman." She wiggled her eyebrows and grinned wickedly.

Carol pulled down the visor mirror and re-fluffed her hair. "They are certainly going to need a lot more help. Honey, when I die, just put a big free sign on everything and let people take it all," Carol said dramatically.

"You know, I don't even like to think about that," Leigha chastised.

"Sweetheart, it happens to us all eventually. But don't worry, I'm not planning on going anywhere for a long time."

I thought about my last conversation with my own mother. I'd called her for her birthday in January. She'd thanked me for the hand-painted, Armenian scarf I'd sent but failed to mention the enclosed card of the llama in polka-dotted under-wear which read, 'Another year older? No Prob-LLAMA. Put on your party pants and celebrate!' I knew the card wouldn't be mantle-worthy in my mother's estimation. She favored let-terpress cards of sentimental Rumi sayings or hand-painted flowers. But the mischievous glint in the llama's eyes called to me, and I couldn't resist.

Leigha pulled up to the Chevron station. I jumped out, excited to fulfill my junk food quest. In my enthusiasm, I pushed the door too hard, hitting an irritated-looking man with a thick white beard. I reactively grabbed his forearm and apologized. He shook me off as if I had leprosy, cursed at me to watch where I was going, and gave me a shove as he walked past.

I stood, shocked by his rudeness, staring after him. He looked scruffy. Dark stains dotted his camo pants, and his black sweatshirt had a big tear in the back. Mr. Beardo-Jerkface stomped over to an old truck with a tarp covering the bed. He set his case of Miller Lite on the open truck gate. Shaking off the guy's negativity, I refocused on more import-ant matters.

I grabbed white cheddar popcorn, Red Vines, cinnamon bears, and three sodas, trying to balance it all like it was my first day at clown school. The temptation of the smoked almonds was too great to resist. I gripped the bag of cinnamon bears between my teeth.

"You want some help with that?" a familiar voice asked from the end of the aisle.

Dread flooded me. I turned very slowly, bracing myself for embarrassment.

Owen strolled down the narrow aisle, flashing a grin so wide, it practically showcased every tooth in his head. "Got the munchies?" He pulled the bag of cinnamon bears from my teeth.

How was it I didn't see Owen once during his first three months in town, and now he was absolutely everywhere in my life? He gave me the once over. I grimaced, knowing what he was seeing. A disaster of a woman, filthy from hair to sneaker, her arms full of junk food. I felt like that girl again, standing on the side of the road with a flat tire and a latte-stained shirt.

"We're doing a dump run," I said lamely. "The line is long, and we've been cleaning out the Stevens' barn for them all morning." I sounded normal enough, plus we were helping people. Extra points to me.

Owen pulled out his phone checking the time. "It's already one. You sure you're going to be ready for me to come over in an hour?"

"It's already one?" I shrieked. There was my familiar weird slipping back in. "I had no idea it was that late already. I guess not. Sorry. You don't really need to come over. I'm almost done anyway." I couldn't stop my rambling. "If you have company, you should totally hang out with them."

Owen looked confused. "Wait, don't you want me to come over? And how do you know I have company?"

"Emily." I cringed. "And it's always nice to hang out, but I don't want you to feel like you have to if you're busy."

"Right. If it's all the same to you, I'd still like to come over and help you finish up. I'll tell you about Ava's visit."

"You don't need to," I jumped in. "Tell me, I mean. Sure, come over. I'll be done with the dump by three. Clover will be happy to see Fizzy," I added.

It was Owen's turn to cringe. "I may have to leave her with Ava. But I'll be there."

"Then Clover will be happy to see you."

He followed me to the front. As I set everything down, my haul spilled across the counter. Pulling the cinnamon bears protectively back from Owen, I added them to the pile.

I paid and grabbed the bulging bag. "See you in a bit," I mumbled into his chest before hurrying out, barely missing a woman with a perky ponytail as I swung the door wide. I really was a menace.

The thought made me glance in the direction of the pump, where Beardo-Jerkface was loading his beer into a cooler. The tarp was folded back just enough to access the ice chest. He dropped a can, and it rolled. As he reached for it, the tarp lifted, and I caught a glimpse of what looked like the tip of an antler and a hoof.

I froze. Could this be the poacher Owen's been looking for? Then his torn black sweatshirt registered, making the hair on my arms stand up. I spun on my heels and rushed back into the store. Owen and I almost collided as he was heading out, and I shoved him inside.

"What are you..."

"That man in the blue pickup at the pump has a deer or elk in his bed," I interrupted. "And he's wearing a black sweatshirt with a piece missing, just like the person who knocked me out."

The amusement vanished from Owen's face. "Get back in the truck with Leigha. Call Dave. Tell him what you told me.

I'll take care of it from here." Side-stepping me, Owen left, striding purposefully toward Beardo-Jerkface.

"What's going on?" Leigha asked as I opened the passenger door.

Handing Carol the bag, I kept my eyes glued to Owen as he walked up to the guy. I quickly filled them in on what was going down, and Leigha immediately called Dave.

Beardo-Jerkface had finished storing his beer and was climbing into his truck when Owen stopped him. Owen gestured towards the bed, and I heard Beardo-Jerkface tell him where to shove it. Owen reached for the tarp, pulling it back enough to reveal a large bull elk. Seizing the distraction, the poacher jumped in the pickup, ready to flee. Without thinking, I sprinted across the small parking lot, stopping in front of his vehicle. I held my hand out like a vigilante crossing guard.

Beardo-Jerkface revved his engine, our eyes locking in a tense standoff. I barely registered Owen shouting before another truck roared behind me—Leigha had swung around, blocking his escape.

A hand gripped my arm and yanked me out from between the trucks. "What were you thinking? He could have run you over," Owen yelled.

"He was going to get away," I shouted back, my adrenaline spike needing an outlet.

"I got his license plate. The police would have picked him up as soon as he left."

"Well, I didn't know that," I fired back.

"We'll talk about this at your place later." His voice was stern. "Please, get back in the truck with Leigha."

"Fine. Dave's on his way," I added sullenly.

We watched Beardo-Jerkface hand his keys over to Owen, all his fight gone. The two talked and the scene, so intense, just moments ago, now seemed tame.

"That was exciting there for a second," Leigha laughed.

"Good thing Libby had a play date," Carol said.

We looked around as if trying to figure out what was next.

"Is that Owen's ex? I heard she was here visiting," Leigha asked.

I followed her gaze to Owen's truck parked on the other side of the pump. A striking woman with curly, red hair sat in the passenger seat, looking back at us. A sick feeling coiled in my stomach.

"How do you know about Ava?" Was I the last to find out about her?

"Emily told me. Is that her? Emily said she's super-model pretty, but I can't tell from this angle?"

I was saved from the conversation by a police cruiser pulling up. Dave got out to talk to Owen and the poacher before walking over to us. Leigha rolled down her window.

"Do I even want to know why you're blocking this guy?"

"Nothing to see here." Leigha waved her hand in the air.

Another police cruiser pulled up.

"Why don't you ladies finish your dump run? We got it from here."

"Sure thing, Officer," Leigha cooed as she leaned through the window to kiss her husband. She pulled the truck out, and we headed for the dump.

It took me a full five songs and half a box of Red Vines for my adrenaline to subside. By the time we made it into the dump, my angst over Ava was replaced with a sugar high, which I used to beat Leigha in an impromptu furniture hurling contest. On the way home, we sang along with Tina to "Proud Mary." And just like Tina, I too would keep on burnin' and keep on churnin'.

Fifteen

If the Olympics gave out medals for efficiency, I would be the one handing them out. I made it home in time for a quick shower and to blow dry my hair. I had a cuddle with Clover, stress-ate the rest of the cinnamon bears, and put on my most flattering work clothes, a fitted long-sleeve black t-shirt with a swooping eagle on it, talons extended, and a pair of paint-splattered jeans that hugged my butt.

To prove to myself that I wasn't waiting for Owen like a dog for a scrap, I cranked The Best of Tina Turner and got busy.

It worked because I was fully absorbed in soldering and the music when Owen pulled up. I was on the ladder, putting the final touches on the second giant can. As he approached, Tina began belting out the climactic chorus of "We Don't Need Another Hero." From the top rung, I raised my fist into the air and chanted along with Tina. Together, we called for "a life beyond the Thunderdome." The song ended. I threw my hand down and bent my head for a dramatic finish.

Owen obligingly clapped from below, and I thanked my vast imaginary audience before climbing down.

"Not sure which is more impressive, your performance or the can," Owen joked.

Tina had worked her magic and my spirit was soaring. "Who says we need to rank them? Can't everything I do just be impressive?" I picked up my phone and turned down the music.

"Sure. But if we're ranking them, I'm most impressed you haven't hurt yourself again if that's what you do on top of the ladder."

"That was nothing." I made a dismissive wave with my hand over my shoulder. "You should see what I do when I hang my Christmas lights. It's truly a nail-biter."

"I've no doubt I'll have 911 on standby and be following you around from the ground with an inflatable Santa at the ready, to catch when you fall off."

An image of me sliding down the roof onto the enormous pillowy belly of Ol' Saint Nick made me chuckle. "You know, that sounds like more of an enticement than a threat? I might need to figure out how to build that."

Owen sighed. "Me and my big mouth."

We faced each other, reflecting back one another's grins. Then a voice whispered, Snap out of it. Remember Ava! And the spell was broken.

I found a pair of large work gloves and tossed them to him. "We should be able to finish this afternoon. You ready to get started?"

For the next hour, we worked without talking much, each of us taking turns picking tunes.

When I put the last weld on the top of the third can, I let out a loud, triumphant cry. "Woo Hoo - DONE!" I circled around, inspecting the twelve-foot-tall columns of patchwork beer and soda cans. I'd created a design on each tower using similarly colored cans, but the result was a bit loose since I had to work with what we'd picked up. As a last-minute touch, I added giant tabs sticking up from the top of each column, crafted from cardboard and metallic paint.

I stepped back, admiring my towering, aluminum babies. They were definitely more Frankenstein's monster than Pygmalion's Galatea, but I loved them.

Owen joined me, throwing an arm around my shoulders. "Good job Ridgeway." Working in the sun had made Owen sweat. He smelled like pine needles and warm, down comforters. His casual affection felt painfully bitter-sweet. I slipped out from under his arm.

"You know, Janet is unique, but her tactics seem to be effective. Look what she got you and the town to do about the trash problem," Owen marveled.

"I suppose. Though, she's just lucky I'm a sucker for a project." I glanced around at my work area. "Would you mind if we used your truck to load the plastic bottles?" I pointed to the overflowing buckets in my garage. "They need to go over to the Unitarian church's parking lot."

"No problem. I've got a tarp behind the driver's seat. If you grab that, I'll get started hauling these out."

I walked over to his truck and pulled the seat forward. The tarp was exactly where he said it would be and I grabbed it. Hiding underneath was the small bucket of rifle casings we'd cleaned up at the makeshift target range. I'd completely forgotten about them. We'd kept the casing separate because I wanted to use them in a different project. I pulled out the bucket and rattled them. I probably needed twice the amount. "Have you found any more target practice spots? I'd like to pick up some more casings."

Owen looked at what I was holding up. "I forgot those were back there. No, but I've been busy with Dave, taking him around to where the elk carcasses were dumped."

I remembered I still wanted to hear what they'd found out. I'd been so busy trying not to talk about Ava and be normal, it'd slipped my mind. "Do you have time for a quick beer after this so you can tell me what you found?"

Owen checked his phone, which had chimed twice since we'd been working. He slid it back into his pocket without answering. Wiping the sweat off his face with the end of his shirt, it rode up exposing a small swath of pale, taut stomach. The sight of his bare skin made tingles in my belly, though it could've also been indigestion from all my gas station snacks. Owen caught me staring and smirked. My body heated with embarrassment, and I quickly looked away.

"Sure, a beer sounds good."

We finished cleaning up, and I made certain not to look at him again as we put things away. I grabbed a couple of bottles and joined Owen in my backyard. He was already seated in his usual spot, his legs stretched out in front of him, his head tilted back against the chair. He looked comfortable and relaxed. Like the way someone who's hanging out with a friend feels, I thought bitterly. When I sat down next to him, a cinnamon-flavored burp quietly bubbled up and out. I flicked an embarrassed glance at him. Owen's eyes stayed closed, and he hadn't seemed to notice. I wondered why he was so sleepy, but on second thought, I was pretty sure I didn't want to know.

"What did you and Dave find?" I asked abruptly.

Owen opened his eyes slowly and turned to me. "Almost nothing, and I mean it literally. It was strange. We went to three different sites where I'd seen carcasses dumped. The bones were gone, and there wasn't a trace left. We got lucky at the last place though. We found a front shoulder blade under a bush, probably dragged there by a coyote or something. There was a bullet still lodged in it."

"No way," I gasped and slapped his bicep in disbelief.

"It doesn't mean anything for sure yet. Dave took it to compare with the bullet that killed Peter. It was from a 7mm, the same caliber that Peter was shot with."

A small tingle went down my neck.

"Weren't the casings we found at the target site also 7mms?"

"Yeah," he paused, thinking. "But that doesn't necessarily mean anything. It's a very popular rifle."

I sat still for a moment, letting the thoughts connect. "Did you know both Janet and the Church's recycling were raided, just like my house? And Janet caught the guy on her trap camera. He was definitely looking for something. What if he was looking for the casings we picked up? Maybe they somehow connect him to Peter's death or, maybe, the poaching?"

Owen asked about Janet's video. "It's definitely suspicious that someone hit all three recycling sites." He echoed my own thoughts. "It's worth mentioning to Dave. In the meantime, if someone is looking for them, I'd feel better if I kept the casings. I'll hand them over to Dave the next time I see him." Owen's phone chimed again, and he ignored it.

"Do you need to get that?" My stomach let out a loud grumble. The beer mixing with cinnamon bears were getting rowdy in my stomach.

"Nah, it can wait. You hungry? We could go into town for dinner. My treat."

As much as it thrilled me that Owen wanted to spend more time with me while Ava was still around, I didn't think my digestive system could handle it. I burped.

"Excuse me." I covered my mouth. "No, I think my gas station buffet might be trying to incite a rebellion."

He grimaced. "Should I go?"

"No," I cried, and my cheeks reddened. I decided to rip the bandage off. "You still haven't told me about Ava."

"You haven't told me how you and Emily became new BFFs," he countered, dodging the question.

"I wouldn't call us BFFs. I still think she's a little scary, but at least she's working with me instead of against me."

"That's for sure. She's become your new hype woman. She put on quite the show when I stopped by for sandwiches with Ava yesterday. Talked about you the entire time we were in the shop. How smart and cute you are, how funny you are, and how half the guys in town are after you. You better be careful. I think she's got a new crush."

If Emily was here right now, I would give her a big hug. The girl was starting to grow on me. "What can I say? People like me."

"True." He gave one of his direct smiles and my stomach clenched, making it gurgle again. "And I think she overcharged me on purpose."

"She did," I chirped. "But you're avoiding the question. What's Ava doing here?"

Owen let out a heavy, full-body sigh and rubbed his face. "She showed up Friday without warning. She sent a text saying she was at my house and wanted to know where Fizzy was."

I had so many questions. Had she visited before? Is that how she knew where he lived? Did he want to see her? Was he happy she was here? Was she here to get back together with Owen? Was she staying? I settled for, "When was the last time you talked to her?"

He rested his head back on the chair again, this time leaving his eyes open to stare into the darkening sky. "We've texted a few times since the breakup. She asked for pictures of Fizzy and I sent them. I was lonely when I first moved here, so the contact was nice. But, I've been busy lately. We haven't texted much in the last month or so. Then out of the blue, she showed up." He sighed again. "She's come for Fizzy."

I straightened. My fight response activated. "What? She can't take her. Fizzy's happy here. She has us." My stomach twisted and I fought the rising nausea. "Burt and Carol walk her. She's Clover's best friend." I hadn't realized how much I cared for the little dog until threatened with her loss. My stomach roiled. "I think I'm going to be sick."

"Maya, nothing's for sure. Ava's here until the end of the week. I'm trying to convince her that Fizzy is better off here with me."

I held up a hand, cutting him off. "No, Owen, I mean I'm going to be sick."

I sprinted to the bathroom, silently vowing to sacrifice my favorite threadbare Green Day t-shirt to any god who'd keep me from vomiting on the floor. The patron saint of angsty teen rock must have been listening because I made it just in time before my stomach's final rebellion. When there was nothing left, I slumped over the toilet, breathing hard. A gentle knock interrupted the sound of my panting.

"Maya? Are you okay?"

"Much better now. Just give me a sec."

There was a long pause. "I'm so sorry to do this, but I have to leave. Ava called and Fizzy's run off. I need to go look for her."

Anger filled my empty stomach. "What? I'm going to help, too," I called through the door, rising from my knees. "You go. I'll call you after I get myself sorted and am on the way."

"Are you sure you feel well enough?"

"I'll be fine. We just need to find her. She's snack-sized. Everything will eat her."

Owen left, and I rinsed my mouth and blew my nose. I loaded Clover into Nell and headed out to join the search.

Owen's text came through as I pulled into his driveway. "Fizzy's ok. She's here."

I sagged in relief, happy Fizzy was safe and glad I wouldn't have to face Owen and Ava together. I sent a quick reply and was about to back out when Owen's front door opened, and the little Houdini herself bounded out. I groaned and put the car in park. I got out and opened the door for Clover. The dogs met in the middle, bouncing and circling each other. Then Fizzy ran over to greet me.

"Hello, you little escape artist," I said, crouching to scratch under her chin. Fizzy stood on her hind legs and licked my face. "I missed you too, girl." Clover nudged Fizzy away and the two took off again.

"I'm sorry to drag you over here, Maya," Owen said, emerging from the front door.

"Where'd you find her?"

"She was here the entire time, asleep hidden behind the recliner. Ava couldn't see her."

A tall, attractive woman in her early thirties with dark red, curly hair ambled out of the house and over to Owen's side. She wore fitted jeans and a dark blue shirt that matched her eyes.

"Hi, I'm Ava. You must be Maya."

I greeted her with a monosyllabic, "Hi."

"Sorry for the false alarm and cutting your evening short."

I had the distinct feeling she was not sorry at all.

"I panicked when I couldn't find Fizzy." We all turned to look at the happy little tornado spinning across the yard, oblivious to the drama she'd caused. "She and your dog get along well," Ava observed.

"It's been really nice for both the dogs since Owen drops her off in the mornings. They keep each other company. It's a great arrangement." I hoped I wasn't laying it on too thick, but I didn't want to lose Fizzy.

"Owen mentioned that. He also said another friend helps walk them. It sounds like quite the little community here."

"We seem to have a system that works pretty well," I said. Catching a faint whiff of puke on my breath, I remembered just how quickly I'd run out of the house. I really needed to get out of here. I called to Clover. "Looks like the crisis is over. I'll let you get on with your evening." I opened the rear door and Clover jumped in.

"I'll see you Saturday with Dave to bring the cans over to the park," Owen said as he came closer.

I climbed into my car, and he reached for my door. I leaned back, trying to keep as much distance between him and my questionable odor.

"You sure you're feeling okay?" he asked in a lower voice. "I don't like sending you off like this."

"I'm great." Owen and I both heard the lie in my voice. I wasn't okay, but it wasn't from too many smokey nuts and cinnamon bears. No, the cause of my heartburn was the hot Red Vine still standing outside watching us. "See you Saturday," I said in a neutral tone, pulling at the door.

He bent, forcing direct eye contact. "I want you to call me if you need anything or if anything suspicious happens."

I nodded enthusiastically, refusing to risk opening my mouth with him this close.

"I mean it."

I nodded again, and he reluctantly let go of the door. I waved to Ava and backed Nell out of this bellyache of an evening.

Sixteen

A dirty blonde, with fire-engine-red lips and a starlet hairdo from the forties, stepped from a middle school play and into Leigha's nail salon and workout studio.

"What are you wearing?" I groused, taking in Emily's mismatched getup. It was like she'd raided a costume shop and borrowed pieces from different decades. She wore a thirties white, button-up blouse, sixties chunky red heels, and a tight, black mini skirt from the eighties. Dangling from her arm was a briefcase so big it could fit the rest of her theatrical cast in it. Completing the look was a tiny, black felt hat perched on the top of her head like a cherry on an over-frosted cupcake.

"What's wrong with what I'm wearing?" Emily tugged the skirt down. "I think I look good."

"You look beautiful, Honey," Carol said diplomatically. "It's just a bit much."

I was less tactful. "You look like a sexy, befuddled, time-traveling secretary."

"I don't know what that means exactly, but thank you for the sexy part." Emily curtsied.

"You were supposed to dress like your normal self, not in some Halloween getup," I reminded her critically.

"I started to get ready but was nervous. I read that red lipstick is supposed to make you feel confident, so I put that on. But the lipstick didn't go with my t-shirt, so I found this blouse. But then that didn't go with my sweatpants. One thing led to another." She held out her arms and winced at her own inability to stop herself. "I guess I may have overdone it a little, didn't I?"

"You think?" I asked sarcastically. "You can't go like that. "Do you have anything normal you can put on?"

"I did bring a change of clothes in case we went somewhere afterward," Emily admitted reluctantly.

"Great! Go change. Unless you come out as a banana in a cowboy hat, it has to be less conspicuous," I muttered under my breath.

Ten minutes later, Emily emerged from the bathroom in jeans, a t-shirt, and white sneakers. Her two columns of rolled hair were gone, replaced by cascading waves, and only a faint red stain remained from the lipstick. She looked like an era appropriate pretty woman. We all let out exclamations of praise and relief.

"I don't know if I can do this. I feel so exposed. I'm not sure if I can pull this off as just me."

"Of course, you can," I countered. "You're the determined woman who throws beverages and starts rumors about STDs."

"Keep it clean, Maya," Burt interrupted my pep talk.

I ignored him. "You followed and threatened me, all in pursuit of snagging a date for your sister's wedding. Heck, you were downright scary at times." I raised my voice triumphantly. "Emily, you can do this. I believe in you."

"I really scared you?" she asked, hesitantly, but not without a hint of pride.

"I was absolutely disconcerted," I affirmed.

"I guess I did do all of that." A smile spread across her face. "But, if I had a little something extra, I know I could do it."

"What are you thinking?" Leigha asked.

Emily eyed the nail station. "A new polish might give me the boost in confidence I need. Something with a little sparkle, maybe with jewels on the tips."

"Done." Leigha pointed to the rack of colors. "Pick your shade and hop up."

I bit my tongue, holding my criticisms of this whole unnecessary delay. It wasn't Emily's fault I hadn't slept well again and had skipped lunch. I needed a snack. "Burt, did you bring any food?" I asked hopefully.

"I didn't know I was supposed to," he said with censure.

"You weren't. I've just come to count on you as a reliable source of nutrition. Sadly, you've let me down today."

"Go into the kitchen and help yourself," Leigha offered.

I wanted coffee and one of Burt's goat cheese scones. I was getting hooked on the stuff. "I think I'll pop down to Rustic Reads for a coffee. Will you call me when you're ready?" I intentionally didn't invite anyone to join me. I wanted to go alone and not subject them to my hangry mood.

The bright spring sun and warm weather were already drawing the first wave of summer tourists. The tables at Rustic Reads were full of families enjoying a late lunch and remote workers on laptops. I took my sandwich and iced latte out to the adjacent Claryce Falls park center, an area with public picnic tables and a stage where local bands played on the weekends. I was looking around for a table in the shade when the motion of a hand waving from the far corner caught my eye.

"Seriously?" I whined, my shoulders sagging. With a smile more grimace than grin, I returned the striking redhead's wave. She flagged me over, and I didn't see an easy way out or even a bush to hide behind. At least I didn't smell bad today. I mean, I hoped I didn't smell bad. I took a deep breath, trying to detect anything. But even if I did, what could I do about it now? Resigned to my fate, I dragged myself toward her like I was walking into a dentist appointment.

"Maya, what a nice surprise. Are you meeting anyone or can you join me?" Ava sounded pleased to see me.

Just because I was jealous of the woman, I didn't need to be an ass. Get over yourself, I told myself, trying to dig deep to summon a better person.

"Sure, thanks." I set my food on the table and folded my legs under the bench seat across from her.

"I'm sorry about the whole thing with Fizzy last night. I panicked when I called her, and she didn't come. I forgot about her superpower to sleep through anything."

I inhaled an apple slice. "That is so true. She once went to sleep under my table with the sander going. When I saw her lying there, I freaked out. I thought I'd somehow killed her. Like, I'd accidentally hit her with a piece of wood. I started yelling and shaking her, and she opened her eyes, yawned, and gave me this look like, 'Why'd you disturb me?' Can you believe she was annoyed with me when she'd practically given me a heart attack?"

Ava threw her head back and laughed, the skin around her eyes crinkling.

"I never told Owen about that," I admitted.

"Your secret's safe with me," Ava smiled. She changed the subject and asked me about the recycling project.

I explained how it all started with Trash Trouper Janet Jackson. And about the giant cans and what we were planning on doing to them at the event.

"I love it! It's artsy, redneck, and socially conscious," she chortled loudly.

I liked Ava's laugh. It was big and unselfconscious. Our conversation flowed easily. And, at some point, I stopped thinking of her as Owen's maybe-ex, the source of my angst, and just as Ava. Was that how Emily felt about me, except more intensely? The thought that I might resemble Emily in bulldozing mode made me shudder.

Curious, I asked Ava to tell me about the crazy things she's seen as an ER and flight nurse.

"There are so many. Let me think for a sec." She pulled her hair up off her face and into a messy ponytail. "Oh, I know. Every Fourth of July, we get at least a couple of bros who think lighting fireworks from their butts is a good idea. And it's always guys—never once has a woman said, 'Hold my beer while I insert a mortar shell.' One ambitious fellow went all out with a Roman Candle, and after surgery, the first thing he asked was, 'Did you see the video? Did I go viral?' Honestly, I could call my autobiography 'Weird Things I've Yanked Out of People's Holes.' After a while, you stop asking why and just focus on getting the fireworks out of their cracks."

We talked easily for a while until my phone buzzed. It was Leigha. They were swinging by with her minivan to pick me up. It was odd they were driving since Chris's office was only a block away. I also noticed Owen had texted me asking how I was feeling today.

"Sorry," I apologized to Ava, indicating my phone. I texted Leigha back with my location. "My friends are picking me up."

"You're a tight-knit group here. I'm glad Owen's found his place in it. He can be kind of a loner if left on his own."

She seemed genuine, and I realized I liked Ava. "I guess I haven't seen that side of him, but we've only been friends for less than a month." My phone buzzed again. "Shoot, they're here." I stuffed the rest of my sandwich into my mouth. "I'm glad we ran into each other," I said around my food, surprising myself when I realized meant it.

"Me, too," Ava said. "Hopefully we'll get to see each other again soon."

I nodded enthusiastically. If Owen was going to be with anyone else, I was glad it was with someone who seemed like a badass.

The side door of Leigha's black Chrysler Pacifica slid open, and a sippy cup rolled out.

"Shoot! Maya, will you grab that?" Leigha called from the front seat.

The cup rolled behind the front wheel. I had to get down on my belly to reach it. "Whatever you do, just stay in park," I commanded. I brushed myself off and climbed around Emily into the third row. "Why are we driving?"

"We wanted to keep out of sight, but be close in case something went wrong," Burt answered.

"What could go wrong? She just goes in and asks to look at a few listings. She gets him to write down directions, and she's out of there. It's not like he's going to leap over his desk and try to strangle her."

"Oh my God, do you think he'll try and strangle me? What if he has a gun? A lot of people have guns around here." Emily was starting to spin out.

"Why would you say that, Maya?" Burt patted Emily gently on the back. "He won't hurt you."

"You're going to do great," Carol reassured her. "And we'll be right here if you need us."

We parked by the main entrance of the converted grain mill in front of the glass studio. Leigha turned in her seat. "Let's run through this one more time."

Emily took a deep breath. "I walk in and introduce myself. I tell him I'm thinking about buying a starter home in the area and ask if he might know of any good options. I'll ask him to print a couple out and to write something down for me." She patted an enormous canvas tote she must have borrowed from Leigha. It looked like the ridiculous briefcase had thankfully been left behind.

"That's perfect," Carol cheered. "You've got this, Honey."

Emily held her hands straight out, gazing at her nails. A bright yellow lightning bolt with a jewel at the tip decorated each index finger. "I've got this," she breathed in. "Wait, how will you know if I get into trouble?" There was a brief pause as we scrambled for a solution.

"Why don't we call your phone, and you can put us on speaker in your bag so we can hear you," I suggested.

"Okay," Emily agreed. "I think that'll work." She took another fortifying breath and nodded. "Ready."

We all did a quick scan to make sure Chris wasn't lurking nearby. Leigha hit the button, and the van's door slid open as Emily stepped out.

I called her phone, and after a few button presses, Emily slid it into her bag. I set my phone face-up on the empty seat so we could all listen in.

"I'm entering the building," her muffled voice announced. "Now I'm walking down the hall, passing Finona's Finds. They have the cutest antique end table with little claw feet."

I rolled my eyes. "Focus, Emily," I whispered.

"I see his office, and the lights are on," her footsteps slowed. "Okay, I'm going in." We heard a knock, then the door creaked open. "Hi there, my name is Emily Lemont.

I shot Leigha a confused look, mouthing, "Lemont?" Emily's last name was Brady.

"I'm thinking of buying a house."

Chris's thoughts must have echoed our own because we heard a mumbled question followed by Emily's awkward laugh.

"That was my last name, but I'm trying out my mother's maiden name now. We don't have any boys in the family, and I think it's important to keep the name alive."

The van was silent as we hung on Emily's every word.

"Is that a dream board? I love making those! Oh my gosh, where did you get these stick-on letters? They're adorable!" Emily chirped.

My irritation skyrocketed as Emily and Chris dove into a passionate discussion about craft stores and their best finds.

"Come on, Emily, focus," Burt willed loudly, finally getting on board the frustration train.

"Oh no, excuse me," Emily's voice sounded panicked. "That must be my, uh, my meditation app. I left it on. Yes, it did say my name. Hearing my name helps me fall asleep. It's very advanced."

Leigha's eyes widened in horrified realization. "Oh, crap—"

We hadn't muted the phone. For a split second we froze, before we all surged into action at once. We lunged for the phone, knocking into one another and fumbling it to the floor. Burt snatched it up, frantically trying to silence us.

"Don't worry, it'll turn itself off in a sec," Emily said pointedly. Acting like nothing had happened, she quickly returned the conversation to their shared passion. "You know, I made my first dream board when I was eleven. It had a lot of pictures of Harry Styles on it. I was certain we were supposed to get married. Did you know he got his start when he auditioned for the X Factor? It's like the British version of America's Got Talent."

Chris didn't seem to be a One Direction fan because he cut her off.

"What am I looking for? Great question. Something with at least three bedrooms, a nice front porch. It has to have an updated kitchen, and a stand-alone tub would be amazing."

I was pretty sure Emily was talking about her dream board again. There was a lot of indistinguishable talking from Chris. Suddenly, a loud male shouted. We jumped to attention, ready to run to Emily's rescue.

"I'm so sorry, I can be so clumsy." Emily's voice filled the minivan, and we all let out a sigh of relief. "Those are really nice trousers. You should rinse them off before they stain."

More mumbling, the sound of a door closing.

"Guys, I just spilled coffee on his pants. I'm grabbing the papers now. Start the van 'cause I'm coming out hot."

Old habits die hard, I thought, recalling my own Emily-sponsored beverage mishap.

A minute later, Emily exploded out of the building at a full sprint.

"Open up," she cried, wrenching the minivan side door open. "Let's go!"

Leigha hesitated, starting to pull out of the parking spot. "Wait, where are we going again?"

"To the Post Office," Burt bellowed, a general rallying his troupes. He leaned around me to look at Emily. "You got his handwriting, right?"

"I did." Emily held up a black leather-bound book like a trophy.

"You took his whole journal?" I yelped. This girl did not understand subtly. "We can't keep that."

"I'm not going back in there right now," she huffed.

"What's done is done," Carol reasoned. "We'll take one thing at a time. Let's compare the writing first, then we'll figure out how to return it."

After the minivan's backup camera gave Leigha the all-clear, she eased us into the world's laziest getaway. We ambled along at fifteen miles per hour down the block and a half to the Post Office building.

"Park around by the Church entrance," Burt commanded.

We piled out and Burt pulled keys from his pocket. "Bev gave me a set after Lynell's fit. This way, I can legitimately say I'm accessing 'the church kitchen.'"

"That was awfully thoughtful of her," I said.

"I told her I'd make her a cheesecake. She's wild for it," he bragged.

"I don't blame her. What you've been doing with goat cheese is practically magic," I said, impressed.

"Thank you, Maya." He beamed. "It means a lot."

We followed him up the stairs like ducklings, single file. As Burt unlocked the kitchen door, I grabbed the suspect board from the office and laid it flat on the table.

"Why am I an ice skate in a melted puddle?" Emily asked, frowning at the drawing under her name.

"Uh, because you were skating on thin ice with me," I lied, not wanting to admit I compared her to a potentially overly competitive sociopath.

"I'm glad we're on solid ground now." She laughed at her joke.

"Okay, let's compare notes." I held my hand out to Emily, who reluctantly handed me the notebook.

I scanned the page, the words slowly sinking in. 'He stood on the bow of his sixty-foot Riviera Sport Yacht, his prominent pectorals gleaming in the Mediterranean sun. Christopher Weller was a self-made man, a real estate mogul, and an international playboy. His yacht boy, Sven, handed the devastatingly handsome Captain Weller his drink before bending to raise his mast.' "Oh no," I yelped, instinctively throwing the journal across the room. "Chris writes nautical fan fiction about himself."

"Seriously, Maya," Burt grumbled. "Quit being so dramatic."

"Do you even know what fan fiction is?" I asked Burt.

"It can't be that bad," he muttered, bending to pick it up. Burt opened the journal, scanned it briefly, then snapped it shut like it bit him. "We'll check the handwriting, then return this immediately."

"Good plan. Find a PG-rated section and cover the rest so no one else has to suffer," I suggested.

"Why don't you do it?" he countered.

"Because I'm dramatic. Remember?" I smirked, knowing Burt was already regretting his words.

"I'll do it," Emily volunteered. "I like fan fiction."

I puckered my lips and furrowed my brows in the "why not" look. "Maybe we can get a group discount at therapy."

"Alright, I've got a safe section." Emily held the journal open, using an old newspaper to censor the rest of Chris's sexy yacht fantasies from view.

Burt placed a photocopied threat next to the journal. I sighed. Just like Emily's writing, it wasn't even close.

"That's it," I declared, uncapping the marker attached to the board. "They don't match, and he has an alibi." I dramatically drew a line across Chris's name and scribbled underneath: Karaoke alibi + wrong handwriting.

The weight of defeat fell heavy on us.

"Well, on the bright side, you can finally file your complaints against him now," I said to Carol, searching for something positive.

"I suppose that's true," Carol agreed.

"Now we just need to get the journal back to Chris and somehow scrub our minds," I shuddered. "Emily, I think you should return it. Say you accidentally grabbed it with the listings."

"I'll just tell him I had sudden diarrhea and rushed home so fast I grabbed the journal by mistake."

"Works for me," I said, with a shrug.

"Anyone else feel like a glass of wine or a beer? First round is on me," Carol offered in an attempt to raise our spirits.

I thought guiltily about the design work I'd been neglecting for the resort. But hey, what was one more day of procrastination? "Sure. Let's do it."

"I'll drive Emily over to Chris's first. We can all meet at Jackie's" Burt directed.

Jackie's Place, a bar/family restaurant, had an enormous outdoor area with lawn games like corn hole, horseshoes, and bocce ball. During the weekdays, it was usually pretty quiet. I got a draft of the newest pilsner from the Claryce Falls Brewing Company. Leigha and Carol each got white wines. We took our drinks outside to the Adirondack chairs to wait in the sun.

Emily and Burt showed up just minutes later, the handoff apparently smoother than expected.

"He wasn't there," Emily said, answering the question we hadn't asked yet. "The door was unlocked, so I just put it back onto his desk." She sounded almost disappointed. Clearly, she was getting a taste for the covert ops life.

"I guess it's a good thing you haven't gotten any more letters lately since we're out of suspects," I mused.

"That's not entirely true," Carol admitted.

"What are you talking about, Mom? You promised me you wouldn't keep things from me again," Leigha chastised her mother. "When did this happen?"

Carol smoothed her floral print blouse over her jeans. "Before everyone gets all worked up, I only found the note this morning. I was waiting to tell you all until we were all together. We didn't need more stress this morning. I found it in this purse I haven't used in days, so who knows when it was slipped in?"

"What did it say?" Leigha demanded.

"It just says, 'Leave. Last Warning'."

"May I see it, please?" I held out my hand for the note, and Carol passed it to me. It was definitely written in the same handwriting as the other notes. There was a distinctive 'e' that crossed over on itself and an upward slant to the 't'. The paper was plain printer paper, the ink an unremarkable black. I handed the note to Burt, who inspected it and passed it on.

"What do we do now?" Emily looked expectantly around at each of us. There was a long silence as we all drew a collective blank.

I sat forward. "When was the last time you used your purse, Carol? Maybe we can make a list of everyone you had any interaction with that day."

Leigha pulled her cell phone out, threading her fingers through the dangling beaded handle attached to it. "I'll take down names."

Carol narrowed down the day she used the purse last to Saturday.

"Let's see, I played with Libby in the morning. Then I briefly went down to the Post Office for cheesecake and coffee."

"Okay, let's start there," I interrupted her. "Who was at the P.O. with you?"

"You and Burt, of course. Bev and Carmen, Purdy, Rita, and Anne all briefly stopped by."

"Got them." Leigha bobbed her head towards the list she was typing.

"What then?" I prompted.

"Then I went back to the house. The four of us went into Hillsburg to get flowers. We ran into Linda again and Dave stopped to talk with that poor man, the father of the boy who was killed."

"Gary Becker," Leigha supplied.

Burt and I exchanged a grim sympathetic look.

"After that, we went home and planted the flowers, made dinner, I read books to Libby and that was the day."

"How many people is that?" Burt asked Leigha.

She counted aloud. "That's twelve people, but if you take us out, it's seven. We already ruled out Linda. Rita and Anne recently got back from New Mexico for the winter. It can't be them, since they weren't here when the other notes were left. That leaves Bev, Carmen, Purdy, and Gary Becker."

"I wasn't anywhere near Mr. Becker when Dave was talking to him. I don't think it was him," Carol offered.

"If we rule out Gary for the time being, that leaves us with three."

"What are their motives?" Burt questioned. The rumble of passing pickup trucks and the cooing of doves amplified around us as we took a moment to think of motives.

Emily was the first to offer a theory. "Carol's an attractive woman for her age. And old women live a lot longer than old men do."

"Where are you going with this?" I cut in before Emily's backhanded compliment gained any more momentum.

"There's already more older women in this town than men. Maybe someone's trying to run off the competition like I was with Maya."

"That motive would rule out Bev and Carmen for obvious reasons." I thought about Purdy and her over-the-top flirting with Burt. "Now that you point it out, I can see Purdy doing something like that. Even you said she's been hitting on you pretty hard, Burt."

"And you obviously like Carol," Emily added tactlessly.

Emily for the first time was making a lot of sense. Purdy was an obvious suspect. I started to form a plan. "You're doing Burt's Kitchen tomorrow, right?"

"If I can get home in time to bake something," Burt confirmed.

"And didn't Purdy want to play cards?"

"Yes," Burt answered wearily.

"Why don't you invite Bev, Carmen, and Purdy for baked goods and cards? We'll get a sample of Purdy's handwriting to compare. Heck, we could get Bev and Carmen's handwriting too, just to rule them out. That's three suspects at once." I smiled, liking the plan. "Just schedule it for after noon, so I can be there."

"Shoot, I have nail appointments all day tomorrow, but I want to come." Leigha frowned.

"Do you want us to wait?" Burt asked.

"No, the sooner we get this figured out, the better."

"I'll call everyone and let them know we're playing cards at twelve-thirty tomorrow." Burt stood up. "I'd better get home and bake something."

My spirit had once again risen, buoyed by a plan of action in place and a new suspect in our sights.

Seventeen

The morning dragged like a soggy piece of toilet paper stuck to the wheel of a senior citizen's walker. By P.O. standards, it was an activity-packed morning, with two people coming in to open new mailboxes and a horde of Amazon package pickups. Yet the anticipation of each upcoming minute chafed like a scratchy tag on an ill-fitting bra. Burt entered through the church entrance at eleven-thirty. He popped his head in to say 'hi' before disappearing into the kitchen.

Fifteen minutes later, Carol arrived. She greeted me before she too dissolved into the quiet unrest. At eleven fifty-five, Sue Parker, who sold antique Avon bottles to eBay buyers in China, walked in with an armload of packages. I willed her to move faster, drumming my fingers on the counter as she triple-checked the address labels on each package. At noon, I put the closed sign out, just in case anyone else tried to get in line. Finally, at ten minutes after twelve, I pulled the metal window down to close the customer counter. I hurried and changed out of my uniform and into a Bob Ross, 'No Mistakes, Just Happy Accidents' t-shirt and a pair of jeans.

Burt staged the kitchen table like a British tea party. A three-tiered dessert stand sat grandly in the center. The mini-rustic Danishes looked like something out of a Better Homes and Gardens magazine spread. Adorable, perfectly square sandwiches filled the middle tier. The platter holding cups, napkins, and a carafe of coffee sat at the ready on the counter. I reached across the table for a Danish, but Burt slapped my hand.

"Wait for everyone to get here. Don't you have any self-control?"

Chastised like a naughty cat, I rubbed my hand, even though it was my ego stinging. "I do to have self-control," I grumbled. "I just didn't realize they were only for show."

"Here," he went over to a box stashed in the corner on the counter and pulled out a plate.

"You can eat the defective ones."

"Defective how?" I asked suspiciously.

"They're perfectly edible."

"Then why are they defective?"

"They don't look as good as the others. Do you want them or not?" He pulled the plastic wrap off and held the plate out to me. As I reached for it, he pulled it back in.

"Don't eat too many and make yourself sick."

"I wouldn't do that," I lied. I happily accepted the peace offering of defectives, and all was forgiven. "When did you have time to make all of these?" I asked, stuffing a bite-sized Danish in my mouth. "Mmm," I moaned in appreciation. "The dough is so flaky."

"I started it yesterday morning. The dough has to chill after each layer of butter you roll into it."

"Shhh, don't spoil this magic for me." I tried one of the sandwiches next. "Is this butternut squash?"

"Yep, with candied sage butter and goat cheese."

"Why didn't you open a bakery, Burt? You're so good," I gushed.

He leaned against the top of the table, considering the question. "Patty did all the cooking when she was alive, so I never had occasion to try it. After she passed, I'd make her apple and pear pie to make the house smell like she was still around. I got tired of eating pie, so I tried my hand at muffins. One day, I realized I was baking just because I enjoyed it."

I walked over and slung my arm over his shoulder. "I will happily eat your defects any day."

He gave me the look he reserved just for me and shook his head as if asking what he always wondered, 'What is wrong with you?' When he pulled away, Burt gave my shoulder a pat.

At twelve twenty-five, Bev wandered in from the church. "Hi everyone. Burt, did you make all this? It looks beautiful. I feel like a Duchess." She took a seat at the table. "Carmen sends her apologies. A new shipment of vegetable starts came in today, and she had to get them out." She pulled her enormous bag off the chair where she'd just hung it. "And before I forget, I wrote that recipe down for the rhubarb cake you asked me for." She handed Burt a piece of notebook paper.

"Thanks, Bev. I've got a couple of big rhubarb plants that I never know what to do with it all. I'm looking forward to making this soon." He waved the recipe at me. "Hey Maya, could you put this away for me?" He handed me the recipe, making meaningful eye contact.

"Sure thing, I'll be right back." I hurried out to the locked backroom where the suspect board was still stored. In the background, I heard Bev ask Carol about her new house. Carol told her about the garage sale and how much help the Stevens needed.

Quickly, I knelt and unfolded the cardboard trifold. I held the recipe up to the threats. The 't' could be a match. The 'e' in the words 'butter' and 'strawberry' were very round with little curls on the ends. It was not a match. My relief surprised me. Even though I never truly believed Bev was guilty, I realized I really didn't want it to be her.

"I'm here and ready to play," Purdy sang out, announcing her entrance.

"We're back here," Carol sang out.

I re-entered, following Purdy into the kitchen. Both Burt and Carol looked at me expectantly. I shook my head and gave a cheery thumbs-down.

Purdy jumped at the sound of me behind her. "Dang, girl, someone needs to put a bell around your neck. Sneaking up on an old gal like that isn't a good idea." She put an orange hand over her heart. "If you know what I mean?"

I apologized. "Did you get a tan?" The toasted carrot glow of her skin confused me. Was it intentional or the result of a radioactive bunny bite?

"I did it myself. Can you believe it? I was going to have it done in Hillsburg, but they wanted fifty-five dollars. I did this..." She stretched out a burnt ocher-colored arm for us to admire, "...for less than ten. I tell you, those salons are running a racket." She smacked her engorged lips to either draw attention to them or because she simply couldn't close her mouth without creating a vacuum seal. Taking in the table, she frowned. "I came to play some cards. How are we going to play with that big wedding decoration hoggin' all the room?"

I cringed. If Purdy had any real romantic designs on Burt, she was going about them the wrong way.

"It's a pastry tower, and I'm sure the pastries taste as good as they look." Carol tried soothing over Purdy's slight. "I can't wait to try them."

"We know, Dear" Purdy said under her breath and winked at me. I didn't acknowledge the quip at Carol's expense, yet I still felt vaguely guilty for not saying something. The moment passed, and I seemed to be the only one who heard it.

"After we fill our plates, I'll move it to the counter," Burt primly stated.

When we were all settled with coffee and treats, Purdy pulled two decks of cards from her purse and a small spiral notebook. "Everyone knows how to play Rummy?" she asked, shuffling the cards like a Vegas dealer.

Bev and I were a little rusty, but after a practice hand, we were ready.

"Okay, it's a five dollar buy-in, five hundred points takes the kitty."

"I didn't realize we were playing for money," Carol protested. "I thought this was a friendly game."

"It is friendly, but money makes it exciting," Purdy grinned wickedly. "I'm sure Burt will spot you if you don't have the cash."

"I have the money," Carol protested.

"Great! Bev, Maya, Burt, pony up, and let's play."

Neither Bev nor I had cash, so Carol covered the three of us. Purdy kept score in her little notebook. I tried peering over at it to peek at her handwriting, but she was protecting the score like a mother bear guarding her cub.

"Why are you rubbernecking?" she snapped at me.

"I want to know what the score is." I lied. She rattled off everyone's points. Purdy held a narrow lead over Carol, followed by, Burt, me, and Bev was last. "I thought for sure Carol would be in the lead after the last round," I mused.

"The numbers tell a different story," Purdy answered tartly. After three more rounds, Purdy won. "Should we make it a ten-dollar buy-in for the next one? Double or nothin'?" she asked, shoveling the cash in like a plump squirrel hoarding a full bird feeder.

"Why not?" I got you ladies covered." Carol stared Purdy down. "Only, I'll keep score this time." She held her hand out for the notebook.

"You don't need to worry about that. I like keeping score." Purdy pulled the notebook closer to her.

"I'm getting more coffee. Can I get anyone something to drink?" I filled Purdy's coffee cup without waiting for a reply. If I could get her to use the bathroom, maybe she'd leave the notebook behind.

"If I drink anymore, I'll be painting the porch at midnight," Bev said, covering the top of her mug with her hand protectively.

"Are you painting your house?" Burt asked.

"No, but I will be if I drink more coffee," she chuckled. "I'd take peppermint tea if you have it and another one of those little Danishes if you please, Maya?"

I flipped the electric kettle on and hoisted the pastry tower over to Bev. How could I get hold of Purdy's handwriting? I was pretty sure Purdy lived somewhere on Blue Agate Street, maybe I could get her to write her address for me. That might be enough. I stared at the little goat cheese and plum-filled pastries, praying for inspiration. If we hadn't met Linda at the farmers market, would any of this have happened? The notes started that day, and where Purdy, while selling her pickles, saw Carol and Burt together for the first time. The cogs clicked into place and my prayers were answered.

"Purdy, are you still selling pickles at the farmers market?"

"Do pigs like mud?"

"I think so. Are they like elephants and use it as a natural sunscreen?"

"Don't know anything about elephants. But I'm selling pickles. Why?"

"I'd like to buy ten or fifteen jars for the recycling event."

"What are you planning with all those pickles?" Bev asked.

"We could do a pickle-eating contest or something. Like, who can eat ten pickles the fastest."

"Sounds like a choking hazard," Bev warned.

"I think it sounds like fun." Purdy countered. "People would love that."

I looked at Burt and Carol and made a nudging motion with my head, prompting them to support me.

"It would be alright if only adults enter," Burt chimed in.

"I think it could be a great addition," Carol championed.

"If you all think it's a good idea, I guess Carmen and I both know the Heimlich maneuver."

"Great, Purdy, can I pick them up this week?"

"You got it, girl," Purdy looked excited.

"Would you write your address down for me?"

"You don't need me to write it down. It's easy to find my place, I'm the orange house on Blue Agate Street."

"I've got a terrible memory," I improvised. "I'd do better if I had your exact address. Would you just write it down for me?" I indicated the little notebook.

"Alright, but you're not gonna need it. She scribbled her address down and handed me the scrap of paper.

I checked the writing for the telltale distinctive letters. My vision tunneled as vertigo struck. Disbelief churned with anger. There they were in blue ink like rodent droppings in a picnic basket. I double-checked the swooping 't' and cross of the 'e'. The writing was scratchy and messy, just like the notes. Emily was right, Purdy was the woman. Now that I held the proof of her guilt in my hand, I didn't know what to do. We'd been so focused on finding the culprit, we never discussed what we would do once we found them. Would a couple of matching letters be enough to catch Purdy like the rat she was? I wish I could call a timeout for a huddle with Carol and Burt.

"Burt, don't you think this food should go in the fridge? Would you help me put these away real quick?" I asked, trying to keep calm.

He opened his mouth to protest, but I gave him a pointed look, flashing the note in my hand. His eyes went wide. "Sure, let me help you with that." He got up quickly, knocking his chair over.

"Can't that wait until after the game?" Purdy was already passing out cards.

"They'll dry out. It'll only take a minute," I stalled. When Burt was standing next to me, I moved in to form a barricade with our backs and showed him the address. "It's a match." I whispered, pointing to the 'e' and 't'.

"Bev, your tea smells so nice, I think I'll get some as well." Carol got up and joined us at the counter.

I showed her the writing and nodded. "What do we do now?" I asked. By the looks on their faces, both of them were as clueless as me.

"Let's go, people," Purdy prodded.

Burt put the pastries back in his large Tupperware. We silently took our seats. I sorted my cards. It was a good hand, half a run and three queens.

The game took on an intense air.

"Things got serious with that ten dollar buy-in," Bev commented.

"It's all in good fun," Purdy made a dismissive flick of her wrist. "Did I tell you I'm going to Alaska in two weeks? One of the gentlemen I've been corresponding with invited me to stay with him. He said I looked like a young Zsa Zsa Gabor in the boudoir photos I sent."

I choked on my coffee.

"I didn't take you for a prude, Maya." Purdy gave me a disproving frown.

"Me, either," I said, wondering if he'd seen the same photo of her I had. "How long are you staying for?"

I didn't buy a return ticket." She winked at me. "If all works out, I may only return to sell my house."

This wasn't making sense. Why try and scare off Carol if she was leaving? Would Purdy be so petty as to vie for all of Burt's attention, even if it was short term? I forgot to lay down my queens and drew a card. It completed my run. Next hand, I would be out. Purdy picked up the long line of cards, adding them to her hand, and only laying down three jacks.

"What are you going to do in Alaska?" I needed more information to make the pieces fit together.

"Hopefully, whatever I want. Kurt, that's his name, Kurt, owns a fishing fleet. He's a wealthy man. Owns a hundred acres, his own home in town, and a hunting cabin."

"How did you find him?" I imagined Purdy on Tinder, her thumb callused from swiping right.

"The internet. I typed in 'single Alaska men' and found this site called Rosebride. It's a mail-order bride site, but the men post their profiles, and you can cast a wide net. I messaged them all, and the fisherman bit." Purdy laughed.

"Rummy," I said, laying down my run and three queens.

"What?" Purdy, fumed. "I was going to go out next hand."

The others counted their cards. Purdy wrote down the scores, repeating them aloud as she transcribed them.

"I think you forgot to subtract these aces here from your points," Carol offered when Purdy announced her score.

"Did I? Oops." Purdy didn't seem grateful for the correction. "I've got to use the little girls' room." She excused herself, taking her purse with her. As soon as the bathroom door clicked shut, the three of us started whispering.

"What's going on?" Bev's voice sounded like cannon fire.

We violently shushed her like a chorus of Madagascar hissing cockroaches.

"Sorry," she whispered back.

'We don't have much time. We'll have to explain later," I said. "Do we confront her? Do we call Dave?"

"How sure are you the handwriting is a match?" Carol asked. "Can you get a sample note we can compare it with?"

Quietly, I ran to the backroom and fumbled with the keys in the lock, my fingers suddenly transformed into ballpark franks. I grabbed a threat off the board, stuffed it in my pocket, and turned to lock up again. Purdy passed me in the hall. Disappointment at our lost opportunity tasted bitter in my throat. Carol was picking up Purdy's little blue notebook as we re-entered the kitchen.

"Put that down," Purdy yelled. In a flurry of frantic action, Purdy rushed Carol. She leaped, launching herself at the notebook in Carol's hand.

Carol snapped it back. Purdy, missing her mark, soared past Carol, belly flopping onto the table. Her momentum propelled her forward, skidding across the surface like a Cheeto-colored seal on a Slip 'N Slide.

I stood frozen in shock, watching the scene play out like a half-priced afternoon matinée. Cards and cups flew in all directions. Dishes shattered on the floor. Purdy desperately grabbed at the table. As she went over the edge headfirst, I was released from my paralysis. I lunged for her. Grabbing Purdy's spindly ankles, I managed to catch her before she hit the floor. For a moment, we were all motionless, except for Purdy, whose torso swayed over the tabletop like a fishing lure above a stream.

I pulled on her legs, trying to reel her back up.

"You trying to give me a hip replacement?" she hollered at me. "Not so hard. I want to keep my legs attached."

"Fine, I'll lower you down," I snapped back. What I really wanted to do was let go. If she was lucky, she'd land on her face and her lips would cushion the blow. I didn't and instead eased her to the ground.

She lay on the wood floor, staring up at the ceiling. "Well, shit," she said and started laughing. "Help me up, I think I may have tweaked my back."

Burt and I bent down and pulled her to a sitting position. After we determined nothing was broken or no more out of place than it was before, we hoisted her into a chair.

"That was exciting," she said, brushing her hands off on her clothes. "Should we play another hand?"

"No!" Burt, Carol, and I all said at the same time.

"Purdy, we need to talk." Carol sounded stern.

"Fine, you caught me. I was cheating." She pulled several cards from her sleeves. "I was hoping to make some extra cash for my trip. Big whoop."

"We also need to talk about this." I pulled the note from my pocket and set it in front of her.

She started to deny knowing what it was, but I cut her off.

"We already know it was you leaving threats for Carol."

"How did you find out?" she asked without remorse, only curiosity.

I presented the address she'd written down for me. "The handwriting is the same."

"Does this mean you don't want to buy all those pickles?"

"No!" My voice rose with indignation. "You slashed Carol's tires!"

"You did what?" Bev squawked. "Purdy, why would you do that? I don't understand what's happening. Will someone please explain?"

"Just calm down. It's not that big of a deal. It was a tire, not tires, and I was never going to do anything to Carol."

"Why would you threaten her then, especially since you're leaving?" I tried to moderate my volume.

"I needed her to back off in case I had to marry Burt."

"What? I wouldn't marry you!" Burt blurted.

"You would have eventually if I'd wanted you to." She waved her hand airily. "But I don't need you anymore. It's a mute point."

"It's moot," Burt corrected.

"Nope, pretty sure it's mute. But, as I was saying, I don't need Burt anymore now that I have this fellow in Alaska. None of this would have happened if it wasn't for the government. It's all their fault. They said they'd take my house if I didn't pay my back taxes. Where am I going to come up with $105,000 on my own?"

"How many years of taxes do you owe?"

"Jim used to do our taxes, and after he died, I didn't bother with them. I haven't heard anything for years. Then, out of the blue, Uncle Sam says, 'Pay up'. So, I needed a plan. I figured now that Burt's retired, he probably has a pretty good nest egg, and he wouldn't mind sharing if we were married."

Burt's face was turning a strange mottled red and purple.

"You were my first choice." She winked at him.

Burt let out an outraged grunt and opened his mouth in what looked like the beginning of a long defense, but Purdy, once started, would not be interrupted.

"Then Carol came along, and the two of you were getting pretty cozy pretty fast. I figured if she left, went back home, that'd clear the field for me. And if it didn't work, then I needed a backup plan. I used my pickle money for a few upgrades." She smacked her lips. "A few sexy photos and it worked. I found myself a new man. He bought me a ticket, business class, so you know he's doing okay for himself." Purdy turned to Carol. "I hope there are no hard feelings."

"You put a screwdriver in my tire and scared my family and me half to death. You better believe there are hard feelings."

"You wouldn't take a hint. I had to up the ante. Do you have any idea how hard it is to stick a screwdriver in a tire? Afterward, though, I did feel kinda bad. I may have sprained my thumb. I'd pay you for the flat, but I don't have any money." Purdy brightened. "I can pay you in pickles now that Maya's backed out of our business arrangement. I've got plenty left."

"You keep your pickles. I don't want them."

"No need to get nasty about it." She turned to Burt. "Did you know your sweet kitten had such sharp claws?"

"You hold on right there," Burt bellowed. "Don't you say one bad thing about Carol."

"Thank you for defending me, but I got this," Carol said. "Purdy, the insurance paid for the tires because it was a crime. I could have you arrested and charged for vandalism and destruction of property."

Purdy opened her mouth to say something, but Carol held up her hand to keep her quiet.

"You're leaving soon. I want to forget this whole thing ever happened. And as long as you really are leaving, I'll forget about the money."

"That's very big-hearted of you, Carol. Burt clearly likes the nice ones over the naughty ones. I can see now I never had a chance." Purdy paused and eyed the floor littered with cards, money, and broken plates. "Can I still keep the cash?" she asked hopefully.

"No!" we all shouted.

"There's no harm in asking," she said. Getting up slowly, Purdy took hold of her purse and swung it over her shoulder. "I guess I'll get going then." She took a step and winced. Putting her hand on her lower back, we watched silently as she slowly made her way out of the room.

Surrounded by the wreckage of the kitchen, we stared at each other.

"I'm still confused." Bev looked dazed. "What really just happened?"

It was over. We'd done it. We'd caught the culprit and Carol was safe. Relief, disbelief, and satisfaction swelled through me as I mentally replayed the last few absurd minutes. I saw Purdy sailing across the table, legs splayed like carrot sticks. I snorted. Then I started to giggle. The tension in my shoulders released, transforming into laughter. Bev's look of stunned bewilderment made me cackle, which set off Carol's laughter. We clutched our sides, our mirth gaining momentum.

Bev and Burt stood stoically, watching us as if we were as crazy as Purdy. When tears started streaming down my face, it was the last straw for Burt. He handed me a tissue. "For heaven's sake, Maya, clean yourself up." Shaking his head, he went for the broom, ready to sweep away the chaos and bring sense to the whole ridiculous fiasco.

Eighteen

S waddled like a panda in my hammock, I was trying to sway my ennui away. I'd sought refuge in my happy place on the hillside after the comedown of solving the mystery of Carol's tormentor. It felt a lot like the letdown after Christmas. The void left by the anticipation, speculation, and scheming, had me seeking comfort. I'd miss our Scooby gang and suspect board. Burt seemed to be feeling the same way. We were both so relieved Carol was safe, but didn't know what to do with ourselves now. He'd come into work today for an hour just to read me the paper.

I suppose it wasn't only Carol's case wrapping up. I'd finished the giant can sculptures, and was between art schemes, I'd settled into my new job, and I missed Owen's visits in the evenings. Twenty minutes, that's how long I'd wallow, then I'd do or think about something else. I closed my eyes and sunk into the surrounding sounds. Clover snored softly under my hammock, yipping occasionally as she chased deer in her sleep. The wind blew in bursts through the treetops like rolling ocean waves, engulfing me as they carried me off to sleep.

"This looks cozy."

I shrieked, scrambling to sit up. Clover jumped to her feet, barking. Owen frantically steadied the hammock, keeping me from being dumped onto the ground.

"Woah, sorry, I didn't mean to scare you. I hadn't realized you both were asleep."

My heart pounded wildly. "What are you doing here?" I demanded.

A look of uncertainty passed over Owen's face. "I was worried because you didn't text me back yesterday. Now I know you're okay, I can shove off."

"Wait. Hold on." Amidst all the drama, I'd forgotten he'd messaged me a couple days ago. It was my turn to apologize. "Sorry about that. It's been, well, it's been a lot lately. I guess I just forgot. But I'm fine." I struggled to sit. It was awkward having a conversation while lying on my back, staring up at him. "If you give me a hand, I'll tell you about it." I held out my arm, and he hauled me to my feet.

"I'm afraid," he teased. "Do I want to hear this?"

"It's really good," I promised. "How'd you find us up here?" My hammock was strung up on a hill amongst a small grove of trees. If you knew to look for it, you could see it from the workshop, but few knew to look.

"I followed your tracks from your garage." He pointed to the trail I'd carved in the ground with my camp table. I'd dragged it up earlier so I could easily reach my tea from the hammock. Sometimes laziness took a little effort.

"Wow, you should be a forest ranger with tracking skills like those," I teased.

We headed back into the house. I topped off my tea and poured a cup for Owen. "Before I wow you with my epic tale of triumph, I want the scoop from you first. Did you catch up with Dave?"

"I did. He took the casings. He'll know by tomorrow if there's a match with the rifle that killed Peter."

"That's a lot faster than I would've thought it'd take. If there's a match, then whoever knocked me off the ladder is probably connected to Peter's death. They could even be the killer."

"Could be." A grim line creased Owen's forehead. "If that's the case, we're lucky the guy didn't kill you."

Sickly tingles reverberated like a plucked string through me. I didn't want to think about it. I changed the topic. "Think you can handle an epic tale of misadventure?" I smiled broadly and rubbed my hands together theatrically.

"I'm sitting on the edge of my seat. What trouble have you gotten yourself into now?" He leaned back in the chair and entwined his fingers behind his head.

I jumped right in, starting with the Chris Weller caper. I described Emily's costume in great detail and provided a play-by-play accounting of our infiltration of Chris's office and his self-love fan fiction. When I got to Purdy's head dive over the table, he stopped me.

"Seriously, Ridgeway, it's been less than forty-eight hours since I last saw you. How do you generate so much drama?" Owen shook his head in wonderment and cocked an eyebrow.

"I don't have to finish my story, you know," I threatened.

"You do. I want to hear every uncomfortable detail of it all." He grinned.

And I melted, but only for a second. I pulled it together and carried on with my story. "...and that's why I forgot to text you," I finally concluded my action-packed tale.

"I'm shocked Dave didn't put a stop to it."

"If he'd known, he would've for sure," I agreed.

Clover nudged my thigh, reminding me that it was her dinner time.

"Sorry, girl, I got swept up in my own story." I moved to fill her bowl, and Owen checked the time on his phone.

"Shoot, I didn't mean to stay this long. Ava's waiting on the hamburger I got in the truck. Do you want to come over for dinner?"

Though I liked Ava, I didn't want to spend time with her and Owen alone. I bowed out, claiming a prior commitment to a maturing meatloaf just two days away from becoming a toxic trashloaf.

"By the way, we're also going to Tamale Wednesday tomorrow. Ava asked me to invite you. Seems like you two hit it off over lunch."

"We did. But are you sure you need to go tomorrow? Maybe you should skip it." Owen looked at me, waiting for me to explain myself. I groaned. "Agh, okay. I'm going to be there with Emily. She roped me into being a practice dummy for her new business venture."

Owen remained silent, encouraging me to continue.

"She wants to start a business doing makeup for proms and weddings and asked if she could practice on me. She's turning it into a whole girls' night thing." I sighed heavily. "We're doing before and after pictures because, evidently, I'm not living up to my 'sextential.'" I used air quotes.

"Your what?" Owen coughed.

"My sextential. According to Emily, I'm not living up to my full potential for sexiness."

He didn't even try to hide his laugh. "And you're willing to let her do this to you? I think you're just fine as you are."

"Uh, thanks, I guess. Anyway, she caught me at a low point in my day. Emily was so excited, I caved. She's like a giant puppy when she isn't being a piranha. But I love this idea even less now that I know you and Ava will be there to witness my assured humiliation. Just promise me one thing?"

"What's that?" Owen asked, clearly amused.

"When you see me, don't laugh in my face, do it solidly behind my back." I walked him out. "Tell Ava I'll see her tomorrow." I leaned my head against the closed door, dreading my impending embarrassment.

Less than twenty-four hours later, Emily catapulted me through her front door. "This is going to be so much fun," she squealed. I felt like we were on a teeter totter of enthusiasm, and she outweighed me by three hundred pounds. "Remember, you promised to let me do anything to you."

"Uh, nope, that definitely doesn't sound like me. I am waaay too distrustful to promise that. I'm pretty sure I agreed to let you try the 'subtle makeup' YouTube tutorial on me. After you promised that I could take it off if I didn't like it."

"But you won't because you'll love it." She took my coat and handed me a prosecco spritzer. Energetic pop filled the room as Emily prepared me for my "before" photo shoot. "Remember to look mildly unhappy, but don't be too obvious about it. Wow, way too much."

"I'm not making an unhappy face yet. That is my normal expression," I protested.

"In that case, it's perfect. Keep it coming."

After my second spritzer, I started letting go and embraced my inner Cosmo quiz taker.

"I want really really long eyelashes, the kind that will make me look like I have cow eyes," I instructed Emily as she took a curler to my lashes.

"Do you mean calf eyes?" Emily giggled.

"No, cow eyes because they're bigger." I reasoned with the impeachable logic of a disbarred judge.

"I'm not going to make you look like a cow. Hold still." She came at me with a new Q-tip looking implement.

"Is that shiny eyeshadow?" I pulled away. "Oh no, I don't do shiny."

"Forget about cows. This is going to make you look like you have colossal squid eyes."

"Ick, why would I want that?"

"Because they have the largest eyes of any living creature. They're the size of a big plate. I saw it in a documentary about deep sea creatures."

"Alright," I gave. "Make me look like a colossal squid."

She squealed and jumped up and down. I appreciated how easily pleased she was. Finally, she stepped back to inspect her creation.

"I have just the outfit I want you to wear."

"Fine, but if it has tentacles, they better match the shadow."

When the transformation was complete, Emily insisted we make "reveal" videos in addition to my "after" pictures. Each of us had to emerge from her bedroom and walk down her hallway into the living room.

"Serve that look! Slay!" Emily cheered as I strutted across her apartment.

"Okay, my turn." She handed me her phone, showing me how it was supposed to be done as she rocked the carpet like a drag queen superstar. "Did you get it?" she asked, taking her phone from me. My camera work must have been okay because she let out a pleased squeal. "Owen is going to pee his pants when he sees you tonight," she said, walking around me for one last inspection.

I stopped in my tracks. "Emily, how did you know Owen is going to be there?"

"Ava came into the store yesterday and I told her how great Tamale Wednesday was. I made it sound like a Claryce Falls must-do event."

"No, no, no. Emily, promise me you will leave Ava and Owen alone. Don't spill any drinks on either of them, don't step on their toes. In fact, promise me you'll stay at least ten feet away from both of them all night."

"Relax, the way you look tonight is all I needed to do. We're both looking so good, maybe I'll end up with clients and a date to my sister's wedding."

I tugged the slinky black cowl neck halter top down to cover my slightly exposed midriff, only to overly expose my mounded cleavage shaped by one of Emily's push-up bras. "I don't know if I can go out in this. I feel kind of sleazy."

"I wore that to vote in. It isn't sleazy. It's hot. Remember, tonight is about maximizing our sextential. If you'd worn those daisy dukes I gave you instead of your jeans, we could have reached your full sextential. They would have looked super sexy with your cowboy boots."

"You gotta stop saying that word. Sextential isn't a real thing. And the Oasis is a family-friendly place. I'm pretty sure those shorts didn't even cover my underwear."

"Whatever, but you're not changing that top," Emily said forcefully, the piranha showing her teeth. "You look great and besides, we need to go now, so there's no time to change." She grabbed my hand and pulled me towards the door. I barely had time to snag my jacket and bag before the lock clicked behind us.

As we walked to the bar, I compulsively adjusted my shirt up and down, trying to find the maximum coverage zone. I wasn't normally shy, but I definitely wasn't used to icing the goods and putting them all out in the display window for others to peruse.

"Stop that," Emily swatted my hands. "Remember, you're representing me, my ability as a makeup artist and stylist. You look good. Quit tugging on your clothes and make me proud."

She was right. If I was going to do this, I'd do it right. I let out a very heavy sigh, pushed my shoulders back, and strutted like a woman on a mission to maximize her sextential.

There was a band playing in the back room, which was unusual for a Wednesday night. "It's Jake, the owner's neighbor's cousin's band. They're from L.A. and they're playing Seattle tomorrow." Emily was clearly in the know, and I was not.

"Looking good, ladies," Angel said as he squeezed by us with plates of tamales in his hands.

"Shoot, I wanted to ask him how much hotter you looked with the makeover. I'm taking a poll and going to post the results on my Facebook page."

"Please don't do that," I groaned. "I don't think my ego is strong enough."

Emily looked pensive. "Find us a seat, and I'll order us beers and tamales from the bar." She bounded off, leaving me standing alone, feeling vulnerable without my creator.

I spotted Owen and Ava at a tall four-top against the wall. They didn't seem to be talking, just eating their tamales and people-watching. Before I could pretend like I hadn't seen them, Ava caught my eye and waved. This night was destined for disaster. Owen turned to see what had caught Ava's attention. I could tell the moment he recognized me because his eyebrows shot up. I don't know if it was from shock, horror, or general disbelief over my transformation. In addition to my mile-long lashes and revealing top, Emily had straightened my hair and sprayed something in it to make it extra shiny. Then she glossed my lips and contoured my already prominent cheekbones. It was a far cry from the wash-and-go, minimal makeup look I usually sported. Before I could second guess my getup any further, a voice called my name.

"Maya, over here!"

I turned and saw Jess Cooper. He was sitting at the same table we'd broken up at three weeks ago. So much had happened since then. It felt more like three months had passed. Jess was with two of his buddies. I think their names were Wes and Carson. I'd met them once at a barbecue at Jess's family farm. He stood up and walked over to me.

"How's it going, Jess?" I asked neutrally.

"Wow, Maya, you look incredible. Do you want to join us?"

I stepped back, avoiding his hand that reached for my bare waist. "Thanks, but I'm meeting some friends over there." I pointed to Owen and Ava, who were watching us.

"Are you sure? I'd buy you a beer."

I declined, saying I really needed to join my friends.

"Okay, save me a dance later. I'll come find you."

"Sure," I said, wishing he wouldn't. I hadn't made it more than ten feet before getting stopped again by Jennifer Clavel, a newly divorced mother of two. She asked for Emily's card after I mentioned who was behind my transformation.

When I finally reached Owen and Ava's high top, I was ready to hide under it. "Don't say anything," I warned them both as I neared.

"You look great," Ava reassured.

"Thank you," Emily said behind me. She set two beers on the table and took a seat. "I've gotten a one hundred percent approval rating so far for Maya's makeover," Emily smugly announced.

"I told you not to tell me," I whined.

"What? I thought you didn't want to hear the bad stuff."

"Are people saying bad things? Wait, don't tell me—I really don't want to know." My hands shot up to cover my ears, causing my tiny blouse to rise. I quickly dropped them and told Emily about the business lead.

"My gosh, it's happening. I knew this was a great idea. Does anyone have a pen?"

I found one in my bag. Emily took it, quickly writing her name and phone number on a napkin. "I'll just be a second." She jumped back off the stool and left to hand out her makeshift business card.

"She has a lot of energy." Ava watched Emily pile Jennifer's hair on top of the woman's head, the transformation consultation already in progress.

"She really does." I explained about Emily's budding business and how I was supposed to be a walking advertisement for her transformative abilities. "From a two to a ten with just a swish of the mascara wand." I used my best infomercial voice.

"You're hardly a two," Owen murmured.

My face heated like a lightning rod in an electrical storm. "Can we please talk about something else? Anything? Ava, what did you do today?"

"I hiked up Pete Lake," Ava said graciously, changing the topic. "The wildflowers are out. It was beautiful up there. But it was a steep hike, and I'm wiped out."

"I haven't been there this year yet, but I love the lake. When it gets really hot in the summer, it's the best place for a swim. We'll have to go."

"I'm not sure if I'll make it back here this summer," Ava confided.

"What do you mean? I thought you were staying."

"Why'd you think that? I told you she was leaving on Friday," Owen said.

"I dunno. Plans can change," I answered noncommittally.

"They can," Ava agreed. She cleared her throat. "I've decided to leave Fizzy here when I leave."

"What? Really? Why?" I tried to modulate my happiness.

"Owen pointed out that she's much better off with him and the arrangement you two have going. And as sad as it makes me, I work twelve-hour shifts which means she's left alone for long stretches at a time, even if I get a dog walker. I love her, which means I have to do what's best for her."

I stood and threw my arms around her shoulders. "We will take good care of her, I promise." Then I remembered my shirt and quickly put my arms back down.

"I'll hold you to it." She patted my arm. "And send me lots of pictures of her being adorable. This one is the worst at it." She pointed an accusing finger at Owen.

"No problem, I'll happily hand over dog photography duties to Maya," he easily capitulated.

Angel put a plate of tamales down on our table and a pitcher of beer. "Jess bought this round."

"Uh, thanks, Angel." I turned to see Jess watching me. I nodded my head to acknowledge the pitcher.

He made a dancing gesture with his arms and mouthed, "Later."

"Who's that?" Owen asked, eyeing Jess with a look like he'd just discovered a week-old fish in his truck.

"Jess Cooper, third-generation apple farmer and the guy who broke up with me the night you and I met in this very bar."

"If you broke up, why's he buying us beer," Owen scowled.

I sighed and rolled my eyes. "Evidently, he's a fan of the makeover too."

"Who wouldn't be?" Emily asked, rejoining us. "He's totally cute. I'd date him." She eyed him like a wolf sizing up a fat piglet.

"Yeah, he's got a good front and back," I agreed. "It's just the middle that's kind of boring."

"I don't mind boring. I'm exciting enough for two people," Emily joked.

I pictured Emily and Jess together and oddly, it worked. "Are you serious? Because if you are, I will absolutely introduce you."

"Do it. Introduce us." Emily bit into a tamale. "But after we eat. What's he like, you know, in the sack?"

"Nope." Owen held up his hand, "I don't want to hear this."

"Too much girl talk for you?" I teased.

"Something like that. Just don't need to hear it."

Emily and I laughed at his discomfort. She held up her beer for a toast. "Here's to makeovers and new starts."

We clinked drinks and got serious about our food.

After Ava's third yawn, she threw her napkin over her plate. "That's it for me. I'm sorry to bail early, but I'm tired. Owen, do you mind if we leave now?"

Owen looked at me, then glanced in Jess's direction and hesitated. Was he jealous, or was it just my wishful thinking? I didn't want him to leave.

"Owen, if you're not ready to go yet, Maya can drop you off, and Ava can take your truck to your place," Emily offered, a mischievous gleam in her eyes. "That way, you can stay and party with us, and Ava can catch up on sleep."

Owen looked questioningly at Ava. "You comfortable getting back to the house on your own? It's pretty much a straight shot."

Ava hesitated, looking between the three of us.

"You can use your phone's map if you're afraid of getting lost," Emily offered sweetly.

Owen pulled keys out of his pocket. "I'd like to stick around and hear the band play a little longer. Is it alright if I get a ride home with you, Maya?"

I tried to come off as casual, nonchalant. "Sure, no problem." I pretended to watch the band in the other room so I wouldn't have to see either Ava's or Owen's reactions.

"Alright, then." Ava didn't have much choice but to agree. "It was fun hanging with you ladies." She stood, taking Owen's keys.

Owen asked her to text him when she got home. We said a final round of goodbyes, and Ava left looking like she was ready for sleep.

No sooner had she left than Jess was filling her empty seat. "You're a lucky man, surrounded by so many beautiful women tonight," he said to Owen.

Owen hooked a hand on the back of my chair. "I am."

"Jess, this is Owen and Emily. Emily's the one responsible for my look tonight."

He complimented her on her excellent work, making Emily glow.

"You ready for that dance yet?" he asked, extending his hand to me.

I hesitated, not wanting to leave Owen.

"Come on, just one." Turning to Owen, he added, "I promise, one song, and then she's all yours again."

Owen stayed silent but looked like he wished Jess would stick a tamale in his tamale hole—or maybe somewhere even less polite.

"Okay, but only one," I said.

Jess grinned. "That's all I'm asking for."

I took his hand and slid out of my chair. Jess led the way, weaving through the tables and chairs, my hand still firmly in his. We stepped onto the floor just as the band struck up a slow ballad. I groaned to myself. Jess was not the one I wanted to be dancing close with right now. I also didn't want him getting the wrong idea. We weren't picking up where we'd left off.

"Don't look so worried," he said, pulling me around to face him. "I know I messed up, and I've probably missed my chance with you."

"Probably," I nodded.

"I'd be lying if I said it didn't hurt a little that you replaced me so quickly."

I fought the triumphant smile trying to spread across my face. He didn't need to know Owen and I weren't together.

"And I know I only have myself to blame," he continued. "I was stressed about money."

"I got that," I said sarcastically.

He cringed. "We have to replace a tractor and our drip irrigation system. We don't have that kind of money. I wasn't sure if we'd pull through. And I felt guilty over every penny I spent when I knew we were so close to losing it all."

Sympathy and irritation twined through me. "I had no idea. Why didn't you tell me?"

"I know." He pressed his lips together, flattening them into a straight line. "Our time together was my escape. I hung out with you to unwind and turn my brain off."

I suppose that's why dating Jess had felt like dating an unplugged toaster most of the time.

"I wish I'd said something too, especially since one of the grants I put in for came through. It's covering all the expenses, plus some farm upgrades over the next three years." He beamed, clearly proud of himself.

"That's incredible. I didn't know you wrote grants either. A man of hidden talents."

He blushed and looked away. "There was a lot I didn't mention. Not on purpose—just because it was nice not to worry for a little while. But I don't like how I left things. I should've told you what was going on. I messed up, and now we're not even friends, are we?"

Any lingering hard feelings I had were two-stepped out by Jess's confession.

"Sure, we're friends. And to prove what a good friend I am," I smirked, "I'll even get you a dance with Emily, the cute blonde at my table. I know for a fact she's looking for a handsome dance partner tonight."

He gave me a tight-lipped smile but agreed. When the song ended, I led our way to the table. I took my seat next to Owen, who immediately rested his arm on my chair.

"I hear you're a good dancer," Jess said to Emily, extending his hand. "Would you do me the honor of this next dance?"

Emily giggled and shot me a quick, questioning glance. I gave her a subtle nod of encouragement.

"The honor is all mine." She jumped up, and they headed out to the dance floor.

"I'm not sure if I just did a really bad thing or a really good thing," I said, watching them twirl across the floor.

Owen furrowed his brows. "You're okay fixing Emily up with that guy? I mean, you're not interested in him anymore? It's not awkward?"

"Nope." I leaned against my chair. Owen's knuckles pressed into my bare skin. He flattened his hand against my back. The feel of his warm, rough palm started my entire nervous system humming.

"You'd be okay if he and Emily got together?"

"Yep." My brain stopped working.

He moved his thumb back and forth, slowly tracing my shoulder blade.

"Ava's really leaving?"

"Yep." He purposely mimicked me.

"And how do you feel about that?" I held my breath.

"I feel just fine. Do you want to dance the next one?"

Yes, I really wanted to dance the next one with Owen. I

wanted to dance, kiss, lick, touch, and everything else with Owen, but not tonight. Not until Ava was gone, and I wasn't dressed like Barbie's party-girl sister, Night-Life Candy. Not until I knew what it meant.

Torturing myself, I pressed back into his touch, mentally palm-slapping my forehead. I took a deep breath. Turning, I looked him in the eyes. "Can I get a rain check on that?" I knew I might be blowing my shot with Owen, but if this was truly my only chance to cross the bridge between friendship and more, it wouldn't be where I wanted to end up anyway.

He slid his hand onto my shoulder, scooting in close to speak softly in my ear. My body's hum was almost deafening. "Maya, you can count on it."

We sat that way for a few more songs, the energy building between us until it was almost tangible, audible. I pretended to listen to the music but heard nothing other than the vibration of closeness. Finally, I knew if I didn't leave, I would act in a way I wasn't ready for. I caught Emily's attention and signaled my intent to leave. She made a shooing motion and wiggled her eyebrows towards Jess.

I stood and Owen helped me with my jacket. His fingers grazed my neck, and I almost lost the battle with my self-control. We were quiet on the way home. I was afraid to speak, afraid of what I would say. When we reached his house, he leaned across the console. I kept my eyes forward. He hesitated and kissed me on the cheek. Without a word, he got out. At his door, he turned and waved goodnight. I released a long exhale. I guess there really was something to be said for reaching your maximum sextential.

Nineteen

Scenes from yesterday evening repeated in my brain. Every time I thought of Owen's thumb rubbing against my skin, a swarm of flaming butterflies took flight in my stomach like acid reflux after Thanksgiving dinner. I needed the reel to stop. None of it meant anything…yet. I still wasn't certain what Owen's and Ava's relationship was. I was also no stranger to the concept of one too many beers and empty flirtation. Distraction was what I needed, but restocking the supplies in the lobby wasn't cutting it. My phone chimed, signaling a new text message. Normally I avoided checking my phone during work, but today I was only too happy to break my rule.

The message was from Dave. He wanted to meet Owen and me at my place. Owen instantly replied he'd be there at three. Something had happened. Dave wasn't a let's-ditch-work-and-hangout kind of guy. It had to be about the bullet casings we found. What if they matched? What would that mean? If they were the same ones used to shoot Peter, then whoever used the target practice site was probably his killer. But whose gun was it? Could it have been Peter's own gun he was shot with it?

"Come grab this door." Purdy, holding a heavy-looking box, was trying to open the door with her foot.

I ran over to hold it for her. "I didn't think I'd see you around here again," I said.

"Why not? You mean because of the business with Carol? That's in the past. I never look back, only forward. It was all a bunch of fuss about nothing."

I wasn't sure if I was impressed or outraged by Purdy's lack of self-consciousness and remorse.

"I know you aren't buying my pickles, but I liked your idea of using them at that little event of yours, and I want to donate them. A peace offering. My way of giving back before I go. Get the other door to the kitchen, before I drop these? I could use some help with the rest of the boxes too."

"Boxes? Wait, how many pickles are you donating?"

"About a hundred jars."

"What? Nope, stop right there. We don't want that many pickles." I could only imagine what Burt would have to bake to get rid of them.

"You better open the door before I drop these. It'll smell like vinegar soup in here for weeks if I lose my grip."

I knew I was being manipulated, but I still opened the door.

She set the box down on the kitchen table with a heavy grunt. "Great, now let's get the others."

This woman had some nerve. "We're not taking any more pickles."

"But Bev said she wanted them all for the festivities."

I called Purdy on her lie. "Then she can come over and help you unload them into the church. I'll just give her a call." I started walking out to the office.

"I might have exaggerated a little." Purdy stopped me. "But I'm moving. What am I supposed to do with them? I can't sell them before I go and I'm not going pay to mail them."

"I don't know. Stick a couple of olives on each side of them and sell them as erotic crudités. Donate them to the food bank. All I know is, you're not leaving anymore here."

Purdy perked up. "That's a great idea. If I donate them, I can write it off on my taxes, mileage too. I needed to get boxes in Hillsburg today anyway. Now the trip's on Uncle Sam!" She seemed tickled. For a woman who owed the IRS a fortune, I was surprised by her knowledge of tax write-offs. "I'm off then." She sang out and waved, "Have a great day now!"

I stared after her. What would it be like to go through the world with that much confidence? I wondered if that's how all charismatic villains were. Maybe, I should take a sentence or two out of the book of Purdy and be bold with Owen.

In the afternoon, waiting for Dave and Owen to arrive, I worked on the golf tournament t-shirt design. At ten 'til three, Dave pulled up in his sheriff's county cruiser into my driveway. The car meant he was definitely here on official police business. I closed my laptop and left my office to go greet him. I'd already made a pot of coffee, especially for Dave, and three cups sat on the table at the ready.

"Heard you all cracked Carol's case," Dave greeted.

"We did," I said neutrally. I wasn't sure how much of the story Dave knew and if I was in trouble or not. "In fact, Purdy came in today to try and drop off a hundred jars of pickles she didn't want to ship."

"That woman is something else, isn't she?"

"A unique bird, I'm glad there's only one of her," I agreed. I pointed to the coffee pot, then the cup with the small creamer and bowl of sugar next to it. "I just made that for you." He poured himself a coffee and sat down at the table.

"Leigha is on me to cut back, but it's the only thing keeping me running right now."

I had a million questions I was dying to ask Dave about Peter, but I wasn't sure if I was off the hook with him yet. "You're not angry with us for looking into the threats on our own, are you?" I picked at the tablecloth. Sitting across from him now, I felt anxious. Dave was a good friend, and I hated to have him ticked off at me.

"No," he sighed. "I wish you guys hadn't done it, but I get it. I talked it out with Carol this morning. I can tell I'm never going to win an argument with that woman. She's so sweet and good intentioned, even when she's wrong, I still feel like the world's biggest jerk for disagreeing."

"I can see that," I chuckled. Now that I knew Dave and I were all right, I wanted to grill him on what he'd found. But I exercised difficult patience and waited. I figured he'd have to go through it all again when Owen showed up.

Dave drank half his coffee, and we chatted about Libby's latest antics and Carol's upcoming departure. I kept checking my phone. Owen was late, and by three-fifteen, I snapped.

"I can't take this small talk anymore. Start talking. What did you find out?"

"I'll wait for Owen to go into details, but what I'm going to tell you needs to stay between us."

"Of course," I nodded.

"We found a match between the rifle casings you and Owen collected, the one embedded in the elk bone we found, and the one that killed Peter."

I let out a long whistle and sat back in my chair. It was all connected to Peter's death, but the full picture still wasn't clear to me. "At Peter's funeral, there was a slideshow with a lot of pictures of him hunting. Did you check the casing against his guns?"

"We did, and those of his father's in case Peter was using one of them. We didn't find a match."

We heard Owen's truck pull up. I headed to the door and stuck my head out. "Hurry, Dave won't give up everything until you get inside."

Owen was in his work khakis and cap. Inside the door, he bent to take off his work boots, but I pushed him in. "Don't worry about the mess. I'll deal with it later." I topped off everyone's coffee while I quickly caught Owen up on what Dave already shared. "So," I said, folding my arms on the table and leaning forward, "What's this mean?"

"It means whoever was digging through the garbage was probably after something you all picked up at the target site. Which means I need to get the team to go through the lot and see if we can find anything. It also means I want all the trash removed from Janet's place and from here. I know you were planning on moving those giant cans of yours this weekend, but I'd like to get them out of here as soon as possible. I don't want to give anyone a reason to come rooting around again."

"I'll make some calls, and we can move the cans this afternoon," Owen said.

"I don't think it's as dire as all that," I reasoned. "I'm sure it can wait until Saturday."

"And why are you so sure about that?" Owen asked heatedly. "This guy already killed someone and sent you to the hospital. If moving those dang cans a couple of days earlier means it might keep you safe, why wouldn't we do it?"

I was surprised by Owen's vehemence.

"Exactly." Dave wrapped his knuckles on the table.

"Listen, I don't need you both ganging up on me. I can't just dump them off in the park. I'll need to call Christina Russet with Parks and Rec and make sure it's okay for us to set them up early."

"I'll go call Christina now," Owen said, walking into the living room. "Hi, Christina, Owen Reece here…"

Dave hauled himself from his seat with a weary sigh. "Let's go take a look at that trash you got out there."

I followed him out to my workshop. "Here it all is," I said, making a grand sweeping gesture.

"Show me what you picked up at the site."

Lined up, the recycling and trash were neatly sorted into five-gallon buckets.

"Everything's pretty mixed up now with trash from other sites. The bullet casings are the only things kept separate because we forgot them in Owen's truck. We picked up a bunch of Butterfingers wrappers and Cool Ranch Doritos bags at the one site. Most of those should be in the garbage bucket." I went over to where I thought the container was.

Dave rubbed a hand down his face. "We can't use any of it as evidence because we can't prove where it came from. But I'll take it with me and look through it. Maybe there's something that might be of help."

I walked around the workshop looking for the garbage we'd collected. "Weird… I can't find the trash pail." I crouched down, peering under my workbench, sifting through the bottles and cans. Dave joined me, lifting anything that might hide the bucket.

Owen stepped into the entry. "Christina's fine with the cans going up tonight. She said she'll swing by in the morning and put up signage promoting the event."

"That's great," I replied distractedly. "Owen, you didn't get rid of the trash we picked up from the target site, did you?"

"No," he answered slowly. "Is it missing?"

"It looks like it. Maybe Burt or one of the others tossed it during the cleanup after my concussion."

I pulled out my phone and fired off a group text. "We'll see what they say." Sliding my phone back into my pocket, I did one last sweep around the shed, scanning every corner.

"What else did you pick up that day?" Dave asked.

I scanned the rest of the collection. "Mostly plastic bottles and beer cans, but I used a lot of them in my sculptures, and I gave the plastic bottles to Bev and Janet for their part of our project. Either way, we rinsed everything we used, so even if I could tell you which ones came from the site, any evidence would've been washed away."

Dave made an unhappy "hmmm" and turned to Owen. "Will you help Maya take the rest of this stuff to the transfer station this afternoon? The sooner we can get this cleared out, the better I'll feel about Maya being here alone."

Dave's request on my behalf irked me. It made me feel like he saw me as weak and vulnerable, two things I was not.

"First, I am not alone. I have Clover. Second, I'm right here, fully capable of taking this to the dump myself. Third–" I paused. "I can't think of a third at the moment, but please quit talking for me and about me like I'm not here."

"No offense intended," Dave said by way of an apology. "It makes me feel better knowing you have help. The idea of someone rummaging around you while you lay unconscious and bleeding makes me protective."

The image he painted gave me cold shivers. "Alright." I softened my stance of total independence. "Thanks for looking out for me." I punched him affectionately in the arm. "And since you're so worried, you can help us load the monster cans onto Owen's truck. With three of us, it shouldn't take long." Though the cans weren't super heavy, their size made them awkward to handle. Still, we managed to get all of them onto Owen's truck bed with the tailgate down.

I loaded Clover and everything else, including stakes and ropes into Nell. Our three-vehicle convoy pulled out like a presidential motorcade. In town, Dave peeled off to meet with Janet while Owen and I continued to the park to set up the cans.

At the park, I found a spot in the shade and let Clover out to pee on things, while Owen backed his truck onto the grass near the installation spot. Our conversation consisted of me giving directions and Owen asking questions as we unloaded, positioned, and secured the cans.

Once we were done, I stepped back to inspect our handy work. "I think they look pretty good," I said, giving us a little pat on the back.

"They do," he agreed. "It's a shame that you're literally throwing all that work away. Well, recycling it, anyway."

"I don't mind, I like the performative element of it all. I think it will be fun to watch them get smashed."

Owen smiled. "It'll certainly be dramatic. I know you can handle it yourself, but do you want help getting rid of the rest of the stuff?"

"Nope, I've got it." I was feeling more awkward the longer we didn't talk about last night. But now that it was just the two of us, all my social skills evaporated like cold sweats in the desert.

"Alright, if you're sure, I'm going to head out. Ava's leaving tomorrow, and we're going fishing on the lake today."

"That right? Seems like she just got here." I tried to sound casual. "Have fun. Tell her goodbye for me." Little fingers of jealousy squeezed my chest. "I better get this stuff to the transfer station before they close." I pointed to my car and got in without waiting for a reply.

Owen was taking Ava, his ex-girlfriend, out on a boat, on the lake for their last evening together. I didn't even know he had a boat. I guess I got my answer to my question about beers and casual flirting. It made me mad and a little sad. Did Owen care so little about our friendship that he'd jeopardize it by flirting with me while he still had unfinished business with Ava? I deserved better.

I fumed as I threw glass bottles into the enormous dumpster. The destruction of shattering glass against metal was satisfying. One by one, I hurled the bottles like baseballs, each crash chipping away at my frustration until only a dull ache remained.

If I were Purdy the supervillain, I'd slip on a sexy saloon girl corset or Emily's barely-there top and invite Owen over. I'd go after what I wanted with both guns firing. But I wasn't Purdy or Emily, and I'd just have to find my own way through.

On the drive home, I opened all of Nell's windows and the sunroof, cranked up the heat to beat the chill, and blasted Elton John's "Rocket Man."

When we reached my place, I checked my phone. Owen had texted, asking if I'd gotten home safely. It seemed we were all a little rattled. I replied, letting him and Dave know the recycling was gone and Clover and I were snug and secure.

I still needed to finish the t-shirt designs for the resort and get the files over to the silk screen shop tonight so they'd have samples ready by Monday. With a microwaved bean burrito and a glass of chocolate milk, I settled down in front of my computer for the evening.

The next morning, I'd barely been at the Stevens' for fifteen minutes, helping set up the yard sale, and Burt had already snapped at me three times.

"Careful with that," Burt growled. "Put those photos in the pile for Maggie to go through for the library exhibit."

We were moving boxes Nancy and Ben had sorted with Carol's help, laying the content out on tables by category.

"Why are you in such a bad mood today?"

"I'm not, you're being sloppy."

I crossed my arms, popped a hip, and stared at him silently with a raised eyebrow.

"What? Don't look at me like that."

I continued to hold my position until he relented. "Fine, maybe I am a little cranky. I tweaked my shoulder last night, taking Owen and his friend fishing."

"You took Owen and Ava out?" I tried to play it cool, but I was like a hungry dog thrown a chicken cutlet of hope.

"We ran into her and Fizzy when we were walking Clover and Greta. We let the dogs play for a bit." Burt rubbed the back of his neck, looking tired. "Somehow, I ended up offering to take her and Owen out fishing. I haven't had my boat out in two years, and it took me all day to get it ready. Pinched my hand getting it hitched." He held up his left hand, showing off the bandage he refused to explain earlier. "We got a late start waiting on Owen. When we finally got to the water, we were out less than an hour before the wind picked up and Ava got too cold. Then, when I was unloading the boat, I tried nudging it back with my shoulder and ended up hurting the dang thing." He rubbed his right shoulder with his bandaged hand.

"It doesn't seem like it was much fun." I tried to sound sympathetic, but my insides were doing a happy dance. Pulling myself out of my selfish glee, I assessed Burt. "And now you're moving boxes with a busted shoulder and hand? Seriously, Burt, just go sit down." I brought a chair over to the table. "You unpack the boxes, and I'll bring them over."

He grumbled but took the seat.

"What did you and Ava talk about while you waited for Owen?" I pumped him for information.

"Why do you want to know?" He narrowed his eyes, looking at me suspiciously.

"No reason. I hung out with her a couple of times, and she seems like an interesting person. I was just wondering what you thought of her." I knew he couldn't resist a direct solicitation of his opinion.

"She's a pretty girl, isn't she? A nice sort, but not one to be tied down. She gave up her apartment, put everything in one of those Pods things. She didn't even know where her next job would be. Can you imagine that?"

I could see how someone like Burt, who'd worked at the same job for decades, might find Ava's travel nurse lifestyle a little reckless.

"She came to see Owen, not just to pick up Fizzy, but because she had nowhere else to go. She was homeless." He shook his head in total bafflement. "Owen better be careful. She's not the kind of gal you marry."

"Did you really just say that?" I asked incredulously. "You're showing your age, and it isn't looking good on you right now." I felt my momentum building. "First, it is not the ambition of every woman to get married. Second, just because Ava doesn't fit some antiquated role of a fifties housewife doesn't mean she can't have successful long-term relationships. And third—" I paused. I was always running out of arguments too quickly. "And third, Ava and Owen aren't even together and if they were, Owen would be lucky to have her." Why was I arguing against my own self-interests here?

"Simmer down. I only meant she doesn't seem like she commits to things, jobs, places, or people. Would you ever give Clover up for some temporary job?"

"No." Some of the steam left my sails.

"You bet you wouldn't. Now, if you're done chewing me out, go get another box."

I lugged several more boxes over to him. "Sorry, I snapped at you," I murmured like an angsty tween.

He nodded his head in the direction of his truck. "There are some cookies in a Tupperware in the passenger seat. Go get them and I'll forgive you." Cookies were always the right answer.

Coming up the Stevens' driveway was a blonde woman, her head sticking out of the car window. She waved as she drove like she was painting the world with sunshine from the seat of her well-loved, bumblebee-yellow Jeep.

"Ah, it's Maggie." Burt smiled and waved back.

"I'll go grab a couple more chairs in case she and Nancy want to go through the photos out here." A loud crash and squawk came from inside the house. I ran in and froze. The living room looked like it'd been ravaged by a tornado. A pile of boxes lay on the floor, their contents disgorged in a violent mosaic of chaos. The room looked like the fallout of a failed Rube Goldberg machine. I tracked the chain reaction of events across the living room, a fallen box had upended a side table which had knocked over a vase that shattered, spraying the floor with shards. In the center stood a dazed-looking Nancy.

"Everything okay in there?" Burt poked his head in.

"I was reaching for my coffee and I must have knocked something over." Nancy's voice shook.

"Don't worry about it," I said. "Maggie just got here. Why don't you both go through the photos outside and I'll clean this up." I cleared a path and offered Nancy my arm. "Careful, you don't trip on these papers." Once I had her safely outside sitting with a new cup of coffee beside Maggie, I left them to it and went back to face the destruction.

Carol, who had come down from the attic, was already sweeping up the broken glass. "We'll need to clean this out of here before we leave." She shook her head, pausing to take in the mess. "They won't be able to walk around in here without falling over something."

Kneeling down, I picked up scattered issues of Field and Stream from the eighties and put them back in a box. A copy lay open, displaying an advertisement showcasing three men with thick Tom Selleck mustaches and rifles. One man aimed a rifle at a deer while the other two looked on. Below were three smaller photos: the first, showcasing their virility, exhibited them in a hot tub with big-haired women; the second featured the men at a shooting range, honing their skills; and the third was simply a steak and potato. The headline read, "Timberline Resort, Where Real Men Go to Be Men."

I thought about the ad and how it compared to the designs for the golf tournament I'd sent off last night and how very different they were. And yet, some things hadn't changed. I remembered a couple of weeks earlier the conversation I'd overheard at Rustic Reads between the bickering couple from Moon River Resort. The woman wanted to blow glass and her husband... My thoughts slowed as I replayed the scene. He wanted to go target shooting with a guy from the Pro Shop. I jumped up. "I got to make a call." I hastily climbed over the mess and made my way to the back porch.

Dave's phone went straight to voicemail. "Dave, it's Maya. I remembered something, a conversation I'd overheard a few weeks ago. I think Peter may have been taking guests from Moon River Resort out target shooting. Not sure if it's helpful or not. Give me a call when you can." I hung up and went back inside.

"Everything all right, Hon?" Carol looked worried.

"All good," I smiled. "I just thought of something I wanted to mention to Dave. Now," I stood with my legs apart and put my hands on my hips like Mr. Clean. "If we're going to get this place put back together, we're going to need some music."

We danced and sorted our way through the disorder until it was all right again.

"Let's go see if there are any more cookies," I suggested, and we went out to join the others in the sun.

Twenty

Lynell came into the P.O. flapping a letter like a flamenco fan. She looked around, eyeing the closed door leading to the hallway. With exaggerated movement, she laid her letter flat on the counter, smoothing it out. "May I use your restroom?" I was pretty certain she wanted to make sure Burt wasn't holding a secret coffee social in the kitchen.

I gestured to the door. "Down the hall, second on the left."

Moments later, she returned. "Have you seen Burt today?" She pretended to look for her wallet. "I wanted to talk to him about maybe doing some baking for the Hummingbird. Gus Winters, one of my regulars, you may remember him, he was here last week. Anyway, he said Burt's cheesecake was the best thing he'd stuck in his mouth. His words, not mine."

I agreed Burt's baking was delicious, and told her I didn't think he'd be coming in.

"I hear he and Leigha's mother are getting pretty friendly."

"If by friendly, you mean that they're friends, then yes. They are friends." I tried to put some censure in my voice, letting her know I was not gossiping about my friends.

"Purdy said they're more than just friends."

I was about to tell her in a polite, professional manner to mind her own business, but she didn't even take a breath before she was onto the next person.

"And speaking of Purdy, did you know she met a man and is moving to Alaska to be with him? She's never even met him in person. I hear it's because she's having some financial troubles. I can believe it with all the work she's had done lately. Have you seen her? I tell you, they'll never get that plastic in my face."

I looked at her blankly. "Do you need a stamp for this letter?"

"Sure, here." Lynell handed me a dollar.

"Do you know when the Stevens are moving out?"

I weighed the harm in telling her. "In a month or two. They're having a huge garage sale this weekend. You should stop by. Burt's there helping out. They have a lot of antiques they need to get rid of."

"Really? I'm looking for a couple of antique tables. Do you think they have any?"

"Probably." I was pretty sure I hadn't seen any, but I wasn't going to tell her. I reached under the counter and pulled out some yard sale fliers I had stashed away.

"Would you be willing to set these at the café counter? You get so many people coming through, and the Stevens could use the help. I know everyone would appreciate it." I was laying it on a bit thick, but if it helped the Stevens, I'd slather it on with a trowel. She eyed the little handouts with suspicion.

"I'm not sure. I understand they went around Chris Weller to sell their place so they wouldn't have to pay him a commission."

My rage flared. "That is not what happened."

"Really? That's what Chris told me."

If I told Lynell what really happened, soon everyone in Claryce Falls would know too. Maybe that wasn't such a bad thing. Maybe, I could use Lynell's love of gossip for good. After all, if Chris could use Lynell to spread a bent tale, I could use her to straighten it out.

"Do you want to know what really happened?"

She crossed her arms on the counter and leaned in. I edited the story for maximum impact and ease of retelling.

"Now we're trying to help them clear out their home so they can be with their children in this last phase of their lives." I ended my story melodramatically.

Lynell clasped her chest as if holding her heart in place. "I had no idea. No idea! And to think Chris is making himself out to be the victim. Give me those." She picked up the pile of fliers. "I'll make sure everyone who comes into the café today gets one."

"That's so kind of you, Lynell. You're really helping out the Stevens." And it was true, even if I was heavy-handed with my praise.

"Anything for a family who's been a cornerstone of Claryce Falls. I'll drop these off at the café, then head over to the garage sale to look for those tables."

"Great plan, good luck garage sale shopping." I finished putting the Friday mail delivery in the boxes and closed up.

After changing into loose jeans and a blue, long-sleeved t-shirt with retro orange and green stripes across the chest and arms, I wheeled Broomhilda out to the street. Though the sun was out, the spring day still held a chill. Pushing off, I headed to join my crew at the Stevens' yard sale. Leigha and Carol did an excellent job posting signs. As I rode, the orange neon posters easily guided the way. I heard Libby's squeals before I rounded the bend and saw a long line of cars. Between the signs and Lynell's promotions, word had gotten out about the sale.

"Hey Maya," Maggie greeted me as she helped load a sewing machine into the back of a woman's car. I flung my leg over Broomhilda and coasted to a stop by the house. I locked my bike to the porch banister to keep it from accidentally being purchased and headed over to see how I could help.

"Where do you want this?" a male voice asked. Owen emerged from the shadows of the barn with a saddle in his arms. Put a cowboy hat on the man and he could've been on the cover of a western romance novel. The book would be called something like Saddle Up for Love, or The Bronc Rider Wore Denim, or Ready to Ride. He was one cowboy I'd head into a sunset with.

"What are you laughing at?" Owen set the saddle on the ground and walked towards me. He let out a high-pitched whistle. Clover, Fizzy, and Buddy charged out of the barn, a run-away train of wagging tails. When they saw me, they barked and charged over for scratches.

I plopped down on the grass and flung open my arms to them. "I was naming the title of the Cowboy Romance novel you'd be on."

"How about, No Spurs, No Service," Leigha suggested. "Or Wrangled by Desire?"

"That's a good one. I'd read it," I said. "It sounds classy and dirty."

"Ladies, really enough," Burt cut us off.

Carol backed him up. "Burt's right, leave the man alone. Besides, the book should clearly be called "The Cowboy of Teanaway Creek.""

"A classic, for sure," I laughed.

"What about "The Rough and Rugged Wrangler?" Owen grinned.

"Are you encouraging them?" Burt was incredulous.

"Know when you're beaten, Burt. Better to just join 'em." Owen wiped his dusty hands on his jeans.

"Now, that's an entirely different kind of book," I joked.

"Maya, enough," Burt scolded. "There are children here."

I looked around to where Libby was happily reading a book to Nancy in the shade, well out of earshot. "Would you say you're–" I deepened my voice to mimic a movie trailer voiceover, "--At The End of Your Rope? Get it? And that was the last one. I promise."

Owen reached his hand down to help me up. I wrapped my fingers around his warm, rough palm and felt the way chocolate chip cookies smell. He hauled me to my feet, and I brushed the dirt off my butt.

"I didn't expect to see you here," I said.

"When Burt took Ava and me fishing, he mentioned you all could use help. So, I'm here."

"Did Ava get off okay?"

"Yep, she left early this morning. Headed for Eureka, California to start her year-long contract." I wanted to know how he felt about it but didn't want to ask with people around. "Fizzy is certainly happy to see Clover," he said, watching the two sniffing for animal trails in the bushes.

That reminded me. "Burt, thanks for picking up Clover and bringing her here."

He nodded in acknowledgment but was too preoccupied looking at belt buckles to say anything.

"I'm here to work, so what can I do?" I helped Owen haul out horse tack and arrange it into a visually pleasing pile. No sooner had we finished than a man from the horseback riding club came by and bought it all. Ben must have given him a great deal because he was quick to load it when he saw someone else looking at the saddles.

By three, business slowed. We came up for a breather and surveyed the impact. At least half the stuff was gone, and the Claryce Falls' historic museum was coming by to look over the rest for their collection.

Ben joined Nancy in the lawn chairs under a big Douglas fir. "I'm pooped out," Nancy declared. "Why don't you throw tarps over all this and call it a day?"

When we were done tying everything down, Carol invited us back to the Lores' for pizza.

Maggie and the Stevens declined to join us. Maggie was anxious to show Jason the photos the Stevens donated to the library. "I know he is going to be as crazy for these as I am. Thank you again." She bent down and gave both Ben and Nancy a hug.

Nancy took Maggie's hand and squeezed it affectionately. "It just tickles us to no end that you're going to display them at the library. Thank you."

Carol phoned in the pizza order before we left.

"Do you want to put your bike in my truck?" Burt asked.

"I'll put it in the back of mine," Owen answered for me. "Maya's on my way. I can drop her off when we're done."

"Suit yourself."

I turned between the men in an exaggerated twist. "I guess you both got that sorted for me. Thanks." I walked over to unlock Broomhilda. Owen followed, his forehead creased.

"Did you want to ride with Burt?"

"No, I appreciate the lift. I was just giving you both a hard time." I liked that he seemed uncertain. Welcome to my world, Buddy.

"You know, sometimes you're hard to read. I can't always tell when you're joking and when you're serious."

"Why can't I do both at the same time? I'm an excellent multitasker." I handed him my helmet and clipped the lock to my bike. "I'm starving. I need to eat." I looked at him straight on. "And I'm serious about that."

I kept the conversation light on the short drive to Leigha's. There wasn't time to get into anything serious. He told me about his fishing misadventure with Burt and Ava. "And on top of everything, Fizzy peed in Ava's suitcase while we were gone. She stayed up late washing all her clothes before she left. I don't know if she even went to sleep because she was gone before I got up today."

Did that mean they weren't sharing a bedroom? This conversation was very interesting.

Leigha handed me plastic plates and glasses to take out to the table. Owen carried the water pitcher and napkins.

Shortly after we'd arrived, Dave got home. He'd grabbed a shower and now looked comfortable drinking a Coke with Libby in his lap. He closed his eyes while she pretended to paint his nails with a dandelion. When he heard me walk out, he opened his eyes and raised an eyebrow. "I saw I missed a call from you. What'd you want?"

"It's about Peter's case. You want to talk about it later?"

He sat up straighter, jostling Libby.

"Daddy, careful," Libby reprimanded. "I almost messed up."

"Sorry Darlin'," he said absently and kissed her on the head. He looked up at me. "What do you have?"

I told him about the conversation I'd overheard. He made a low humming sound, processing the potential implications.

"I'll stop by the resort on Monday and talk to people. That's a good lead. Nice work."

"I'm just sorry I didn't think of it sooner."

"You remembered it now. That's all that matters. Did you find out what happened to that missing trash?" Dave asked.

"Nope, I looked around for it again and the others said they didn't throw anything out."

"Interesting." Dave paused, thinking. "I'm glad you got the rest of the stuff out of your place."

Leigha and Carol walked out carrying pizza and salad.

"You aren't talking about work, are you?" Leigha warned. "You need a break. You're off duty, Officer."

"Yes, Ma'am," he said, lifting Libby off his lap to get up and kiss his wife. Dave was true to his word. Nothing related to Peter's death was mentioned again the rest of the night.

When the yard lights turned on, Libby crawled onto my lap, and we snuggled up cozy in an Adirondack chair. The gathering was a perfect way to end a crazy week. I must have fallen asleep because I woke when Dave gently lifted a dozing Libby off me.

"You ready to go?" Owen asked quietly.

"I am," I said through a yawn as I stretched.

In the truck, Owen cranked the heat and turned the radio on low. Clover's head lay on my thigh, and Fizzy curled against me on the other side. I rested my head on the seat.

"You awake?" Owen asked hesitantly.

"Kind of."

"I'm fishing tomorrow with a guy from work."

"Nice," I said, only half paying attention

"Do you have plans Monday?"

"Don't know."

Owen paused. "If you're free, do you want to watch a movie? At your place. Or we could do it at mine if you want."

Drowsiness made me slow to answer and a moment later Owen added, "I'll even pick up dinner – your choice."

I stifled a big yawn, using the corner of my sleeve. "Sure, but no horror flicks or greasy Chinese."

He chuckled softly. "I think I can manage that." Owen reached out, his hand next to mine on Clover. His fingers brushed against my fingers as he scratched her.

Clover stretched out with a contented sigh, reflecting my own feelings. The warm darkness wrapped around us, a silent comfort, as we made our way together through the night.

Twenty-One

I was done in by coffee and toast. Two staples of an American breakfast brought me to my knees and then flat on my backside. I sat on the floor, holding my ankle, waiting for the pain to ebb, so I could tell if I'd broken the dang thing or just severely sprained it. Adding insult to injury, my pajama pants were soaked with my much-needed coffee. The piece of toast I'd slipped on lay next to me, looking annoyingly innocent and edible. Clover licked the butter smeared across the kitchen tile. I tossed the toast to her. Vengeance would be mine—the bread was going down.

After a few minutes of feeling pathetic and sorry for myself, I prodded the rapidly swelling ankle and determined it was probably a sprain. Growing up playing sports and being somewhat less coordinated than some, I was no stranger to sprains. In fact, I injured myself often enough, I preemptively had a sprain kit at the ready. I pulled myself up, wincing when I put pressure on the injured ankle and hopped to the freezer. I pulled out a large cold pack and longingly eyed the half-pot of coffee. If I had to sit for twenty minutes with an ice pack, I would at least have my caffeine. I rooted around the cupboard, standing on one leg like a stork with a bad case of bedhead until I found a travel mug.

I filled it and made sure the lid didn't leak. Grabbing my ice pack, I hopped over to the couch and got myself situated. Waiting while my phone timer counted down twenty minutes, I watched cartoons and caffeinated myself. I texted Burt and Carol letting them know I'd be late to the Stevens and why. Burt told me to stay home—they didn't need me. I felt both relieved and guilty.

Accepting my home-bound fate, the only goal I set for myself was rounding up a day's worth of snacks, ibuprofen, sports wraps, books, a notebook, and my laptop. Clover and I settled into the couch, me spread out on one end and her curled up on the other. Both of us ready for our lazy day.

On Monday, a large purple bruise cradled the underside of my ankle. It still felt more like someone had driven over it with a tractor and not that I'd been ambushed by a slippery slice of bread. With a full day ahead, I wrapped it with a stretchy bandage and found a sneaker wide enough to fit my swollen foot. After work at the post office, I needed to swing by the printers in Hillsburg to pick up the sample hats and t-shirts, then take them to the resort for Elby's final approval. I breathed in deeply, channeling my inner warrior princess, and hobbled my way out into the day.

I kept my foot propped up most of the morning at work, and the drive to Hillsburg afterward was easy enough. To reward myself for making it, I treated myself to Remmy's Drive-Thru for a burger and strawberry shake. It was a special indulgence, and I was savoring every bite and slurp.

The hoovering of my straw against the empty shake cup synced perfectly with my arrival at the resort's main lodge. I limped my way to the counter and asked for Elby. By now, the pain meds were wearing off, and I was living on the sugar rush of my shake alone. I waited, leaning against the counter and facing the grand room. It was a space designed to slap you in the face with Pacific Northwest majesty. The vaulted, wood-planked ceilings rose three stories high. The far wall was lined with windows, showcasing sweeping views of the forest. Beyond the trees, the rugged Cascade Mountains stretched into the distance, their snow-capped peaks visible on the horizon. On any other day I'm sure it would be very impressive, but today I would've preferred the view of my TV and a beer. When the receptionist returned, he said I'd just missed Elby, but thought she'd headed down to the Pro Shop. I grunted at him and slowly made my way back out to Nell.

At the Pro Shop I experienced a deep sense of regret that I didn't play golf so I could chuck my clubs through, the shop's window. The doors were locked and a handwritten note was taped to it: "Gone to Collect a Broken Cart - Back Soon." On the course, between the pond and trees, I saw Jay working. I considered waiting, but I wanted to get home to clean up before Owen came over. Even if Elby wasn't here, I could leave the sample gear with Jay. I slung the bag with the t-shirts and cap over my shoulder and painfully made my way out to him. About three-quarters of the way, I regretted my decision. A golf cart was hitched to the back of Jay's enormous new truck. He was getting in as I approached.

Seeing me, Jay rolled down his window and propped his forearm out. "What are you doing out here?"

"Dropping off merch for the tournament." I patted the bag. "I was hoping to find Elby at the Pro Shop, but I keep missing her. Can I leave it with you to give to her?"

"Okay, I'm headed in. If you don't mind the mess in here," he said, indicating the cab, "I'll give you a ride."

I walked around the front and opened the passenger side door. An empty Mountain Dew bottle rolled out onto the ground, and I bent to pick it up. Straightening, my eyes swept over the debris strewn across the floorboard: bright yellow Butterfingers wrappers and Cool Ranch Doritos bags lay like coiled snakes among the trash, ready to strike. I froze.

Icy pinpoints pricked my spine. My heart quickened, each beat drumming louder than the next in my ears.

Jay followed my gaze to the mess. His friendly smile slipped, replaced with something darker—wariness, maybe?

"Just kick that stuff over and get in," he said, his voice flat, the warmth gone.

Every instinct screamed at me to run. I forced a smile, but my muscles felt stiff, locked in place. "You know," I said, trying to sound casual, "I think I changed my mind. It's such a nice day. I'll walk and wait for Elby."

"Nah," his tone sharpened. "You should let me give you a ride. It's not safe to walk the course. You might get hit by a stray ball. I wouldn't want anything to happen to you."

The hairs on my neck stood up. No one else was in sight. The course was deserted.

"It looks clear to me." I swallowed hard. "Besides, I'm kind of a neat freak. Messes make me...uncomfortable. I'll catch you back at the shop."

I shut the passenger side door and started walking. My pulse raced, each step an eternity. The trees, my closest refuge, were behind me, but they felt too far away. The truck engine revved. Out of the corner of my eye, I watched as Jay made an enormous U-turn, the golf cart rattling behind precariously. I felt the vibration of the engine in my bones as it grew louder, following me. My muscles tightened, ready to leap.

The truck passed me, a tsunami of relief flooded me, and I almost cried. But then it stopped.

The world narrowed, my breath suspended in my throat. Slowly, I reached for my phone.

Jay leaned out the window, his expression neutral. "Maya, get in the truck. I can see you're limping. Let me give you a ride."

My legs wobbled. "Nope, all good, thanks." I waved him away, plastering on false cheeriness. "I'll see you up there in a minute."

We held our position, sizing each other up. The seconds stretched.

"I know you think you know something, Maya, but you don't. Get in the truck now, and I'll explain." His voice dropped, sharp and commanding.

A spark of fear ignited like a firecracker inside of me. I exploded, bolting across the greens, heading for the trees.

"Damn it! Maya, stop!" Jay yelled. The truck spun out, and I heard a loud crash, like the golf cart toppling.

I pushed harder, ignoring the shooting pain in my ankle.

"I didn't hurt Peter. It wasn't me. He was my best friend." Jay's voice rang through the air, desperate, but I kept running.

"I don't want to hurt you, Maya."

The trees were close now. Just a little further. I poured every remaining ounce of willpower into my legs, begging them to move faster. I crashed through the undergrowth, branches clawing at my clothes, my sneakers catching on the tangled roots. I couldn't stop. Couldn't look back. My toe snagged on a root, and suddenly, I was airborne.

I hit the ground hard. Agony exploded through my leg as my injured ankle twisted beneath me. A muffled scream escaped my throat. Behind me, the truck skidded to a stop, the door slamming shut. Panic surged through me like electricity. Frantically, I clawed at the ground searching for anything I could use to defend myself.

I found a thick branch and forced myself to stand. Agony shot up my leg. I leaned against a tree, gripping the branch like a lifeline. I wasn't able to run away, so I was going to have to fight. I fumbled my phone and dialed with shaking hands.

"911, what's your emergency?" the operator's voice asked.

I raised my voice loud and steady, even as I fought my panic. "I'm calling the police, Jay. Don't do anything you'll regret. They'll be at the golf course any minute." I hoped the operator was listening and understood. "They'll see my car at the Pro Shop and your truck on the greens parked by the trees. They'll know we're in the grove together. Just stay back."

A heavy silence followed, broken only by the crunch of footsteps approaching through the undergrowth. "Maya, don't do that, please. Let me explain." Jay sounded desperate.

My breath shook. I tried to steady it, slowly exhaling, willing my fear to reshape into something sharper, more dangerous. I was a cornered wolverine, ready to fight with everything I had. Teeth bared, I braced myself. I wasn't going down without a fight.

Jay crashed through the shrubs and halted when he saw me. He moved cautiously towards me like a man approaching a rabid animal. His hands were raised, palms out. "Maya, listen to me. It was an accident. I didn't shoot Peter." He swallowed, eyes darting to the phone in my hand. "It was a resort guest. Some rich tech guy from Bellevue. We were out shooting, and Peter ran out to set a target. The guy was still firing and… and he hit Peter. It was an accident."

I gripped the branch tighter, my knuckles white. His words were rushing now, frantic.

"The guy gave me money to keep quiet. A lot of it. I didn't mean for any of this to happen. Just put the phone down, and we can talk this through. We can share the money, okay? Please, Maya, I don't want to hurt you."

"But you already did. Didn't you, Jay? You gave me a concussion."

He inched closer, his eyes focused on my phone. "I got trapped in there. I panicked. You hit your head, and there was so much blood. I lost it."

"You left me to bleed out while you went through my workshop," I growled.

"It's all out of control," Jay moaned, holding his head. "I thought you were dead."

"You didn't even check to see if I was still breathing. That's cold Jay."

"There was nothing I could do, and I needed to find all the stuff you picked up from our target practice. Give me the phone and we can talk about this."

"Did you use your gun to kill Peter?"

"You're not listening. I didn't kill him. It was the guy from Bellevue. He was using Peter's rifle. Come on, Maya. This won't bring Peter back, and I have money. Just let it go."

"Where's the gun now?" I tried to keep him talking, buying time for help to arrive.

"Hand me the phone, and I'll tell you."

I flicked the speakerphone on and tossed it a few feet away onto the ground.

"There, you want the phone so bad, go get it."

His eyes darted between me and the cell. Slowly, he bent, reaching for it. The moment his gaze dropped, I struck. I swung the branch with all the strength left in me. The impact cracked across his back. He hit the ground screaming. Jay rolled, and I swung again. Just as the branch was about to connect, his leg shot out, slamming into my ribs. The force knocked me to the ground, but not before my strike landed on the side of his head.

We both lay still, breathless. Fire flared along my side, leaving me paralyzed with pain. I stared up at the treetops as white spots flickered across my vision. I let the initial shock pass and forced myself to move, pulling t-shirts from the bag tangled around me. Crawling towards Jay, I dragged the branch behind me, ready to hit him if he attacked. I saw his chest rise and fall in shallow breaths, blood trickling down his forehead. Nothing else moved.

Trembling, I tied his wrists together using the shirts then knotted his shoelaces. My ribs screamed at me to stop moving, but I had to finish this.

I searched for the phone under Jay and held it to my ear. "Hello? Are you still there?" My voice trembled.

"I'm here, Ma'am. Are you alright?"

"I think so. I'm at the Moon River Resort Golf Course." I gasped, trying to describe my location.

"There is an officer at the resort. He's on his way to you now. Stay on the line with me."

A siren wail bounced off the trees. Beside me, Jay groaned, his face twisted in pain as blood ran across his forehead. He turned his cheek into the dirt, sobbing. "It's all a mess... Peter's gone, and I messed up so bad..."

I didn't know what the real story was, and I didn't care. I heard a car skid to a stop and the siren cut out. Dave's voice bellowed my name.

"We're over here," I yelled.

"Maya," panic was thick in his voice.

"I'm here," I hollered back in the world's worst game of Marco Polo ever played.

Dave crashed through the shrubs, diving to his knees next to me. "Are you okay?"

"Mostly," I answered honestly. "I think he got it worse."

Dave moved to where Jay lay and inspected my makeshift cuffs. "Are these t-shirts?" he asked with what I liked to imagine was awe and reverence at my ingenuity.

"It's what I had." I shrugged, immediately regretting the movement. "Jay was there when Peter was shot. The candy wrappers we picked up were his. I don't know the full story, but he does. He's also the guy who knocked me out."

Dave pulled Jay into a sitting position and replaced the t-shirts with real handcuffs. He helped Jay to his feet. But when Dave let go, Jay almost toppled over again.

"His shoelaces are tied together, too." I pointed at Jay's feet. Dave took out a knife and sliced the laces free.

"Are you okay here for a minute while I get him to the car and stop this bleeding?"

"I'm not going anywhere," I said with a false glibness.

Moments later, Dave returned for me. He helped me out of the woods and to his car, where we rested on its hood until a steady EMT named Tova showed up. She taped my ribs and ankle and loaded me into the ambulance.

At the hospital, Dave waited while I had x-rays of my injured bits taken. I was sprained and bruised, but nothing was broken.

My phone chimed with a text from Owen asking me if I wanted anything special from the Thai restaurant for dinner. I had lost all perspective. It was as if two worlds were running in parallel. There was the normal one I generally lived in, which had no idea I'd stepped out of it. And the Bizarro world where I'm chased by men in trucks and fight off potential murderers on a golf course with a stick. The Bizarro world knew about the normal world, but the normal world didn't know about the other yet.

I texted back. "Will be late. At hospital now - all good." My phone immediately rang. I looked at Dave standing next to me and showed him the screen with Owen's name. "Would you mind telling him I'm okay? I'm just too tired to talk about it all right now."

He nodded, took the phone, and stepped away to have my conversation for me while I finished filling out my paperwork.

When Dave dropped me off at home, Owen was there waiting for me.

"I'll take your keys and have someone drop your car off for you tonight, okay?" Dave held out his hand.

I gave him a big hug. "Thanks for coming to my rescue."

He put an arm around my shoulders.

"You'd pretty much rescued yourself by the time I got there. If I hadn't already been at the lodge following up on your lead, you would've had him in a jail cell with your feet up on the desk by the time I'd gotten to you." He released me. "Now, go eat dinner with this guy and relax." Dave let himself out.

"You know there're easier ways of getting out of spending time with me than brawling with criminals." Owen carried two plates mounded with food over to the coffee table.

"If only you were better at taking hints, I wouldn't have to resort to such drastic measures." I smiled.

"Do you need help over?"

"No, I got it."

He ignored me and carefully slid an arm around my waist. I leaned into him, his warmth a reassuring presence. "I don't know which parts of me are bruised and which parts are sore because I haven't sprinted like that since high school. You should have seen me out there. I was like Usain Bolt or Flo-Jo streaking over the greens."

"I'm not ready to laugh about what just happened to you, Maya. Give me time to catch up." He stopped us and turned to wrap me in a hug. "I need you to stop getting hurt like this." He rested his face on the top of my head. "You said you wouldn't make this a habit. Remember?"

"Owen?" My voice was high with question.

"Yes, Maya?"

"Are you and Ava together?"

"What?" Surprise was evident in his voice.

I didn't care if I was being tactless or if the timing was off. I was all out of careful and awkward today. My adrenaline had worn off, and I was feeling very raw. "You heard me. What happened to you and Ava during her visit?"

"Nothing like you seem to be thinking. We aren't back together." I waited for him to continue. "She came to get Fizzy, and I suppose to see if there was something still there between us, and she got her answer."

"Which is?" I raised my eyebrow pointedly.

"Which is that I've moved on." He took my chin in his hand and tilted my head up. He waited for me to look him in the eyes. "I'm already pretty hung up on someone else."

A slow smile as wide as Texas spread across my face. "Good," I said. Then I hesitated. "Wait, you mean me, right?"

He rolled his eyes. With his other hand, he reached up and gently cupped my face. He bent his head slowly towards mine and whispered across my lips. "Yes, Maya, I mean you."

I stretched up and kissed him. Gravity shifted, pulling us towards each other. My hands wove into his hair. He let go of my face, wrapping his arm around my waist to eliminate the last of the space between us. A sudden pain shot out from my rib cage, and I cried out.

Owen immediately released me. "Crap, I'm so sorry. I got carried away."

I laughed, instantly causing me to moan. "We both did."

"Here." He held out his arm. "I promise to behave myself for the rest of the evening."

"That doesn't sound very exciting," I said and grinned.

"Maya," he groaned and pressed his forehead against mine. "You've had enough excitement for one day. I need you to behave for the rest of the night, too." He straightened and helped me the remaining distance to the couch. When I was settled with my ankle wrapped in ice packs on a pillow tower, Owen handed me my food. He let me choose whatever I wanted to watch without comment. After the excitement of my day, I wanted the pastoral pleasantry and culinary comfort of the *Great British Bake Off*. I looked over at Owen sitting next to me and down at Clover and Fizzy curled up beside him. Deep contentment flooded me. I was out of the Bizarro world and back to the exact place I wanted to be.

Twenty-Two

"I brought treats for the hero. Two kinds of tarts, a sweet goat cheese and blackberry jam, and a savory turkey with herb goat cheese." Burt held a large paper bag out in front of him as he entered the post office.

"Burt, don't call me that." I was feeling like a smothered kitten, over manhandled by its adopted gorilla mother. After the rest of the Lore household heard about my golf course brawl, Leigha, Carol, and Libby came over for a mandatory girls' night. Right before they left for Libby's bedtime, Burt showed up in his small RV and parked it outside my house. "Just in case the doctors missed something," he'd be right there.

And now, only five hours since I'd left him, here he was again. Yes, I was stiff and sore, but I wasn't some glass princess. And today, my involvement in the "incident" reached some of the general Claryce Falls public. There'd been a steady stream of gossip-seekers. I didn't blame people for wanting to know what happened, but I wasn't supposed to talk about it yet. Plus, I'd slept poorly, which meant I got easily irritated over other people's annoyance with me for holding out on the salacious details. I'd spent most of the day mildly frustrated with the world.

I needed to go home, curl up with Clover, and take a nap. Instead, when I closed up, I had to head straight to the church parking lot to stuff nets with the last of the plastic bottles. There were still a million loose ends to finish up for the Campground Opening Celebration this weekend, and I was going to be busy up until the big day.

I was also pretty disappointed I wouldn't be able to ride Broomhilda in the mile-long bottle-pull ride from the park to the recycling plant. But it wasn't like they needed me. All the kids from the fifth and sixth-grade classes were riding their bikes and pulling the nets their classes stuffed. The local bike shop offered free rentals to kids without bikes, and they even had a couple of large tricycles for those who hadn't learned to ride yet. It was going to be quite the spectacle. Even Leigha was riding with Libby on the back of her bike.

"Have you talked to Dave today?" Burt called from the kitchen, where he was making coffee.

I hollered back that I hadn't and asked why.

He walked out reading from his phone. "And I suppose you haven't looked at the breaking news from the Hillsburg Herald?"

I gave him a look, conveying my answer.

Leaning against the counter, he cleared his voice. "Bellevue man arrested in connection with the death of Claryce Falls man. Robert Hathem, from Bellevue, Washington, was taken into custody late Tuesday night in connection with the murder of Peter Becker, twenty-two, of Claryce Falls, Washington. Authorities detained Hathem for questioning after Becker's body was discovered in Teanaway State Forest on Sunday, April tenth."

Suddenly it clicked. "Burt, I know who Robert Hathem is. I've seen him. Twice! Once with his wife at the bookstore, and again when he almost ran me down outside the glass studio." I felt cold all over. It was the same day Peter was shot. He dragged his wife out of her glass class. What if it was right after he'd shot Peter?"

"Do you really think it was the same guy?"

"I do," I said. It made me sick to think I'd been that close to Peter's killer and never knew it. "Maybe Dave would've caught him sooner if I'd just put the pieces together faster. If I had, then the whole nightmare showdown with Jay and me wouldn't have happened."

"You can't think like that," Burt said. "They'd still be looking for them if you hadn't put two and two together with the candy wrappers."

"I don't know." I still felt guilty, like I had failed. "What else does it say?"

"A hiker's dog found the body, sparking an investigation that led to Hathem's arrest." Burt read on. "Jay Whippler, twenty-one, was also detained following an incident at the Moon River Resort golf course on Monday, May eight. Both men are suspected of involvement in the shooting.

Authorities allege that Robert Hathem accidentally shot Peter Becker with Becker's own rifle while Becker was resetting a target. Instead of reporting the incident, Hathem is accused of bribing Jay Whippler to help hide both the body and the weapon and cover up the death. Whippler's involvement became clearer after he was arrested following an altercation at a golf course, further linking him to the crime.

Whippler and Becker were employees at the Moon River Resort Golf Course. Investigators revealed that both men were involved in a scheme that included taking guests out for target shooting and engaging in illegal elk hunting.

The arrests have sent shockwaves through the Claryce Falls community as more details of the case continue to emerge." Burt made a disgruntled huff. "They don't even mention you in this, and you're the one that broke the case."

"I don't mind one bit." Dave warned me it was only a matter of time before my name showed up in the press. "The whole thing makes me sad. Jay isn't evil, he's just young and stupid."

"Most people who do stupid things aren't evil." Burt agreed. "But our lives are shaped by the decisions we make at critical moments. Jay made a lot of poor decisions recently."

We both stood silently, overwhelmed by the waste of three lives.

"Burt, you here?" The floorboards in the hallway creaked as Bev made her way in. "I'm praying that's coffee I smell. And please tell me you brought treats because we've got a lot of work to get done this afternoon." And just like that, the normal world surged ahead.

Today was the day. The sun was bright, the air was clear. A crowd of women, men, kids, and dogs crowded behind a cord chanting "Drop the ball! Drop the ball!" In front of them, rising like shiny totems to beverage consumption and recycling, my three giant aluminum cans glinted in the light. Sherman, who was manning his old crane, raised the small wrecking ball above the shortest of my three can sculptures.

When the ball was positioned directly above it, he opened the crane door and leaned out. "I can't hear you," Sherman called, egging the crowd on.

The crowd took up the challenge and yelled their demands even louder. I laughed, marveling at Sherman's showmanship.

Owen draped his arm around my shoulders, grinning. "Ready to see all your hard work flattened like a pancake?"

I beamed up at him. "I can't wait. They're fulfilling their destiny." I slid my arm around his waist and turned back to the crane. Excitement zinged through me.

Leigha poked me in the thigh, her eyes narrowing at Owen and me. Her unspoken question was clear: 'When did this happen?'

I winked at her, turning back to the spectacle. As the crane's ball descended with a satisfying crunch, the crowd erupted into cheers. The can crumpled into a jagged, fat disk. Sherman gave the ball a couple of final, triumphant drops, and the crowd's applause roared. He repeated the theatrics twice more, giving in to the crowd's demands to drop the ball.

When all giant cans were squashed into lumpy aluminum pancakes, they were loaded onto bike carts. We wandered over to the picnic area. Carol and I snagged a couple of free tables, and I rested my ankle with her while everyone else went to grab lunch from the food trucks.

"This turned out to be an absolute hoot," Carol said, her eyes sparkling. "You all did an amazing job."

"I'm thrilled," I agreed, chuckling. "And did you see Maggie win the speed pickle-eating contest? Her jaw was a pickle sawmill!" I laughed again, recalling how Maggie had daintily dabbed at her mouth with a paper towel, followed by an enormous belch. The crowd loved it.

"Hi, you two." Emily slid into the spot next to Carol, with Jess trailing behind, carrying two plates piled high with fried chicken and mac and cheese.

Jess greeted us with a warm smile before setting the plates down and taking a seat next to Emily.

"Thank you." Emily leaned over and kissed Jess on the cheek. "You're the sweetest." She turned to me and mouthed, "He's so hot."

I stifled a laugh--looked like I was a pretty good matchmaker.

Soon everyone was back, loaded with food and drinks. Burt took a seat across from Carol and Owen scooted in close to me, our thighs touching. Dave, finally able to take the day off, pulled over another table for the Lores to spill onto. I waved Jason and Maggie over to join our party.

The spring warmth made everything taste better. We stuffed ourselves with pot stickers, nachos, and strawberry shortcake. Kids twirled near the stage, their little feet out of synch as they danced to Bev's playlist, piping through the portable speaker. Janet stepped up to the stage and the music cut off. Since the project all started with her, we'd decided Janet should be the one to announce how much recycling we'd collected. Bev worked with Janet on her talking points, and we made her practice her speech in front of us.

The mic squealed as Janet pulled it from the stand. "We are lucky to live in Claryce Falls, surrounded by forests..." She was doing great, sticking to the script. Speaking about how we all needed to pitch in and pick up trash, even other people's. But then, mid-sentence, she went silent. Her eyes locked on a target, like an eagle spotting a sunbathing bunny.

"Hey, you." She pointed, at a man holding a small boy. "You with the kid and green shirt. Stop!"

He was talking to the kid and didn't notice all the eyes on him. Someone tapped the guy on the shoulder and motioned to Janet, who was still tracking him with her finger, like a crossbow with her sight set on him.

"You recycle cans." Janet scolded. "You don't throw them away. Go recycle it."

The man looked confused and chuckled uncomfortably.

"I saw you throw your soda can in the trash. Go put it in recycling. I'll wait here all day."

His wife emerged from the crowd, taking the toddler from his arms. The man shuffled back to the trash, plucked the can out, and tossed it into the recycling like he was making a free throw. The shot aroused a round of small, awkward cheers.

"It's people like you–" Janet started again, but Bev, swooped in and snagged the microphone.

"Thank you both for the live demonstration of being mindful of our waste." Bev grinned as she side-stepped Janet, who tried to grab the mic back. Christina Russet from Parks and Rec ran up and firmly escorted Janet from the stage.

Bev finished the speech, thanking the grade schools who participated. Then, to my surprise, she gave me a special thanks. My face went bright red when the crowd cheered for me and my can sculptures.

"Now, eat up and enjoy the food!" Bev finished, quickly turning the tunes back on before any more soda can drama could break out.

Resting my chin in my hands, I gazed at my row of friends, a wave of love and gratitude flowing through me.

"What're you grinning at?" Owen's knee bumped mine.

I looked him square on, my heart full. "I want to take you on a date. What do you say about that?"

"I'd say it's about time. I've been playing hard to get for a month now. I was starting to lose hope." He winked at me.

"Ah, that's where you went wrong." I slipped my hand into his. "I like them easy to get."

He leaned in, his breath tickling my ear. "I can be easy for you."

My cheeks flamed, and I was about to respond when Leigha interrupted with a dramatic gesture.

"You two, enough flirting. It's time for the bike ride." She wiped Libby's mouth and led her over to the bikes.

Owen rose, holding out his hand to me. "Come on." He grinned, eyes sparkling with mischief. "I've got a surprise for you."

"What is it?" My stomach butterflies were on full flutter duty.

"Only one way to find out." He entwined our fingers and led me over to the row of bikes lined up with nets stuffed with bottles attached to them. "I know you were disappointed you couldn't ride, so…" He pointed to a large tricycle with a makeshift seat on the back where the basket used to be. "I worked with Shane at the bike shop, and he's letting us borrow this."

"You're going to peddle us there?" I felt tears sting my sinuses. "That is so sweet." I couldn't look at him, or I might embarrass myself.

"Hop on," he said, his face glowing with happiness.

I was a total goner for him. I climbed onto the seat, facing backward, my heart soaring.

Owen handed me a helmet with a grin. "Better put this on. I don't think your brain can handle any more knocks." The first group of riders took off down the trail, the nets bouncing behind them. "Here we go. You ready?"

"Heck yeah," I cried. I was ready for the ride. Ready for adventure. Ready for whatever crazy road and surprises awaited us next.

Acknowledgements

There aren't enough dancing animal GIFs on the internet to express my appreciation for my sister, Lynnette, and my mother, Yvette, who let me reread scenes to them countless times. I can now concede that a banana in a cowboy hat may be funnier than an aardvark in a bedazzled jumpsuit (though I'm still not entirely convinced).

My infinite gratitude to my top-notch advance readers and their invaluable feedback: Anne, Gail, Melissa, Nora, Sara, and Tami—the best friends, family, and co-conspirators a gal could ask for. Thanks to Dawn for her generous guidance and advice; to Robert and Roz, from whose shelter this book arose; and to my editor, Stacey Goitia. You all helped make this book what it is!

Stay Connected!

Loved this book? Don't miss exclusive updates, sneak peeks of upcoming releases, and behind-the-scenes insights!

Join the Eve Barnes newsletter community for fun content, special giveaways, and the latest news delivered straight to your inbox.

Sign up today and become part of our story!

www.evebarneswrites.com

Thank you for your support!